THE PERFECT SONG

THE PERFECT SONG

Damon

iUniverse, Inc.
New York Lincoln Shanghai

The Perfect Song

iUniverse, Inc.

For information address:
iUniverse, Inc.
2021 Pine Lake Road, Suite 100
Lincoln, NE 68512
www.iuniverse.com

www.perfectsong.net

ISBN: 0-595-31274-8

Printed in the United States of America

To my family

Foreword

The skinny man shivered in the woods waiting for dawn so he could snatch a million-dollar scrap of paper rejected by a maniac.

It was an odd life, playing anonymous janitor to a shadowy, international genius.

But what the hell, a man had to have *some* kind of occupation in life. Poul scratched his balding head and shoved his long skinny hands back into his pockets. He kept his eyes closed to shut out the utter blackness of the forest. He was a city man, and even after a year-and-a-half following this *guy*, whoever he was, Poul couldn't get used to rural America. He liked being surrounded by buildings, concrete, traffic hums and exhaust smells. He didn't feel comfortable with people, but he liked the ambiance of them around him.

He hated raw earth and was afraid of animals. While he didn't quite believe that nature should be totally conquered, he had a strong conviction that it should be kept in its place, relegated to such areas as small gardens, manicured fruit orchards and foreign countries.

However, money was money and you found it where you could. He leaned down and picked up another paper. He was going to be *rich*!

CHAPTER 1

Poul was tall, lanky. If someone spray-painted him green, he would resemble a praying mantis. He had tried his hand at a variety of jobs over the past 10 years. He had also tried marriage. Nothing seemed to click until recently when his job as a morgue janitor and his marriage ended at the same time.

It was at that depressing cycle of a thoroughly aimless life that Poul knew he needed a goal. Some direction. All his life he had wanted to be rich enough to not have to work for somebody else. He wanted to be independent enough to choose his own girlfriends and cars. Time wasn't going to wait for him. He had to take action.

So with no possessions or personal commitments, he set off in quest of money. If he wandered long enough, they would find each other. He knew that. This was America, land of discovery and overnight success. Humming and sniffing, he headed off in no particular direction. He scratched his chin and chuckled to himself. Damn, it felt good to be free.

No more smell of formaldehyde and unresponsive company. No more wife whining about unpaid bills. Freedom and money.

America.

Damn!

Mendel stopped in a clearing, dropped his bag and sat down. He pulled the dark hair from his eyes and ears and shoved it behind his back. He was no closer to finding the perfect song than he was when he set out two years ago.

He was tired and discouraged. A faded denim sleeve flapped loosely around his wrist.

As the sun began to set, his large, dark eyes turned to the bag beside him. He stood up, yanked it open and dumped its contents. Dozens of songs cascaded lightly onto the grass. He leaned down and picked up single sheets from the crinkled marshmallow pile, studied a few and tossed them.

"Junk! Just junk!" He pulled at his beard, then dug out the stubborn sheets that had clung to the bag as if in a desperate bid for survival. They were bits of the Bird Songs. He had spent months studying birds, watching them, listening to how they voiced rhythmic dialects, trying to be them until, in a burst of energy that settled into a steady volcanic flow, he wrote wild songs, hard songs, loud, crazy songs that flew in all directions and threatened to tear a listener apart with the sound of air, cries and clouds rushing past the ears. The bird music soared forth with a hum of joy controlled only by the slight confines of thin skin and flexible feathers. They were spacious, swooping songs sailing through the atmosphere where no obstacles forced you to veer from your path, where you fought air currents, then rode them a half mile above the earth with your wings straight out to the side of each eye, where tops of century old trees shrank to the size of dandelion buds…where nothing affronted the senses in this rush of pure freedom.

While writing, Mendel had reveled in a kind of madness. He had become the birds, flying upward, soaring through an endless sky, skimming over patches of fields and forests and farms that resembled the tattered quilt he'd slept in as a boy. Closer to the sun by only a few hundred feet, he saw it so large and bright it took up half the sky in its unfiltered radiance.

He dove and felt the power and control, the precise relationship demanded between eye and muscle to drift down and land gently on a willow branch or hurtle earthward at a mole, snatch it and push again upward.

The grace and freedom of bird life led him even further into energy patterns and exploding forces that lay beyond the rough barriers of the senses. Mendel wrote songs that would require an orchestra composed of madmen, maniacs, rapists, and terrorists. These frenetic musicians would be conducted by lovesick Kamikaze pilots, renegade astronauts and unpublished poets.

These were songs of suppressed energy released in torrents before the conservative rationality of consciousness could grab control and rinse carmine to blotchy pink. They were songs of cloven-hooved angels swinging sky-length swords above the masses of people whose heads bent down in desperate prayer; songs of albatrossed men plunging through maelstroms of the self into lands where seabirds screamed and babies warred with demonic fury.

Mendel read the songs and flung them. Dozens of sheets, like slight, crippled birds, fluttered behind him into the distance. With the exception of a few which might have some potential, the songs were gone, flipping in the breeze, catching on bushes and fading from sight with the setting sun.

The years he had spent wandering, studying, gathering and writing, now were behind him with this final severance. And with this little death, Mendel's energy turned to anger. Even God's rage can't compare with self-anger. God annihilates. The self tortures mercilessly. Van Gogh knew it. Baudelaire made the journey once or twice. Hemingway could have filled in some blanks before he loaded his gun and turned it inward. Blast away the pain! All the agonies of the world's events are teacup tempests compared to the gnawing hell of one tortured soul.

Good lines, Mendel thought. He pulled out a piece of paper and wrote them down. As soon as he finished, his anger returned. He grabbed a stick and whipped the papers on the ground, sending them in all directions. The scraps reacted like men. Some scattered at the stick's fury. Some lay and took the beating while others hid in the dimming light of dusk.

Exhausted, Mendel flung the stick and sat down again by his bag. The act had been a matter of purging, something all men, civilizations and even worlds indulge in occasionally. He used the now diminished song bag for a pillow and fell asleep, knowing he would rise tomorrow and continue his quest for the perfect song.

Many idle men and some of who have made an academic occupation of it have questioned whether one man's action can change the world. Adam might give a discouraged but heartfelt nod. Plato would hedge his bets. Jung would dismiss it and argue that fate, destiny and even "willful" actions can often be reduced to synchronicity, a fairly common fusion that each day helps create marriages, business partnerships, babies, minor revolutions and major revelations.

As Mendel trudged down from the mountain the next morning, eyes on the humpy Appalachian ridges, Poul headed up the other side. He walked slowly, scratching his ribs and trying to devise a plan to package dead leaves into fireplace logs. The plan would serve a twofold purpose: it would make him rich, and it would rid the world of natural waste. Look at them, he thought, scuffing along, dirty little things lying here by the tons just rotting back into the damp, smelly earth. Nature's dirty dump.

It was in this position in time, space and mental composition that Poul spied one of the crumpled song pages. Like a rooster pecking at a shiny object, Poul bent his long frame into a bony jackknife and picked it up. "Hmm. Strange." He scratched at his earlobe as he studied the musical notes. He looked around and began leisurely gathering up the discarded papers. He just might be onto something, he thought. It wasn't like an isolated mountain to be harboring such oddball items.

Jung described synchronicity as a "meaningful coincidence," as opposed to a "chance grouping." Synchronicity, he continued, is not cause and effect but a "falling together in time," time itself being so elastic that it can be expanded forever or reduced to the vanishing point. In later years, Poul would often wonder if he would have found the papers had his aimless wanderings taken him a mere 50 feet to the right or left. Or, what if he hadn't left the morgue and his marriage until a week later? Or what if the songwriter had been a man of a milder temper and saved the songs, (or of a more cynical nature and burned them?)

Poul concluded in the years to come that there are nothing but "if's" when humans are involved.

What happened did happen and it affected the lives of nearly everybody in the civilized world.

As he gathered the papers, Poul became so involved in tracking and collecting them that time did indeed seem to disappear. Before he realized it, the sun had quietly eased into the horizon's awesome girdle and he found himself trapped in dusk's new world.

"Damn!" His pale skin chalked even whiter as a new reality imposed itself. "I'm lost. Jesus-barefoot-Christ…. I'm lost." His reedy voice faded into his churning stomach. He tested several directions, panicked, and ran. A tree leaped forward and knocked him flat. Warm blood leisurely trickled from his beakish nose. He lay back on the dirty ground as stars partied in his eyeballs. He knew he was beat. He was not going to be sucker punched by another invisible tree.

When the bleeding slowed, he crawled cautiously to what felt like a large, neutral pine tree. Strange rustlings, rattlings and calls that seemed to emanate from neither man nor beast gave birth to themselves and grew in the flora-clad blackness. Poul cringed against the tree, lowered his head and covered his ears.

"Dear God, save me from all this and I'll be the most faithful damned servant you've had since Job." Then he cursed himself. "Damn me! I do everything goddamn wrong. My whole life is a wrong turn. Now I'm lost in this God forsaken nature and I'm gonna die for a bunch of paper scraps. Christ, I hate dirt. Where's a streetlight when you need it?"

With his bloody face imbedded between his knees, Poul scratched the back of his neck, cursed, prayed and felt time expand with malicious elasticity. Morning seemed an eternity arriving.

CHAPTER 2

He must have dozed because Poul, who had never experienced dawn, missed this one, too. Joyous to be alive and rid of those awful night noises, he slowly stretched his legs. He gathered up his pages and limped back to the cheap motel he'd found the day before.

After breakfast he laid the songs out on the bed and studied them in these safer confines of the dirty beige room with the cheap painting of a 12-point buck staring with big black eyes. Poul circled above the pages like a one-man posse, walking around the bed and looking at them from different angles, nodding his head, sniffing and scratching nervously. "Hmm. Yes, yes." He lit a cigarette and chewed at his lower lip between puffs.

He took the painting down. He didn't like woods or wild things. Then he spent the rest of the day in his room, smoking, drinking coffee and wondering what to do with this mysterious gift. He wished he understood music. It *felt* like he had something good. Late that night he put the papers in a box. Then, vowing never to venture outdoors if it might mean being caught by night again, he crawled into bed and fell asleep.

If Poul knew how drastically the little box of papers would alter his life, he might have thrown them away and returned to his leaf marketing study. If he knew the songs would make him one of the wealthiest men in the United States, he would have laughed and mentally spent the money in a thousand newly rich ways. If he had known he would never use his millions, he may have become suicidal.

But Poul didn't throw away the songs and to almost the last day of his life he was never really sure if he came out on the top side of his hunch.

❦   ❦   ❦

The songs' original owner was perhaps the most imprisoned free man on earth. He had left home in his early twenties after spending the better part of his youth in the small town library reading everything from Aristotle to the rather lean selection of late 20th century works.

He spent every non-reading moment studying the guitar, piano and harmonica, the three instruments available in his small farm home. He studied songs with the meticulous greed of a bee poring over the season's last goldenrod. He played songs forward, backward, at different speeds and with different interpretations. He shoved himself inside them and burst them outward like melodic bombs.

By the time he hit his second decade, Mendel had read all he could ingest. He had also taken music as far as he could. He realized that he could not a find a song, the combinations of notes, chords and rhythm that was perfect. He began writing songs but quickly discovered that he didn't have the needed experience in writing or life. So with a canvas bag full of blank paper, a few pencils and the clothes he wore, Mendel simply left home to find life and write songs.

Eventually, he was sure, he would find the perfect song.

On his own, he quickly shed himself of time's burden. It was shelved in the same mental category as a chicken drumstick. It was something that for him was once solid and substantial, but was now only a thought. Time was a toxin invented by man who then gorged himself on it then wept when it was gone. Mendel went on a lifetime fast. Now, free of the false need for security and money, Mendel roamed, spending an entire season if he wished, studying the life of leaves from green bud to brown crust.

But within this new freedom, he was manacled by his drive to find the perfect song. He didn't care if it were published or heard by others. He just needed to find its parts and bring it to life. His gray bag bulging, Mendel walked. He avoided other humans. He scribbled a lot. Inside he was a seething sponge, gathering data, emotions, thoughts, fusing, synthesizing and with intermittent volcanic gushes, pouring forth dozens of songs at a time.

Right now he was on his hands and knees, one cheek to the ground, watching a grub inch its slimy way across the dirt to a slate chunk at a swamp's edge. He kept his eyes fixed on this little odyssey that took the grub over two dead maple leaves, 28 blades of grass, and two small rocks formed from layered semicircles of some form of carbon.

At one point Mendel stood up and frightened a hungry crow. The bird perched in a tree and cawed out a fury of obscenities at this human interruption. Mendel laughed. "Go find another! This one is helping me do research!" The crow screamed again and flew off.

Mendel made a note about a crow's temper. Nasty.

When the grub found its destination under a stone, Mendel, who had been lying on his stomach, turned over. "I wonder what something so slow thinks about?" He closed his eyes and placed himself in the grub world.

That night he wrote.

❧   ❧   ❧

Yes, if the songs were to be exploited, it must be legal. Poul could never be a crook. This trait was not of his choice. It, and numerous other neurotic mind bumps were due in part to Miss White, his Sunday School teacher. When Poul was five, he lifted six pennies from the collection plate. In his young mind, it seemed not like stealing but sharing the wealth of the Kingdom.

But the dour old Miss White, a woman who was never young and ever childless, thought differently when she caught little Poul with his pocket full of the Lord's change. Her hard blue eyes were plunked like flint buttons in a face whose lips formed a granite slit in a square jaw. As she looked down at him, little Poul knew he was in very deep shit. In later years, Poul often shook his head and said that women like Miss White should not be displayed to little children and unstable adults.

It was during her sermons that Poul developed the nervous habit of scratching and sniffing. Miss White introduced Poul and his friends to the Walls of Jericho, Sodom and Gomorrah, Babylong (as Poul understood it), and the Serpent Satan, among other tales of violence, evil and destruction. She had one favorite story, which she hauled out every six months.

"Today," she always began, "we will study Genesis, Chapter Seven." Then she'd pause, looking at each child's innocent expression. She'd take a slow, deep breath and in a tinny voice that could penetrate concrete, say dramatically, "The Flood." It sent chills down the kids' backs and the old woman judged her effectiveness by whether or not at least one child asked to go to the potty.

Then she would stand so the semi-paralyzed children had to follow the tight black dress up to her icy little eyes.

"And the children of God (which she pronounced "Gawd" in the tradition of many ostentatiously pious Christians to show their status above a common layman who just says "God"). "And the Children of God were eeevilll." She held her Good Book against her flat chest. "They imbibed themselves in eevilll ways…imbedding themselves in lechery, deecbouchery, alcohol, and sinful statues." She'd close her eyes. "And worst of all, they would lay down with men and women they were not married to." That seemed to bother her most of all, which was a mystery to the little Poul. If you're tired, you lay down. What does it matter if you're married?

"They were wicked fools!" Miss White would raise her hand, fingers stretched heavenward as the children prayed for God to send in their mothers. "Our Lord Gawd would not have this and grew sore angry and came drown from His almighty throne and said unto Noah: 'Noah, my children are exceedingly bad, *exceedingly* bad and I shall punish them verily with my Wrath and Fury. I am going to kill them all!'" Miss White would then glance with furious satisfaction at the terrified young faces. "But you have been good, Noah," she said now in a low voice, confident and smug in her role as God. "You have obeyed and feared me. Build an ark and collect a pair of animals so they can be saved and…flourish."

The woman took a long, slow breath that seemed to roar like a brimstone factory in the silent church basement. "And when the ark was finished, God made it rain forty days and forty nights and oh, oh, those wicked people cried in terror as the waters rose around them. And they cried out: "Dear God! Please have mercy! Don't kill us! Don't let us die!" But the rains continued and the waters rose until it covered them like fat wicked rats. Men, women, children and every living thing were soon dead, except for Noah, his family and his animals."

In Poul's mind, if only one family on the whole earth was good enough to live, God had some big improvements to make as a creator and role model. Here's a god who lays out a rule saying "thou shall not kill," then wipes out every living thing on the planet.

Obviously, omniscience isn't everything.

The rest of the story was short, being a general cursory outline of the dove and new beginnings. Miss White's primary purpose was to impress upon the children the exacting wages of ongoing sin. She also meant to let them know they'd better keep an eye on their friends and neighbors, because in the end, everybody pays.

When the teacher caught little Poul with the pennies, her expression was a mixture of malice, glee and Christian anger. Forgiveness was, of course, out of the question. That afternoon she made Poul memorize the Ten Command-ments and then recite them five hundred times. There was no way for him to cheat. She sat and listened to him, making a check after each complete recita-tion, then drew a circle around each set of 10 checks, then a line through each set of 10 circles.

The Ten Commandments were indelibly, infernally scrolled in mental cur-sive in the boy's brain, never to lose their power should he live to be a thousand years old. Sunday School made Poul a very nervous child.

In later years, he decided that God's punishment to adventurous children was to feed them to aging virgins in black dresses. And though he'd indulged in many small misdemeanors over the years, he had never stolen again, and never would. Miss White made a mess of his mind, but she'd straightened him out on stealing.

As it stood in his mind right now, the mountain had given him the songs. He knew an author was lurking about somewhere, but before he could make any kind of move, he decided to see just what the songs were, if anything. He took a bus to Syracuse, NY, to see his nephew Carl, a struggling young com-poser. The young man had recently earned his master's degree and worked as a musician in a small club and gave private lessons to spoiled children to support himself while he wrote.

He greeted Poul courteously. They barely knew each other. "You said you had some songs?" He asked, after the quick formalities.

Poul nodded and sniffed. "Yeah. I wanted to get your opinion."

Carl took the bundle. Though he was only 26, Carl's blonde hair was thin and receding. Must be in the damned family, Poul thought. "I can only give them a quick run through," Carl said. "I've got a lesson, then a gig downtown later."

Poul nodded and scratched the corner of his mouth. "That's all I wanted. "Thanks."

Carl played through a few compositions before the doorbell rang and a scowling boy with a stiff walk and a piano book stalked in. "Be right with you, Woody. Sit down over there," Carl said without looking up. The boy stared at the floor, dropped his book and plopped into the chair. Poul smiled uneasily at Woody who responded by flipping Poul the bird.

Carl ran through several songs before he stopped with an odd smile that contained pleasure and confusion. "A couple are a little rough, but there's some really good stuff here. A lot of power." He turned back to the last piece. "A lot of power," he said to himself, studying the arrangement. "I didn't know you wrote, Uncle Poul," he mumbled, lost in the notes on the sheet.

"Uh, I've just been fooling around. Boredom takes you in funny directions, I guess." He forced a quiet chuckle. "They're ok, huh?"

Carl nodded slowly. "I...there's something hypnotic about them...I..." He stopped, shaking his head to break the spell of the music. "I'm sorry. I have to give this lesson. I know a publisher in New York. He's one of the best. Send the songs with a letter using my name." He wrote out the name and address on the back of one of the sheets.

"Thanks for taking the time, Carl. I know you're busy."

"So they're yours, eh?" Carl asked rhetorically, as he escorted his uncle to the door. "They're really amazing. Let me know how you make out." They shook hands and said goodbye.

Had the young man just been polite and encouraging? No, there was too much surprise and awe in his voice. And his hands kept returning to the keys to finger out different passages, trying different interpretations, maybe trying to memorize them for his own use.... Poul's paranoia had always been a key to his survival. It had given his life a desultory edge, but it had also served to keep his senses sharp.

No, Carl wasn't bullshitting. He really liked the songs.

Acting swiftly for the first time in his life, Poul sent the songs to Carl's publisher friend, J.B. Beasely III, a young, ambitious businessman becoming well known for his ability to pick new talent, his maverick style of promotion and marketing, and his honesty.

Beasely had a reputation as a hard driver who left a lot of bodies by the wayside. The bodies were not victims of attacks, but rather those who could not or would not keep up with his frenetic pace and ability to read popular taste, a talent that was based as much on intuition as professionalism. It was widely known in publishing circles that Beasely's goal was to become the industry's top publisher, and nothing short of death would stop him. He was intensely hated and highly respected.

CHAPTER 3

❀

The phone rang six times before Poul picked up the receiver and very quietly said "hello." It was his experience, what with bill collectors, a greedy ex-wife and unfriendly relatives, that phone calls bearing good news were one of life's rarities.

"I'm looking for Poul." The authoritative voice was clear and direct.

Poul sniffed nervously and said, "That's me."

"This is J. W. Beasely." Poul's throat tightened and he bit his lower lip. He felt like a man being politely garroted. "Beasely, the publisher." Poul tried to get a word squeezed through his choking throat. "In New York! You sent me your frigging songs!"

"Yesh," Poul squeaked. He scratched at his throat. Open up! He cursed silently.

"Listen, we're both busy men," the voice said. "I want the songs you sent." Poul's brain circuit panel crackled, threatening a red alert. His ears were experiencing auditory mirage syndrome. He nodded. "You want them...."

"Yes. They're wild, a little—no, a lot—on the far side. Different than anything being done today. But my gut feeling says there's potential. I want to take a gamble on them." Poul nodded. "Look, we need to meet but to tell you the truth, I'd like to see more material...see if you can maintain the momentum. If it has the same power as what I've got in front of me, we're in business." Poul nodded again, staring at something he couldn't see.

"Listen," the voice continued, "I'm sending you a five thousand dollar advance. It's in the mail. We'll talk contracts later. You're living in a motel, right?"

Poul nodded, trying to make some kind of sound that could be interpreted as human. He sniffed, cleared his throat. "Yes. A motel. I'm…on the road. Uh, you said, five thousand…dollars?"

"It's what I think is fair. You're an unknown and this is very different stuff, but I have a feeling. I've got enough for a 10-song disc and I'm going to go with it. But I want enough for a quick follow-up if it sells. If it does, we'll talk money." There was an uneasy pause. "You can send me more songs, right?"

Poul nodded as if they were talking face to face, then caught himself. "Yes, uh, yes! Sure." He swallowed. "More…."

"I know this creative stuff takes time, but the sooner you can send me a new batch, the better. I'm having arrangements done of what I have right now. The disc could be out in just a few weeks."

A large, invisible hand reached inside Poul's stomach and squeezed hard, cutting out Poul's breath and forcing his heart to glop up toward his throat. What if the real writer saw the disc? Poul would not only be ruined and broke before he had a chance to be rich, he would have a permanent room in the iron bar motel.

"Don't use my name," he said quietly. "It has to be anonymous." There was a silence. Beasely's voice, when it returned was a monotone of disbelief. "I've never heard of an artist not wanting his name—"

"Please! It's very important. I'm…real introverted and my doctor says exposure could cause me to get, uh, suicidal. Worst case I could stop writing songs. And I'm writing as therapy." He scratched at his chest. "I'm a very bad case."

He could almost hear Beasely cursing under his breath. "Ok," he said finally. "Jesus, this is…artists usually have egos the size of…okay, okay…This time. But only because we're not emphasizing the artist as much as the art. We'll have to talk about this before I release anything else. If it sells…Christ, I think I'm crazy."

"Thanks, Mr. Beasely."

The publisher regained his ambushed authority and said briskly, "When you have more songs, bring them in person. Good talking with you." He hung up and Poul studied the phone, this bearer of incredible messages. Jesus Christ, he was about to be rich! Rich! Money by mail via some sodden songs lying on the dirty ground—making him filthy rich! Ha ha haa!

But through the melody of greenbacks wafting before his unblinking eye came the wicked reminder that the songs belonged to some really anonymous crackpot who was probably still cavorting around that grimy forest scribbling and tossing away a fortune. At least Poul hoped so.

It was bothersome that the songs Beasely had weren't exactly Poul's to sell. But he would deal with that later. After all, he did find them. They were on state forest land in a free country. He was merely doing his job as a citizen picking up litter. Someone else probably would have thrown them away. Yes, he found them and…. A feeling of illness crept like a gentle, expanding flu into his body. How in God's name would he find more songs? How do you ask for a million-in-one chance twice? If he didn't find more, the game was over.

It was a quest in a land full of mines. If he found no more songs, he was finished. If the real author found out, he was finished. No, the author had relinquished the material. Still…. "Oh, damn," he moaned, rocking back and forth on his bony butt, feeling alone. He could feel the hairs along the sides of his head loosen as he scratched at them. "I'm going to be a bald con with a nervous condition," he thought. But, he thought, he would be a hairless, aging vagrant if he didn't at least try to seek out more songs.

He kicked at a bed leg. Why did life always get complicated? "God damn it!"

Money was being sent to him by a man he never met for some songs he'd found, songs written by someone totally unknown. Through the night he tossed in bed. God knew he didn't steal those pennies in church and He knew Poul wasn't stealing now, he told himself. He was sharing, making a commodity available. He was nothing more than a recycler, a retailer, giving something Party One didn't want to Party Two who did want it. And Party Two was paying him. So what if Beasely thought he was the author? Poul would rectify that in the future. Somehow.

As the sun washed out the night, so too did it seem to clean up his stream of consciousness. He rose, nervous and exhausted, packed a small bag and headed out the motel door to his future, praying that he could find more songs which meant nothing to him.

Nothing but money and freedom.

❧   ❧   ❧

Wandering through the woods, he kicked leaves, turned rocks and tripped over hidden roots. "Damn stuff ought to be caged!" He mumbled and cursed as he traipsed the mountain. Mental conflicts and lack of sleep made his nerves raw. There had to be, he told himself, a composer in this mass of trees, field grass and rocks, and Poul had to find him. It was that simple. There was a hunter and a huntee. Reduced to that simplicity, Poul was able to keep his feet moving and his eyes on the ground. Whenever the complexities of money, morals, ownership and basic truthfulness sneaked into his mind, he chased them out again. A hunter and a target. That's all.

Survival.

He found nothing. His second night in the forest was no easier than the night he discovered the papers. He was exhausted but whenever he dozed some rotten animal or a formless thing made a sound and woke him. He did not like nights without the comforting structure of rooms, streets and other concrete geometries. This damned nature was totally without form or any sense of purpose at all—and it was filled with wild things.

When the morning light returned, however, the thoughts of riches drove him on. The end of the second day silently greeted the empty-handed man. He felt himself near tears at the prospect of yet another night alone in the woods. He built a clumsy fire, cooked some soup, then crawled under a bush after first beating it to scare away snakes.

For all the good it did. Fears rose like organic tombstones fertilized by the fecund darkness. His mind gave shapes to the sounds around him—a bear ready to maul him and eat his innards as he screamed his way to death; snakes slithering into his trousers to get warm and biting him with his first move.

There was no end to the monsters. Fortunately there was an end to night. The next morning, cold, stiff, and nearly delirious with lack of sleep, he vowed to quit. He found a small stream and drank. He ate the last of his granola bars. Then, cursing himself, his luck, and everything outside every city limit, he began walking.

It appeared as a mirage when he first spotted it. A little white, fragile, mocking mirage. He continued toward it, a scrap of paper scuttling softly over the landscape. When something in his mind convinced him that it was real, he broke into a shaky trot, then began running. A stone shot up in his path in front of his foot and he landed solidly on his face.

"Suvabithh," he mumbled, spitting out bits of grass. He pushed himself up painfully. Limping toward the paper, and wiping his mouth with a scrawny, quivering hand, he knew his nervous system was on the verge of total bankruptcy. He had to leave soon. "Lousy forests. Dirty, messy places…big, rotting junkyard of dead wood and deer shit!"

He reached the paper and picked it up, his tired, cynical mind not caring anymore if it were a song or a Big Mac wrapper. He smoothed it out and as he did, the notes unfolded as if by magic. He sat down on the ground without taking his eyes off it. As he studied it, each note seemed to melt away the delirium, the fears, and despair that had increasingly littered his mind.

"This is it! I've found it!" He yelled. "There *are* more! Oh God, I'm saved!" Yes, he could write more songs for Beasely! He could be rich!

He kissed the paper, then wiped the tears of joy from his eyes to study it better. Yes, there was no mistaking the hurried marks of a hand scurrying to keep up with the rushing mind. The silver black sheen of worn pencil, the lines of poetry under the hasty notes, and footnotes scribbled all around the edges. This was his man!

Though he found no other papers that afternoon, he knew there were more. He didn't know how he knew. He just knew. His night was blanketed by dreams of floating on warm, white pillow clouds in a sapphire sky and beautiful women in black satin dresses with diamonds, provided by Poul, draping their collarbones. Nights of love and laughter.

He awoke damp and shivering and stood up as soon as his stiff legs would allow. He brushed off stems and leaf bits and scratched his neck. His whole body itched. He was anxious to find more songs and get the hell out of here.

During his first three days of searching, Poul had devised a strategy should he find a song. He now put his plan into action. He began walking in widening circles until he found another paper, then another and another, until he established a paper trail in this wilderness. Creating a pattern he would follow for a long time, Poul stooped to snatch up a paper with one eye on it and the other eye searching for the next one.

During the ensuing days of the hunt, Poul thought about thousands of things, but primary on his obsessed mind were three thoughts:

-A fervent hope that the creator of these songs didn't discover him;

-The blatancy of the creator's rejection of the works and therefore the obvious claim to ownership Poul could make to them;

-The potential for the rich and happy life he was reaping in his gathering efforts.

The third thought always made him laugh with a sense of incredible luck and quiet victory. Success was as simple as picking litter!

By the end of the sixth day, Poul again began to despair for another reason. There seemed to be no end to the papers. They just kept appearing as he moved. He was exhausted. His food supply had run out two days before and he was forced to munch on strange plants, hoping none were poisonous. His clothes were ruined with mud, sweat, dew and sun. His sharp face was stubbled with a beard growth that itched constantly. He was living like an animal…with diarrhea. And he hadn't had a full night's sleep in a week. Nature was not a pleasant bedfellow.

That night he lay down, knowing he had to return to his motel or not return at all. His strength would not hold out much longer.

The morning light, to the attentive, always seems to bring some little gift. Now that Poul had nearly convinced himself that the songs were being manufactured by a band of invisible tune-crazed trolls, he found Mendel.

The man sat in a small clearing in the distance, hunched forward, head-on his chest, beard falling toward his crotch. He appeared to be in some kind of meditation.

"I'll be damned," Poul whispered. His heart kicked into fourth gear at the sight of the man. Poul had hit the end of the trail. He had come to the source.

Now what? In emergencies, the mind takes over and works swiftly, tromping over such obstacles as philosophies, moral and ethical questions and the possible consequences of various actions.

Poul hid.

A few minutes later the man came to life, his hairy head popping up from his chest as the arms reached for paper and pencil. He furiously scribbled on the paper, sat and studied it, then wrote again.

This went on for hours. Poul watched. The man was, Poul concluded, mad.

While he wrote, he threw all his energies into slamming marks on the paper, his dark hair fairly trembling with the might of his outpouring. Each time he stopped writing, he remained as still as an ancient philosopher who has busted beyond the constraining concepts of time and mortal life. When he lit into the paper again, his actions were those of a condemned man who raced against the dwindling hours to put down the last note.

The man was now on his twelfth page. After studying it, he quietly cursed, crumpled the paper and flung it. He repeated the process throughout the day, with the exception of a few pages that he stuffed into his bag.

Poul sat with his back against the tree in the distance, munched a grass stalk and watched the man create "his" songs and make him richer with each violent rejection. As he leisurely absorbed the man's image and actions, he smiled. Life never looked better, its beauty and promise never so glorious.

Life truly was a song. Poul thought of his nephew in his little apartment, who moved at the pace of a tranquilized turtle compared to this madman before him.

"Carl," he smiled to himself. "You want to know where real art is created? It happens in the middle of some big, dirty woods by a nut who hasn't had a haircut or new clothes in years, a man who writes songs then throws them away like stale peanuts. Carl, you ought to get out and see more of the real world. Heh heh."

Poul estimated the man to be about his age, maybe a year or two older.

It was hard to tell from the distance. All he could make out from the man's profile was the straight, proud nose that protruded rebelliously from the mass of dark hair and beard. He could, however, almost feel the waves of energy and frustration that emanated from the man as he struggled to translate what was in his mind onto paper.

Poul sighed and leaned his head back against the pine tree as he watched this man compose the rest of Poul's life.

"Keep on tossing those pages friend," he thought. "I'll clean up after you. Heh heh. What a team…."

CHAPTER 4

The crow's brash caws were like a file scraping open a rusty can as it helped sweep negative energies from the atmosphere. Mendel listened until the crow headed elsewhere. Then he lit a fire. He filled his pan with water and boiled fresh mushrooms and milkweed leaves. When he finished eating, he watched the orange flames draw inward, thin and small, licking out with weakening fury. Occasionally a flame shot out above the rest, in futile defiance of its fate. When the final flame fell backward into smoldering nothingness, Mendel bent over the ashes. He idly wondered where fire went when it was gone. He looked at once playful and serious, as a child does when the doll it has brought to life recedes back into doll hood, closing off its wonderful dimension.

Mendel slowly covered the warm ashes and stared at the sky that dappled blue above the maple, oak and ironwood leaves. The warm, heavy smell of chicken, by some process of olfactory ghostliness entered his head. He saw his mother, thin and gentle, always smiling sadly, stirring the pot like a humble artist, creating a new work of recyclable art. Reminded of all he did not have, he packed his bag and moved on. There were so many missing parts to the song, and each time he wrote, he felt he was only at the beginning.

It was as though the perfect song were a rain drop that fell and exploded into thousands of droplets, each of which fragmented into thousands more individual dots of moisture. And each of these broke into millions of atoms that were absorbed into everything he saw, felt, heard, smelled, tasted and thought. How does one collect all those parts and reassemble them when even a whole lifetime is but a fragment, an atom in the world which itself is but a fragment of a raindrop in a vast universe?

When Mendel disappeared over the hill, Poul cautiously moved in and picked up the papers. He scanned through them, moving his lips to the rhythm of the poetry beneath the notes.

"Hmm. Fine looking little tune here. Damn fine." Within a couple of months, Poul had memorized the man's habits, general speed and travel pattern. It was time to head back. He scratched his chest and back of his neck. Near as he could tell, he'd been tailing the writer a couple of years. Whenever he was near a town, he'd called Beasely to let him know he was still working. But, he realized now, he hadn't called in several months.

His whole body was crawling with dirt and assorted bits of nature that seemed to assume a new life inside his clothes. But soon he would have a bath and would be clean and rich. He was going home to clean up. Heh heh. "Beasley, baby, here I come. Your little genius has picked up some new inspiration! Ha!" Yes, he could picture it all now. A bath, a cigarette, a little something from the top shelf. Wasn't life grandly orchestrated?

❧   ❧   ❧

It felt great to back in civilization! Ah, Manhattan, city of cities, center of all that's wealthy! Home of Wall Street! Cars lined nose-to-bumper! Horns of all pitches honking in a music that Poul understood! Taxi drivers yelling in funny languages! This, by God, was *life*! Poul knelt down and kissed the sidewalk.

"Welcome to America," a passerby said, thinking Poul was a new immigrant.

"Thank you." Poul breathed in the smog-laced exhaust fumes with joy, weaving around people on the crowded sidewalk until he found the building containing the Beasely offices. As he rode the elevator to the 25th floor, the quick stares of business people in their tailored outfits made him self-conscious. He realized he should have taken the time to buy some new clothes and get a haircut. But he had been in too much of a hurry to get out of the mountains, and to deliver the songs to the publisher.

He entered the office suite, a ragged sight with torn, dirty clothes, and smelling musty. His beard, small dark eyes and bald head gave him the appearance of a maniacal prophet. The filthy canvas bag slung over his shoulder rounded out the picture.

A young brunette, with a picture perfect look that takes two morning hours to achieve, surveyed the grizzled, skulking man. Her disgust and fear were obvious. "I'm afraid you have the wrong office." Her words slid toward him on tiny cubes of ice. "I'm going to have to ask you to—"

He spoke quickly before he lost his nerve and ran from this iron angel. "I'd like to see Mr. Beasely. I'm—"

"That's impossible," she said, reaching for the phone.

"—Poul."

The secretary froze. She slowly drew her hand from the phone. "Poul?" She asked in a suddenly timid voice. He nodded, tentatively. "The…composer Poul?" He hesitated, shocked by the title. Then he nodded again. "The one who writes the songs?" He shrugged and nodded. Now it was her turn to feel intimidated and her face reddened with the silliness of the last question.

She stood up and Poul swallowed. She could easily be one of the women in his many dreams on the mountain. She was beautiful and built in a way that could make a man forget such small matters as time and power and maybe even money.

She was also smart and businesslike, realizing that saying anything more would be chancing inanity again. "Mr. Beasely has been waiting for you." She opened the door behind her and disappeared inside. Poul heard her whisper "He's here!" like an excited high school girl. A moment later she reappeared and opened the door, motioning Poul inside.

He cleared his throat and mumbled his thanks and she said, "You're welcome, sir," as he stepped inside. I'm in Oz, he thought, finding himself on a plush gold carpet in a room of teakwood walls decorated with gold records, autographed photos of recording stars and shelves with gold and silver mementos. In the middle of the room, behind a large oak desk stood a small man in a custom-tailored beige suit. The thick blonde hair and deep blues eyes gave an intense, commanding air to the otherwise bland, round face. He stepped around the desk with his hand outstretched. "Poul! So happy to meet you finally. "I'm J.B. Beasely III." They shook hands. It was obvious by his quick, sure motions that the young publisher was a hard driving man who would never be content with just having. For him, life was the process of getting, with all its intricacies of business, personal relationships and strategies.

He motioned to the chairs and coffee table at the side of the office. "Sit down. Relax. You look like you've had adventures in Never-Never Land and barely survived to tell about it."

Poul sat down. He had never experienced a leather chair before. It was good.

Beasely stared at the spindly, dirty man with unabashed curiosity, until Poul sniffed and shifted uncomfortably. Beasely realized his impropriety and broke his gaze. "I'm sorry! It's just that I've been waiting so long to meet you." He pulled out a long thin cigar from a leather case and lit it. He paced before Poul with a nervous energy.

"You're just as I pictured!" Then he laughed. "Of course you are! I called your nephew Carl and asked for a description so I'd know you. Listen, call me J.B. All my friends do. Ok?" He puffed his cigar, shooting smoke from the corner of his mouth like a coal-burning engine gathering speed for an uphill run. "So where the hell have you been? I've been worried sick! Tried to call, no answer. Sent a messenger. Nobody home. I thought I'd lost you."

He spoke as if they'd known each other for years. Poul nodded, thinking the man was as intense and crazy as the loony songwriter he'd just chased through the mountains. Something about the publisher grated on Poul—the energy maybe, the need to talk, deal, command—but he also liked the man. He seemed like an honest guy and that was enough.

"Thanks for your concern, Mr. Beasely."

"J.B." Poul smiled and nodded. Beasely laughed. "Concern is an understatement. Poul, you are fast becoming one of the hottest composers in the country." He waved his cigar in the air as if it were a magic wand opening a new world. "There's no question but what you will be *the* hottest in a short time with the, uh, new material?"

He made a short jab with the cigar wand at the bag. His expression was a strange combination of boyish wonder, polite inquiry and lust. Poul nodded and patted the bag. Beasely smiled.

The lovely secretary entered with a tray of coffee and pastries. "I thought you might like these," she said to neither man in particular.

"Thank you Sharon. That was very thoughtful," Beasely said.

He sat down in the chair beside Poul and poured the coffee. "As you know, your records are selling around the country and picking up speed at an incredible pace. I don't have the figures in my head, but I can get them. I've never seen anything like it! Listen, Poul, I've been in the business for 15 years and my dad was in it for 30, and I'd stake my whole firm on the hunch that you'll be bigger than—hell—*anybody*! His deep blue eyes were windy sea excited. He looked straight into Poul's face. Poul didn't like to look at anybody head-on and picked at the hole in his ragged jeans.

Beasely continued talking, telling Poul how he'd inherited the firm when his father, a laconic, pipe smoking Liszt lover, died of cardiac apathy, which his son interpreted as heartbreak, or at least a loss of hope.

"Dad always waited for The Big One—an artist who would take him from a small, can't-complain business to a major label that commanded respect," he said. He puffed reflectively on the cigar before his eyes grew hard. "But a nice, philosophical gentleman doesn't make it in this business." He began pacing. "Young artists flocked to the company to cut their first record. If they had potential, larger companies sneaked in like filthy coyotes and bought the artist. Then they'd push 'em, burn 'em out, even kill 'em."

"They killed them?" Poul said, puzzled.

"Figuratively, sure! Hell, an occasional fatality—drug overdose the most common...suicide...plane crashes. Keeps a certain mystique about the whole business. Look at the icons the companies—and the public forged: Morrison, Joplin, Hendrix, Kobain! Occasional death is just good business."

Mentioning his father made Beasely pause. He looked over at the portrait of the man with the kind face and gentle eyes. His father was simply too friendly and easy-going to succeed. His wife, Beasely's mom, tired of him and flew away with a French publisher of eroticism and the old man died a few years later. The young Beasely took over with a vow to become the largest in the business. And no one would push him around.

The vow was for his father, but his ambition was powered by that generator of so much human activity—fear. It was the fear of failure, disguised, as with so many men, as the positive desire for success. His father died a failure—a very nice man, but a failure. Beasely III would die a success or clawing his way toward it.

Poul slowly ate a donut, fighting his sugar-starved body's commands to gobble it whole. He also knew that keeping his mouth full would give him time to assimilate all this. He had not given any thought to the process of becoming rich, which in this case was the production and promotion of records. He had lived his miserable existence these past couple years solely on Beasley's promise that he would give Poul a lot more money for more songs.

Finally he cleared his mouth and said. "So the first batch of, uh, records, is selling well, eh? That's great to hear. What does that mean in terms of—"

"Royalties?"

Poul nodded. He was thankful for the interruption. He was about to say "money." Royalties was much more businesslike.

Beasely looked puzzled a minute, then nodded with sudden understanding. "Of course, you haven't been home. We've sent you a second check for $10,000, and a third for another $10,000. It's not much but it's early. The word is spreading like wildfire and we can't keep it stocked. We've stepped up production and we're widening distribution. There'll be more."

Poul nodded, rubbing his chin in wonder. Beasely pointed to the bag on floor. "How are these? Is there a theme like the last batch?"

Poul's stomach did a belly flop. He pulled a cigarette from the tray and quickly lit it, praying that the nicotine would still his quivering hands. Damn! What in hell had he been thinking about all that time in the woods? He had waltzed in here dirty, smelly and totally unprepared. He must have an asshole for a brain.

He took a deep drag on the cigarette. "Well, they're a little rough...I don't really think about themes. The stuff—songs—just kind of appear, and I, mm grab them before they get away." He took another drag and dug at his ear. "They're like a gift and I don't really try to analyze too much, you know?" Please say you know, he mentally pleaded to Beasely as he knocked ashes into the ashtray. Please say something. He gathered his courage and turned to look at Beasely who was nodding.

"I understand. In fact, you hit it right on the head. An artist's job is to create, not to analyze." Then, almost to himself, he said, "I should have realized. The incredible passion of the first batch, that you don't stop to think about...and yet the songs are so—what?—*precise* in their passion..." He broke the thought with a wave of his hands, jumped up and rushed to the intercom on the desk. "Send the Poul staff up and tell the studio musicians to be ready tomorrow."

Poul's voice squeaked. "Poul staff?" What region of the Twilight Zone had he walked into?

Beasely relit his cigar, took a puff and smiled. "I knew you'd be back with more songs. And I told you, I'm betting my existence on you, Poul. We're going to be big."

Clouds of smoke trailed behind him as he renewed his pacing. "You're one of those extremely rare geniuses in history with the good fortune of having the right timing. The public loves you. And they're buying your art while you're still alive and young enough to enjoy it. That doesn't happen often, at least not with good art. Now, I'll take some of the credit, between you and me. I assembled a hell of a batch of the best arrangers and musicians to interpret the material. In short, it's paying off and—" Beasely stopped and studied Poul with a look of mild alarm. "You're awfully pale. You're sweating. Maybe a touch of the flu. I'll call a doctor."

"No!" Poul leaned back in the leather chair feeling nauseous and weak. "I'll be ok. Really. I guess I haven't eaten much lately. Been working awful hard. And all this is new and scary."

Beasely nodded, then smiled and grabbed the phone. "Miss Stone…" A little later the beautiful secretary brought in steak, potatoes, green peas, pie and orange juice. Poul shook his head in disbelief. When his angel of nourishment began cutting up the steak and feeding him, he succumbed fully to this new world. Yes, being a songwriter was worth every second of the suffering. He chewed the tender meat and watched the silky blouse-covered mounds rise and fall before him with the perfumed rhythm of their own special song.

In the following days and nights, Beasely and Poul were together constantly. The publisher bought Poul new clothes, found him an apartment, took him to the best restaurants and to the studios where the second album was being constructed from the scraps of paper. Each day brought new reports of the debut album continually picking up sales. Poul was learning a lot, fast, about the business side of music. The people in the business—especially Beasely—ate, drank and slept music.

Poul loved it all.

But though the hectic days and melodic nights were fun, the forest and the real artist weighed on Poul. As the months passed, Beasely kept harping for more songs to meet his next deadline. For Poul, that meant returning to the forest, wallowing through that filth, lying awake nights, and worrying about animals. It meant living like one hunted himself as he foraged, constantly bending over to pick up songs and keeping his eye open for the composer, angry landowners, and rattlesnakes. Everytime he thought about returning, the now well-dressed, slightly heavier Poul broke out into hives, chained smoked and itched.

One night they sat in a small, expensive restaurant that Beasely frequented. Poul finished his meal of sirloin and mushrooms sautéed in delicate sauce of butter imported from Switzerland and white wine. The waiter hovered about them, seeming to read their every desire. God, this was the life!

"Beasely, cities are God's gift to civilization," he said, lighting a cigarette. "It's what He had in mind since the Old Testament."

"I've never known anything but New York," Beasely said. "I mean I spend some time in L.A. But all the rest…they're consumers."

Poul nodded, relaxed, more contented than he ever could have imagined.

He knew he had to go back. If he quit now, he could live modestly for a few years off the royalties that were mounting. If he gathered more songs, and they were as popular, he could become a millionaire within the space of a few years.

Besides, dirty as it was, it was his job.

A few days later Beasely flew Poul to Los Angeles where he'd hired an orchestra to play a demo set of the first songs. "I wanted a live orchestra so you can get the full effect of your work," he explained. He shook his head, causing his blond hair to slightly shake. "I know no group of humans can match the power and scope of your vision, but I think we'll come real close."

The orchestra took off on the second movement of the Bird Songs. Poul was so overwhelmed with the works that for awhile he forgot that he hadn't written them, so in tune were they with inner feelings he rarely expressed and often dismissed. The works carried such a power, grace and defiance of the earth and its gravitational chains that he felt he himself could soar into the heavens in total Mercurial freedom.

When the movement ended, both men were still. Poul was speechless, still struggling to return from the sky to solid ground. Beasely, too, wore an expression of distance and contented hypnosis. Finally he sighed and turned to Poul. "What do you think?"

"Fantastic," Poul nodded.

"A fairly accurate translation then?" Beasely asked like a boy waiting for approval.

Poul nodded. "Oh, yeah. You hit it."

Beasely relit his cigar which had gone out during the performance. "The next set contains material that you just brought back. I haven't heard this stuff myself. The men sat back and listened. The songs were about leaves, birth, lust, rain, aging and dying. They were pretty, but quieter than the bird songs. There was a gentleness about them. There was much about harmony and the necessary violence of survival, but the violence carried no anger or bitterness, nor even understanding—just acceptance. The only sadness was the moment a dead leaf was finally ripped from its limb by the wind and fluttered helplessly downward, accepting its transition as it landed upon its bed of earth. The song tore through the hard facades of the two listeners, and they wept.

When the set was finished and he knew he could speak without his voice cracking, Poul said, "You did a wonderful job."

Beasely blew his nose and sighed. "Thank you."

On the return flight to New York, Poul lit a cigarette and nearly said, "I don't know that much about music—the business part." He exhaled, mentally warning himself to be more careful. "New York is full of musicians, Beasely. Why did you go to California for them?" Beasely smiled, his round face looking at once innocent and wise. "LA is the only place where we could find musicians desperate, wild and crazy enough to truly interpret the anarchy of the music. If you knew the background of some of those guys—and women—who just played for you, you wouldn't have entered the place without a machine gun and a dozen bodyguards."

Poul nodded and leaned back, thankful for ignorance.

"I don't want to push you, but when can we plan on more songs?"

Poul thought a moment and shrugged, wondering how long it would take to track down his man and if there would be anything to pick up "When I find—the, uh, inspiration. You know what I mean." Shit. He wondered if he subconsciously wanted to get caught.

Beasely was silent, staring out the plane window. Did he catch the slip? Poul felt uneasy. Finally Beasely cleared his throat. "I'm trying to figure out the promotion timing. I'd like to have an estimate—if it's possible," he added almost apologetically.

Poul nodded again, wondering not if he were in over his head but how far over. "Let me think on it."

"Ok."

Poul crushed out his cigarette and dug at his thigh. Somewhere, 14,000 feet below, the crazy man was writing, he hoped. The immediate danger of getting caught had passed and Poul slid back into semi-confidence. Yes, he was sure the man was writing. He had to be. Poul's career depended on it. Hell, so did this crazy artist's career depend on it. I've made him what he is today, Poul thought. He'd be nowhere without me.

Beasely puffed on his unlit cigar, still working out promotion strategies. "Oh yeah, about using your name this time. How do you want—"

"No!" Poul was yanked from his reverie. "No," he said more quietly. "I'm sorry, I can't...Not yet."

"Why not, for God's sakes?" Beasely's round face showed confusion and anger.

Poul thought quickly. "I'm afraid of being found out." It was the most honest statement he'd made yet about the music.

Beasely took a gulp of his scotch straight up. The drone of the planes engines covered their silence. "I don't know if I can go any further without a name, a live composer."

"You have to, Beasely."

"It will hurt us both, everything."

"You said the music speaks for itself."

"I need promotional material. You can't promote what doesn't exist!" Beasely squeezed his glass to control his anger.

Poul looked him directly in the eye. "Work with what you've got this time." The tone of his voice said there was no room for an answer.

The next 1,000 miles were flown in silence as the plane pushed heavily through the darkness.

CHAPTER 5

Poul found the artist a few hundred miles west of where he had left him. It had taken several months to pick up the paper trail and collect the material that led to the man.

Now that he knew the man's location, Poul doubled back to make sure he hadn't missed any papers. As he continued his search, he thought about introducing himself and telling the fellow his songs were selling fast and that patches of devoted, almost fanatical followers were springing up around the country, trying to establish the identity of the mysterious, faceless, nameless genius.

In fact, that's what Beasely was worried about. "In everything, there is a void," he told Poul at dinner one night. "If you don't fill the void with what you want, others will fill it in, and in every case, it won't be what *you* want. Good marketing is creating an image and filling the void with it, then convincing people they need or want it. In this case we don't have to convince them. But you're killing me Poul, with this mystery bullshit."

Maybe he was right, but Poul had no choice until he could figure out an alternative. To him, taking the songs uninvited was ethically questionable, but manageable. He would not take credit for another man's work, however. He was tempted, certainly, but the image of the horrible Miss White loomed in his mind. Getting caught was the most humiliating thing in the world.

He thought of introducing himself to this crazy guy, but he didn't. If the man was happy with his work, he wouldn't be throwing it away, Poul reasoned. There was also the very real possibility that if the artist learned of his success, he might just stop writing and enjoy his money and fame and be ruined. Or the sudden shock of the success, coupled with the culture shock of re-entry into society might even mentally impair the man, who was obviously high strung, sensitive and half crazy anyway.

Poul shuddered at the thought. Yes, the man might very well fall over the edge and kill himself. Artists did that, Poul knew. He'd heard stories of artists, wiping their brain slate clean with artillery, leaping with a single bound off tall bridges, spilling their guts with Hari Carving swords.

They were a strange bunch. It must be hell to be an artist, Poul thought. They didn't need religion to give them a Satan. They were their own worst enemies. No, he kept concluding, scratching his neck and shaking his head with a mature air of responsible deliberation. To tell the man at this point about his success could ruin both their careers.

There's a time and place for everything.

❀   ❀   ❀

His bag hanging heavily on his slightly stooping shoulder, Mendel continued westward. To any of the few strangers he met, Mendel was simply a hobo, a ragged anachronism looking for a bowl of soup and a slow train.

He wandered seemingly without direction, his tattered, colorless clothes flapping freely about him. The feature that distinguished him from other wanderers was the large, dark eyes that fastened their gaze upon their subject with undisguised curiosity and total concentration. The many people who briefly saw him in early years remembered the eyes. Later, when Mendel's fame had spread, these people described him to reporters, collectors, and bounty hunters as a man who just was. They spoke of his gentle, quiet countenance that contrasted almost unnaturally with the powerful eyes that bore into subjects with an innocent but intense openness. A few of the more highly-strung witnesses said that after talking with them for just a few minutes, Mendel knew their very souls.

Once his supposed powers were amplified and reported on, thousands of spiritually undirected souls would seek him out. This would cause a natural backlash of egotists to also search him out. Both groups would want something. The first would want his words; the second would want his life.

Mendel stopped in the Midwest and listened to its music. He lay for weeks on the grassy plains and absorbed the grumble of the huge tractors in the cornfields, the laborers' grunts and the sound of the farmer's hand brushing the sweat from his forehead.

He took particular notice of the children's playful yelling in the fields and on the one-and-a-half lane dirt roads. The sounds were rich and full-bodied, flowing outward until they disappeared into the expansive sky. What a contrast, he thought, to the yelling of children in cities like Chicago. Their sounds rang sharp and hollow and beat themselves to cacophonic shreds against the concrete that closed around them. Mendel gathered choruses from the stout, middle-aged housewives fixing supper, and the music of the clean wind that whooshed in a sonorous sighs over the wheat fields' amber waves. He gathered the men's curses that sprang from their lungs in earthy rhythms, and swirled with the sad bawling cattle and short heavy grunts of pigs snuffling through the world with snouts groundward.

He listened to the sounds of the Methodist ministers who spoke of Heaven in quiet, gentle voices, and to the hymns that wafted from the small white churches and rose upward with an age-old confidence that goodness is, after all is said and done, its own reward.

From these notes he wrote strong, clean songs full of clear rhythms and coursing blood, the acrid sweet odor of dark manure mingling with the heavy dampness of springtime sod, the sound of ebullient oaths ringing pure in the unpolluted air, and the simple blessing spoken over the supper table heavy with food.

The songs were his best yet, he felt. He had paired the richness of human blood with the soil's deep texture. He had fused the cold clarity of creek water with the steaming pungent piss of the horse and cow. He had captured the tension of the hand's muscle as it gripped the tractor wheel that directed the plow—now and generations ago. "Seeds and sweat," he wrote in his notebook.

One day he passed an old farmer taking a break to have some ice tea from his thermos. Mendel wrote down the man's summation of his life. "Drink, sweat and pee."

He spent weeks in an abandoned barn full of soft sounds of pigeons and worked on the songs, loving the land and the people and the songs' essence so much that he was tempted to stop writing, give his brain a pat on the rump and send it out to pasture. He would spend the rest of his life working with his hands and trusting to nature for the rest, just like his father had.

Poul spent his nights shivering in the sprawling cornfield that Mendel was now forming into poetry. The sword-like leaves rattled against each other like an endless graveyard of hyper tense skeletons. Poul's enthusiasm for his prey was about as bubbly as a dust bowl.

"What the hell am I still doing here?" He muttered at the ears of corn. The top of his head was freezing. He had read somewhere that 60 percent of your body heat goes right out the top of your head. Why he didn't bring a hat was beyond him. The few hairs left on the top were going to freeze and fall off.

"What's he doing out here? Batch of smelly farmers cussing out animals, pouring that sickening slop in trays for a bunch of pigs. *Real* pigs for Christ's sakes. What kind of man spends his life serving a pig?" He stopped. Christ, he was picking up scraps left by a man writing about men who waited on swine. Life was too absurd.

"Beasely's going to be sorely disappointed with this batch," he thought, "If the madman ever lets them go." He pulled his coat up around his neck and shuddered each time the corn rattled. "I hate dirt!" He scratched his cheek. He had shaved off his beard in New York to look civilized again. Now it was back and itching constantly. "I hate dirt and everything that comes out of it…except food. Jesus, what I wouldn't give for some ham and eggs…."

That night Poul developed a theory that he would amend, improve upon and resort to in distressful times throughout his life. It was this: Eden began in fact as a lovely resort complex with revolving bars, room service and heated pools, all surrounded by geometric concrete walks, streets, courtyards with a tasteful few plants for effect, and no weather. When Adam and Eve received their walking papers, they were sent from Paradise into nature to sweat their asses off in this God-awful dirt. Sex being their only pleasurable diversion from work and toil, they begot some troublesome kids who begot others, who continued begetting until they worked their procreative tricks down to Miss White and this crazy, song-flinging fool who was now holed up in a barn writing about animals.

How far we have come from Eden, he thought sadly.

Well, as for himself, he would simply send his mind back to his snug little Eastside apartment and look out over the city while he sipped his wine and listened to the music of the traffic and sirens and fully appreciate God's concrete beauty. He fell asleep and dreamed.

The wind-driven rain was tearing down in oblique gray sheets when Mendel woke. He was glad for the crops, which had been begging for water. He felt good with himself, too, having nearly captured to his satisfaction the songs of the land around him. Nearly.

He spent the day going over the material, shaking his head and driving himself into a bad mood. It all seemed so fresh and full when he first wrote it. Now almost everything seemed, if not shallow, then anemic compared to what he had felt and what he heard in his mind when he wrote it.

He felt as if he were on a road, both sides of which were bare and it was up to him to create the Everything on both sides, and though he had done his best, there were still large chunks of nothingness. Some areas were gaping holes that laughed with wide, toothless mouths at his lack of experience and his inability. Some gaps—like a missing fruit fly or a fallen raven feather lying half buried in a rusting sluice pipe—just seemed too endless to ever fill in.

To make matters worse, some of his created parts were misshapen, deformed, mangled from birth by a rushing creator who had neither the microscopic nor the sweeping vision of natural design to complete the structure. Nothing he did met the expectations of his mind. Nothing he did matched the intensity of emotions he felt when he wrote it. Drivel!

He jumped up, and for a moment stared at the barn boards, shiny with years of scuffing leather boots, sliding, bristly hay bales and brooms pushing loose hay to bawling black and white Guernseys. "Damn it!" He yelled. The pigeons in the loft whirred about the barn's top with the explosion of his voice. He pushed open the barn door and stood back as the furious wind blew the papers around the empty mow, sucking them haphazardly into the vast storm outside. He picked up some that the wind missed and tossed them out the second story door, wishing he could throw his tears and this insane drive into the wind with them.

Later, when the rain stopped, he stepped outside and watched a page somersault across the grass and impale itself on the rusty tine of an unused hay rake. "Who am I kidding?" He wondered. "Everything is a song and nothing is perfect."

He picked up a rock to heave it, but was captured by the pink and silver speckle of the granite chunk. He ran his fingers over the coarse skin of a broken side and for an instant felt its pulse and breath in his hand.

He pictured the millions of atoms inside the rock that moved so much slower than his own. Time, for a rock, moves slowly, taking millions of years to form and millions of years to decompose. He found this rock in the middle of its million-year instant in eternity. He felt as frail and fleeting as a bubble rising from a rushing stream and popping in the air. Ha! To the rock, Mendel's entire life was an eye blink, his grasp on it nothing more than the merest tip of a fleeting shadow of a buried memory. Who was he to hurl this stone, which, in its age-old wisdom had watched all life come and go?

Rocks don't hurl things in rage. Only man disrupts the world in vain efforts to quell the disunity of his inner world. Mendel laid the rock carefully back in its place.

Later, a patch of sun broke out over the area. He glanced up at the sky and saw a group of swallows, tiny and black in the distance, soar in inexplicable, magnificent unison over the fields. Each had a motion of its own and all had one motion. He packed his bag and followed the cloud-mottled sun on its silent path westward.

❧   ❧   ❧

Hundreds of crinkled papers fluttered like shell-shocked seagulls, flapping in fright with every minor movement of the breeze. And Poul danced in rage. "Damn damn damn! They were in a barn! A safe, dry *barn*! Why did he have to *do* that?" He fell on the muddy ground and beat it with his fists.

Later, when he knew the man was long gone, a soaked and miserable Poul scuttled in widening circles, plucking papers from the cornstalk leaves, tree limbs, and mud holes. "Bastard," he mumbled. "Dumb bastard. Shouldn't have a right to pull this crap. He could have cut me a break this time. Spoiled damned kid is what he is…."

By the end of the week, Poul was too exhausted to even curse. He had to save all his energy for his work. By day he concentrated solely on the paper chase. At night, however, he allowed himself the luxury of a new and favorite mental picture. It was of himself, good old Poul, standing squarely behind the eccentric ragamuffin. When the picture was solidly formed in his mind he smiled and gave the guy a good swift kick in the ass.

He had hoped to have all the papers collected within a few weeks and head back to the sanctuary of Beasely's office and his new apartment. But the wind and nature seemed to agree on making him work overtime for his money. He followed the papers into barnyards and sported with sows while rummaging for worn, pig spattered sheets of music and lyrics. He chased them into chilly farm ponds full of sickening mud and slimy things that slithered with cold-blooded depravity up his pant legs in the dark waters.

He chased them for 16 months, running from Kansas to Minnesota to Illinois where he spent four hellish winter months trying to spot the graying paper in the blinding snow. He rushed through Iowa and finally landed in a farmer's chicken coop.

According to his calculations, the coop or its vicinity should hold the last sheet. It should be, he figured, the missing page four of the third group of songs. He wanted desperately to say to hell with it, but he didn't dare.

He searched through the close, musty half-light, plucking scores of white feathers until he spotted the tip end of something that reached out forlornly through the squishy grayish glop that layered the floor. He dropped to his knees in the chicken shit and dug, ignoring his utter hatred of the smell, sight and cackling sound of the place. It had to be the song. It had to be it, he told himself. It had to be—

"Whatarya doin', fella?"

In a minor but extremely frightening moment of total unity, Poul jerked his head up to find his eyeballs perfectly framed by the end of a double-barrel shotgun. God, it was big.

He hauled up a swift silent prayer. "Oh Lord, not now, not in middle age when I'm about to become a respected millionaire and a damn fine person. If I live I'll be generous and kind and You'll be so proud of me. Don't let my brain be shot out in a chicken coop."

"Uh…don't shoot," he said gently. "I'm a good Christian. I fear God…and you." The farmer behind the long gun was small and built solid, with a gray stubble of whiskers poking out his hickory bark cheeks, one of which bulged with a wad of tobacco. His worn overalls were spotted with chicken shit and tobacco juice.

"Yer breakin' my eggs."

Poul looked around cautiously, his small weasel eyes darting about for injured merchandise. The man was right. Shit. He looked up again, slowly, and fought the furious urge to scratch his head while he still had a head to scratch.

"I'm sorry. I didn't mean—"

"Yer trespassin', too." The farmer flipped the wad inside his cheek with his tongue. "I could shoot ya fer that. It's all legal as long as yer whole body's layin' on my property. That's the law." The man's deadpan expression didn't change except for a slight eyebrow raise on the word "law." Like a visual period. Law. Period. Boom. Dead. Bye-bye Poul.

Poul had always had respect for farmers, figuring anyone who worked in all this crap to grow food must have some good in him. But this guy appeared to be a dispassionate killer.

"Don't shoot me," he said gently. "I was just chasing some music. I lost it, you see. Look." He dug the paper out of the dung and held it up. "See?"

The man turned his head and spat out a huge glob of brown saliva. "You broke my eggs and yer trespassin." He paused. "And yer crazy."

Poul nodded as he carefully raised the paper.

"See? It's a song. I had to find it." The farmer cocked his head as he studied the paper. Slowly he lowered his gun. Poul was so relieved he jumped up, frightening the hens who cackled and fluttered, falling from their perches like lopsided bowling balls. More eggs spilled from the nests and smashed on the floor. The farmer set his gun against the wall and ran to the chickens. "There, there. Bebe, Ethel, Francis, Gertie. Settle down. Nice girls. Maybelle, Tootie, come on now. There there."

He quieted them and returned to Poul who stood proudly holding up the brown, torn page that dripped with raw scrambled egg. The end of a long search.

"I got a good mind to blow yer empty head off, friend," the farmer said through is clenched mahagony teeth.

"No. No need for that," Poul said, scraping paper. "I'll get out of here. Sorry about the mess."

The farmer stared at Poul and rubbed his jaw with a red, calloused hand. He knew that no matter how hard he studied, he would see the same thing: a bald, bearded nut from some city standing in chicken shit and raving about a hunk of paper.

"Listen, I owe you some money for the eggs, and for scaring the, uh, girls."

The farmer nodded and spat again. He rubbed his chin and thought it over. It seemed to take forever to Poul. "I figure about three bucks for the eggs and fifty for the stress on the gals. They're nervous types. Might need some counselin'…and I'm sure they ain't gonna lay right for a week or so." He thought a minute. "Kick in a few more for me storin' that page for ya."

Poul nodded. "Fair enough. He dug in his wallet and pulled out three twenties. He had five of them for emergencies. The farmer took them and nodded with a faint smile. "If you think you ever might have more papers in here, come to the house and knock first. I'll give you a hand." Poul stared at him, realizing finally that the man was making a joke. He laughed politely. "Must be one valuable piece of paper, eh?"

Poul nodded. "It's worth what I paid."

They shook hands and Poul left to get back to New York, dump the songs and see if he could find the crazy composer. They had been separated nearly two years. The last Poul knew, the man was heading west. He wondered how many dozens of songs the artist had thrown away since he last saw him. Wearied by the question, he erased it from his mind.

As he wandered, he often made himself sick to his stomach wondering if the music's popularity had worn off by now and Beasely on to other projects. No. Beasely knew his field and said the songs would keep growing in popularity. Beasely knew.

Poul patted his bundle of songs. Everything would be okay. He had his life, which could have been lost back in the chicken coop, and, yes, he had almost forgotten. He had a little gem worth, heh heh heh, a major fortune.

He found it a year ago along a dirt road. It was a little piece of paper, a letter, or part of one. It said something about searching for songs and that his quest continued. It was signed "Mendel."

Nothing more.

Just Mendel.

The madman had a name.

CHAPTER 6

J.W. Beasely's 'composer,' if he is a real man, is a genius, who, though early in his career, can be compared to Shakespeare for the depth and breadth of his vision, to say nothing of his almost mystical understanding of nature.

Beasely laid the article down with a worried half smile. Gray smoke slowly swirled around his head as he walked over to this desk and pulled up his data base. Although the figures showed Poul's music at the top and holding fairly strong, it was past time to make a new move. He paced and worried about the composer for over a year. The idiot had just disappeared! Then Beasely received a telegram saying a new collection would be arriving shortly. That was seven months ago.

Here he was publishing material, finding the just right recording artists, overseeing the arrangements and sessions—all for a composer who was like air! His stomach felt queasy a lot anymore. He began to have blood pressure problems. He drank more at night so he could sleep, but even in sleep the skinny man haunted his dreams.

Beasely puffed on his cigar. The company's strong position in the market would weaken soon. The three albums, "Nature's Violent Whisper," "Springtime," and "Soaring", had done very well, especially "Soaring," which shot six singles to the top five on the Adult Contemporary, three of which crossed over to the Top 40. He had never seen anything like it. No one else in the industry had either.

Critics hailed the music as the work of a genius, of someone who would take a secure place beside Wagner, Beethoven, Leiber and Stoller. Another, after a long analysis, threw up his hands, said the music transcended all classifications and should be enjoyed for the singular art that it was.

"Soaring" was voted one of the top five songs of the decade.

And Beasely Publishing had broken into the Fortune 500 List.

He stared at the charts and poured a drink. He nodded to himself, knowing he couldn't wait any longer. The anonymity had worked like a nice mystery story, whetting the public's imagination until the suspense was almost unbearable. Each album held only its title, the song titles and production credits. Not even the musicians were listed. Writing credits said simply: "By an American composer." Americans take their entertainment seriously though, and listeners, critics and journalists were now demanding information. The Enquirer offered a $10,000 reward for information leading to the composer's identity. Other media quietly investigated nearly every angle of Beasely Publishing, hoping to find a clue. They found none and Beasely knew it was just a matter of time before there would be a backlash.

It was time to create a story. He would call in his artists and have them re-create Poul, give him some hair, flesh him out and have the PR department write up a couple mock interviews.

The strategy would have to be very carefully executed so that the real Poul would be kept out of sight forever. Beasely shook his head with a smirk. Who would think that scrawny bald guy with beady eyes, a bad smell and that damnable need to scratch his body would ever be capable of creating the century's greatest music?

The plan should meet with Poul's approval, Beasely thought. After all the guy didn't want to be in the spotlight. And that was fine. This would give him more time to create. How many artists had succumbed to public attention and let their art fall apart?

Whether or not Poul showed up, Beasely planned to introduce him to the world shortly. Sorry Poul, he thought. Business is business.

Shades of red pulsed in the rocks and sands of the Arizona twilight. Mendel sat cross-legged in the stillness. The red-rimmed boulders and glowing sands radiated an energy too subtle for man to see, but not to feel. Mendel had spent the past three months here learning stillness, learning to feel the quiet vibrations of an invisible life, a past life that existed all around him.

He had written little. He had done almost nothing but learn to exist in this sparse land of old prayers and dormant, whispering gods. Dusk. Crimson fading to black like the sun dried blood of 10,000 fallen warriors. Finally he heard the beat, faint, like a newborn's heart, then he saw. Shadow forms of ancient tribes danced to the muted drums that thumped like mastadonian heartbeats. Men danced and droned prayers, accepting energy from the flaming deity that ruled the land.

He was suddenly overcome with fright and loneliness. He drew his knees up to his chest and swayed slightly to the beat. "I'm alone," he thought. "Alone in the desert, alone among echoing spirits in an empty burning land. There is nowhere to turn. Redness and blackness. Red turning black. Black consuming red. I'm surrounded by spirits but alone."

Fear burned into his mind like the radiation of an exploding sun as the forms of men became solid and danced around him. They saw him; he could feel it. They saw him!

He wanted to jump and run, but he knew he could not escape the wrath of the copper-hued presences. The faster he ran the faster he would burn, crackle and sizzle into a smoldering cinder in the sand's omniscient fires. He was alone in the world with no exit. All paths led in concentric circles back to the self. His mind bounced from hugeness to minuteness, back and forth until he felt himself pulsating like the dark energy flowing from the throbbing drums. He fought to keep from screaming, knowing if he did it would only amplify the madness that beat with unrelenting rhythm against his brain, that another scream would follow, and another, each growing louder and more desperate until he tore at his throat and choked on his own thickening shrieks.

His head grew lighter and lighter until he became weightless and slid out of himself, leaving the emotion-ridden shell that holds the mind heavily to earth. He floated upward and looked at his body without compassion.

Freed of the physical, his mind lost its fear. He turned from his body and began searching. He watched the men beneath him passionately enact ancient rituals that he dimly recognized somehow, somewhere in the prehistoric pockets of a mind liberated from the narrow focus of consciousness. The campfire flicked on the burned faces as they danced in the moon's chilly glow. Silver and red. Red and black. Stark lands with sharp edges. Dark forms gathering a deep, rich nocturnal mother energy that swelled upon itself. If he returned to his body at this moment, he would go mad with terror, for he suddenly realized the truth of it all.

He was looking at his own mind.

A huge bird, hovering in the black sky, fell to the earth in carmine flames and exploded with a screaming hiss. A silver serpent with ruby eyes grasped its tail between travertine fangs and spun with a granite grin, lighting the heavens with a circle of white fire. The drums increased tempo and volume driving into his soul. He felt joyfully alive with terror for an instant that seemed to last forever. He was alive as never before, staring into the face of myth given flesh.

The serpent faded quietly into the moon and despite himself, Mendel was drawn back toward the body that lay crumpled in the cooling sand. His dispassion for his body gradually became a concern as he re-entered the still form cell-by-cell. He struggled to breathe in this heavy, sad, clay form and forced himself to lift his hand that seemed like a leaden albatross.

He concentrated hard on his hand, knowing that he must pull himself fully back from this other consciousness. There was no halfway. It was truly do or die. The cliché amused him and the fact that he felt humor strengthened his return. Dark-haired maidens warm with lust swayed at the sides of his vision begging him to turn his head, to just release himself and go with them. They promised to show him a song of love, formlessness and freedom. He held his gaze on his hand, studying the fingers, the lines on them and the bits of dull red dust imbedded in those lines. He felt another presence above him. It was a tall, strong man holding a scroll, and on the scroll was a song. "Come," the man said in Mendel's mind. "It may be the song you're searching for."

"It's only part of it," Mendel thought while trying to grasp this new dimension.

The man smiled and nodded. "Yes, but it may be a very important part."

Mendel felt his grasp on himself slipping with the temptation. "All parts are important parts," he said in his mind.

"I don't have time," the man said, losing patience.

"There is no time," Mendel answered.

The man seemed to swell to twice his size in magnificent anger before he burst out laughing. With a mighty heave he hurled the scroll into the starlit heavens. Mendel could not tell whether the scroll with the important song burst into flames or whether he was seeing a falling star. The man smiled, like a teacher proud of his student. "You are wiser than you think, Mendel. There are no unimportant parts."

Without knowing it, Mendel began writing. He was back. He was writing. That's all he knew....

He awoke the next afternoon and looked over the songs. He felt twinges of the terror he had experienced. He felt the excitement of his brush with the living myths and a little feeling of humble victory in resisting temptation.

When he finished, Mendel sat back, vaguely satisfied with the songs, but feeling distant from them as loneliness began filling him again. God, he had spoken to no one in months. He had had no real relationships in what was probably years.

He suddenly grabbed his notebook and began writing. "I'm alone because I chose to be. All of us are alone and no number of friends or loved ones can enter that aloneness. They help us hide it from ourselves, but in moments, in dreams, we know we are alone. We know."

He gathered up his things and walked. Being alone is neither good nor bad, he thought. He stopped and shook some sand from his shoe. As individuals, we create our universe by what we accept from the world's infinite offerings, and by what we reject. There is no other truth, no other way.

He knelt to put his shoe on and gave way to tears. No amount of understanding or realizing could erase the fact that being alone is the hardest thing a human can bear. Pain can be suffered. One can blame other humans or gods for frustrations and failures. But when one feels his aloneness, the world is a mirror reflecting a tiny, naked individual.

He closed his eyes and followed his loneliness until his mind focused on a dot encompassed by fleshy blankness. The dot grew and assumed shapes for him until he realized its message. "I am the continual creation of myself," he mumbled. He said it over and over in a quiet chant, and with each footstep the song of the ancestors faded back into the stillness of the softly shifting sands.

Behind him, the rejected papers clung to the bushes and cacti like manna shards.

❋   ❋   ❋

Poul was nearly a scarecrow. His sunburned skin hung like loose red rubber on his small bones and his bald spot peeled in hunks. The Gucci shoes Beasely picked out for him flopped loosely, their shriveled tongues wagging in weary desolation. Poul mentally kicked himself for miscalculating Mendel's intentions by about two hundred miles and wasting a month in New Mexico. He had trudged across plains, around some desolate mountains where Billy the

Kid caused so many problems, and even climbed an ancient, mile high volcano to survey the flat, beige land below him. No Mendel.

He veered south, giving himself one more week and that was it. "To hell with him. I'm a busy man. I've got money to make, places to see, women to meet," he told himself.

What he finally found made him sick. He snatched a piece of paper wrapped with weary masochism around a small cactus. Suddenly feeling tired, lonely and weak, his hands started shaking. "I can't take it," he groaned. "I just can't." He jammed the paper back onto the spines, impaling his finger in the process. He screamed in pain, then quickly looked around to see if anyone heard him.

He shook his head at the pathetic joke. Who would hear him? This place was barren! Why the hell Mendel would spend time here was beyond him. It didn't matter. To hell with him. "To hell with you, you bastard!" He screamed. "I can't take anymore!"

He picked up his bag and headed out as fast as the frazzled Gucci twins would allow.

CHAPTER 7

"You're alive! Oh, Christ it's good to see you, Poul!" Beasely rushed over and threw his arms around the emaciated song-gatherer, then stepped back. He shook his head. "I don't know what you do or where you go, but it sure doesn't look good for your health. Aren't there better surroundings to find your inspiration? Jesus, man, you look like you've been in a concentration camp!"

"That would be easier than living the free life in America," Poul said. He dropped his bag on the floor and his body in the leather chair in the corner. He glanced with disgust at himself in the mirror. He was caked with mud, dust, sand, and the residue of chicken coops, pig sties and forests. He was a walking collection of America's waste.

"I'd like food, lots of food, and a cold beer, Beaze."

"Sure. Yeah, you look like you could use a good steak. Maybe two." He turned to the telephone, glancing at the bag. No, control yourself, he thought. There's time.

"Aren't there restaurants outside New York?" He asked lightly.

Poul rubbed his eyes. "There isn't *anything* outside New York. Just dirt in more forms than you can imagine."

He opened the window and took another deep breath of New York air. He listened to the music of the low growling tractor trailers and wailing sirens. He studied with love and appreciation the gray concrete and plate glass windows of the high rise across the street. "God is concrete," he said to himself.

When the food arrived—del Monaco rare, lobster swimming in garlic butter lightly seasoned with garlic, a cup of artichoke soup garnished with curled parsley flakes, and steamed vegetables—Beasely sat back and lit a cigar. Poul had aged considerably. The lines on the man's face had deepened. He had lost more hair and gray threaded his beard. "Your choice of locations appears to be killing you."

Poul chewed the steak like a starving beast and swallowed. "You're telling me. I don't know how much more I can take."

Poul offered nothing more and continued the steady process of cutting, biting, chewing and swallowing. Beasely puffed his cigar and stared out the window at Manhattan, his Manhattan. He loved it more than any woman he ever met. He looked far below at the limousines against the curbs. Manhattan was power, money and movement.

Finally, Poul sat back, full. He lit a cigarette to visions of the papers lying in the desert. He burped and tried to put them out of his mind.

Beasely turned back from the window and smiled, excited. "Lots of news, Poul. You've had eight songs go Top 40. Three of them are gold. Gold!" He waved his cigar and looked at the ceiling as if he could see the gold spread across it. "Can you believe that? Critics are calling you a one-man phenomenon—you. No," he corrected himself, rubbing the wet end of the cigar thoughtfully against his lip. "They're calling the 'faceless writer' a phenomenon. Which is the reason—" he hesitated and cleared his throat. "Which is the reason we've got to enter the next marketing phase." He glanced at the confused Poul and sped on before he lost his momentum and courage.

"We're going to release your name." He held his cigar up for silence. "I know you don't like it. I know that. But hear me out. The moment is right. Actually, I have to admit, it worked like a charm keeping you anonymous on the first three albums. But now we have to go for it. You'll be—" Poul raised a scrawny, quivering hand, knowing he might be signaling financial suicide.

"You can't," he said quietly.

Beasely nodded. "Poul, I understand your feelings, but it's too late. We've already—"

"I'm not—"

"Started the strategy—"

"The composer."

The silence was so sudden it startled both of the men. It was a great line that could only have worked with these two men at this particular moment of all moments in history. Poul had been waiting for two years for it. He had dreaded it as he savored it. He had rehearsed it. He had played the scene a thousand times in his mind. To have it finally done, in reality, gave him a feeling of relief and freedom he would not have traded for anything.

Beasely's face was blank and white. He stepped in a daze toward his desk and put his hand out to steady himself. "Not funny."

"No joke." Poul felt somehow in control of the scene now. And in fact, as he realized months ago, he *was* in control. And he would explain all this to Beasely, who would have to accept it. "I'm serious, Beaze. Another man writes the songs and throws them away. I collect them and bring them here. You arrange them and make recordings. People buy them and everybody's happy. It's really as simple as that." He sniffed. "Crazy, maybe, but simple."

His head now shaking slowly, Beasely poured a large drink to stop the Coltraine rhythm of his heart beat. "Everything I've worked for," he muttered hoarsely. Christ, even his voice didn't work. Nor did his hand, which was ambushed by a palsy. Poul jumped up and held the glass of liquor up to the publisher's mouth.

"Everything you worked for is just fine," Poul said soothingly. He was afraid Beasely was going to have a heart attack and then all would be lost. "Take a deep breath and another drink and we'll talk this little problem over."

When he had regained his composure, Beasely sat down. When he found his voice again, he began the questions. Poul explained in several different ways what he told Beasely at the beginning. Poul willed himself to be patient. He knew there'd be some kind of scene.

Now, with a couple stiff ones inside him, Beasely puffed at his cigar. "I don't believe this! I just don't. No. No! It's so preposterous that I have to believe it." He turned to the weathered figure still in the chair. "But either way, Poul, you're a goddamned liar. If this is the truth, you're a goddamned liar.

Poul stood up. He took a deep breath but his patience had been exploded by the accusation. He stepped over toward Beasely, his small eyes bright with anger. "Don't you ever call me a liar, you son-of-a-bitch! I let you believe what you wanted, but I didn't lie. I've just told you the whole truth—"

"Out of fear!"

"Out of a sense of what's right!"

Now Beasely was up and they confronted each other face-to-face. "What's right is the truth!"

"Up till now there was no truth," Poul said. "The songs existed by themselves. You're the one who wants to attach a name to them! Why? To meet a demand and sell even more!"

"I think you bought into that concept, too."

Poul threw up his hands in frustration. He nodded. "I did…but they're not my songs and I won't take credit for them."

"But you'll take the money."

Poul sighed. "I can't explain it. This all got much bigger than anyone planned. All I know is the composer must be left alone."

Sensing his partner's weakness, Beasely quietly pounced. "I should have you arrested."

It was, of course, the wrong thing to say.

All the months of traveling, the loneliness, the emotional highs and lows, to say nothing of the damned weather, all came together in an adrenalin power surge that threatened to explode. Poul grabbed Beasely by the shirt with a strength that both surprised and frightened the publisher.

More frightening was the strained smile, and in the beady eyes the glitter of madness. "Arrest me, you damned fool. I bring you the greatest art of the century, so you've been telling me, and make you 'king of publishers,' or whatever it is that's so important to you. I go out there in that damned dirt and sleep with things you've never even *heard* of. I bust my ass gathering up these, these *scraps*, and your lousy thanks is to threaten me! You stupid, self-righteous son-of-a-bitch!" He leaned in until their noses nearly touched. "I'd say you have some key decisions to make real soon, partner."

Poul released his grip. The two stared at each other until Poul finally turned away. Beasely nodded to himself, knowing that Poul, indeed, did hold the cards.

One of the great questions of Beasley's career presented itself and demanded an answer. Beasely had prided himself on his honesty. Some employees might think him cheap and competitors felt he was ruthless, but no one ever questioned his integrity. Now he found he was in partnership with a thief—obviously one of the best in the business.

But Poul was the key to the composer, at least for now. Maybe the story was true, surreal as it appeared. Beasely, Inc. was moving upward at a healthy, steady pace. He couldn't take a fall now.

If the true artist found out that Beasely had been getting rich off his songs, then the publisher would work out a fair settlement and a contract for future material. He'd set Poul packing with a healthy severance check. The attendant publicity would boost sales more than ever.

Ok. Everything was alright. "You're right, Poul. We're in this together."

Poul looked at Beasely, lit a cigarette and smiled. "You're a hell of a businessman, Bease." They shook hands, cautiously, quickly. A truce.

That night at dinner Beasely sat fascinated as a cleaned-up Poul regaled him with the story of his discovery, his adventures and the description of this oddball genius composer. With the large meal and three glasses of wine, Poul had forgotten the recorder that was taping his stories. Beasely would turn the tapes over to the PR department who would shape this wonderful legend—hell, an entire myth. He would absolutely rock the music world with this bombshell.

"So anyway," Poul continued. "The first couple years I couldn't have told you the guy's name if I had wanted to. Then, in the Northwest, Idaho, I think—ha!—who'd ever think you could make a significant discovery in Idaho, even if it is kind of pretty—for a rural area….Anyway, I was picking papers by day and putting them together at night and found this."

He pulled a hunk of paper, taped in the middle and carefully folded and handed it to his colleague. Beasely opened it, his mind filled with images of this possessed artist. The paper read: "…life. But still searching. There is nothing else in life but the search. Love, Mendel."

Somehow, holding the letter written in a hasty, graceful scrawl, the man came to life before him. Beasely blinked away tears.

"I figure it was a letter he was writing to someone," Poul continued. "Like everything else, he was dissatisfied with it, tore it up and tossed it. Or maybe he realized he didn't have a stamp. The guy doesn't have a damned cent, judging from the rags he wears."

"Mendel," Beasely said softly. "*Men*del…Mendel." His tongue savored the name. "It has a nice ring. Easy to remember. He's real…." He rubbed the butt end of his cigar lazily across his lower lip. "Tell me again what he looks like. Everything you can."

Poul nodded, understanding. But as he thought back over the countless hours he'd spent watching the man, he realized he'd never seen Mendel up close or from the front. He was always on the guy's backside.

"I'm guessing at a lot of it." He scratched his thigh thoughtfully and Beasely again counted his blessings that he wouldn't have to use Poul's homely mug for the promotion. As he recreated and created Mendel's image, Poul almost believed that he was absolutely accurate. "His eyes must be fairly large and gentle. He has a lot of compassion."

"There must be some anger there too," Beasely added. "Judging from the wildness of some of the material in the Nature and Bird albums. He's angry and driven."

"Yeah, but remember, there's some gentle stuff too. Hell, there's a 15 minute number on the travels of a slug or something."

"Grub."

"It's small and slimy," Poul shuddered.

They continued to create the man's image until Poul could think no more. They took a cab to Poul's apartment. "Get a good night's sleep, partner," Beasely said. "You deserve it." Both men smiled and shook hands, this time more warmly.

Beasely, feeling more alive than he had in years, returned to his office and called his public relations director, not knowing or caring that it was 1 a.m. "I need you right now, Bob. If my hunch is correct we're going to have to double your staff and you're going to head one of the most spectacular campaigns of this century."

He hung up and gazed out the window at the city. Before he's even unveiled, Mendel is the most listened to and talked about songwriter in the country. A publisher's dream and it was all happening to him. He thought of his father and brushed away tears. "Ah, Dad, if you could only see this."

He poured a drink and waited for Bob. As large as his dreams were, Beasely, like Poul, had no idea how the announcement of Mendel's name would change the world, or how Mendel would change them.

Poul awoke again with images of the Arizona papers, cactus-crucified, bird-pecked and sand-buried. They filled his mind with paperwork no pencil-pushing bureaucrat could ever handle. When he'd first found the material in that awful, silent land, he'd convinced himself that they would weather fine in the dry air. He would spend a month or so to recuperate and then return for them.

Then Beasely informed Poul that the songs to date had made him a millionaire. The release of the new material would multiply his earnings. That meant the Arizona papers were worth—it was beyond imagining. They fluttered in his mind now, gasping with pleas for rescue from the wretched red dust.

Shit.

"Poul, this material is great stuff! Maybe the best yet, in a different kind of way. It's rich, deep, pure!" Beasely paced excitedly in the smoke-filled office.

"Great. You sit in your nice office listening to music while everyone else does the work. I'd be happy too, if I were you." Poul bit his lip and his face reddened as Beasely's angelic smile melted into hurt. "I'm sorry, Bease. It's just the last couple years…and I've got to leave. There are more papers that I left in…uh, left behind. If I don't go now, they're going to disappear."

Beasely nodded, happy to hear there was more. He tried to cover his feelings with a look of concern for Poul. "I understand."

Poul studied the publisher. "So do I."

Beasely shrugged it off.

"Listen, if you can, get back for the announcement. It'll be a major event. I don't want you to miss it."

"When is it?"

"In four weeks."

"I'll try."

"Can I send some people to help you?"

"No!" Poul was surprised at the speed and intensity of his answer. "No," he said more quietly. "I'll be okay." He stood up and they shook hands. He grabbed a handful of cigarettes.

"See you as soon as I can."

Beasely nodded, his mind on the announcement.

Poul wondered why didn't he allow Beasely to form a team to help. Hell, he had enough money to hire the National Guard to pick up papers. No. He didn't want anyone else in on the deal.

That wasn't all of it, he knew. It was more than just money now. It was a need to finish something that he'd started for once in his life. That was it. He itched his nose. That was part of it. All he knew was that it was the white papers that infested his dreams lately, not the greenbacks. And maybe it was Mendel himself. Mendel had him hooked. The bastard really knew how to make Poul's life miserable.

❦   ❦   ❦

California's energy drew him like a gigantic magnet. It grew stronger with each step until he finally stopped to control this crazy pull. He rested at the perimeter and let the energy into him a little at a time, building an osmotic psychic balance. What a place! Highway madness! Humans speeding about like mushy cannonballs. Colors, sounds and shallow thoughts all packaged in a whirling energy of new colors, sounds and smells. People here were born in motion, sped through their lives on eight-lane highways and attended to their dead at quick-stop funeral parlors. The art of the state was pit-stop tacos and packaged prayers, generic enough for everyday use and a minimum loss of time. Whew! No Indian ghosts here....

It was worse than he had feared. Poul shook his head and slammed his bag down. "God, I'll be months." He walked, kicked the sand for buried sheets and checked every cactus until his hands were swollen with their poison. The Palo Verde and cholla were the worst, literally entwining the sheets in their spines and refusing to let go, as if they recognized the hymns to them and clutched the sheets as their own.

Lost in fantasies about developing an electric machete, Poul reached for a sheet wedged under a rock. The stone buzzed, which puzzled him. He knew little about nature, but he was almost certain stones couldn't buzz. Then in a flash of primordial recognition he jerked back as the rattlesnake lunged upward, its fangs narrowly missing his hand. "Vicious little bastard!"

Shaken, he smoked three cigarettes until the quivering subsided. Then he marked the rock. He gathered more papers until nightfall. In the morning, while the snake was lethargic with the cold, he cautiously removed the paper.

"You sneaky little side winding son-of-a-bitch. It's mine now!"

Beasely worked 18 hours a day to meet his deadline. The moment was vital. He timed the announcement down to the minute, knowing that the afternoon papers would want to print the news the day of the announcement to compete with the broadcast media. Then they'd put it on the website for the rest of the world.

If everything was synchronized, it would go off without a hitch. And if it did, with the new CD hitting the stores in the next two days, he would have on his hands the largest first-day sales in history. And it was all up from there, snowballing on itself. The strategy was a top secret, with only Bob, his PR man, in on it. The rest of his top level executives, confused by his secretive actions and maybe a little jealous, spread the rumor that he was losing his sanity. The crazy fart was working all hours, sleeping in his office, having changes of clothes brought to him. The word filtered down through the ranks of Beasely, Inc. His office, it was said, had turned permanently blue from the cigar smoke.

Empty scotch bottles rolled out into the hallway. His blonde hair was turning white.

Not all of this was true, of course.

CHAPTER 8

✿

At first, California seemed to Mendel like a songwriter's dream. So many bits to find and translate! He picked up the sensuous physical song of the warm Pacific, the constant sunshine and groomed, tanned bodies. Nowhere else had he found such vitality and exuberance, all revolving around sun and self. He listened to the honking boats in the San Diego harbor and absorbed the brilliant primary colors of the succulents that set the Spanish style houses aglow.

He sucked in the wisps and textures of the Indians and the aggressive echoing spirit of the early Spaniards who left their names scattered on oceans and boulevards. He caught the vibrations of the song of the Mexican. He walked north and tried capturing the celluloid melody of Los Angeles that roared in a garble of millions of dream songs. Some even sounded familiar, almost as if he'd worked on them at one time.

Without realizing how he'd arrived, Mendel found himself in Disneyland.

Wandering around in this new world, he felt like a child again, recalling the Mickey Mouse Club on his parents' black and white TV. He remembered watching the opening of Disneyland and his childhood fantasy of someday being here. Here he was now in a world of happy dreams, Redenbacher popcorn and Mickey himself who posed for pictures with visitors from around the planet.

Children laughed, parents smiled. Age became what it truly was, an artificial line of demarcation that turned deadly when people stepped back into the daily world and believed in it. This was a dimension that existed somewhere between Christmas and nirvana. For the first time since he had begun his quest, Mendel hummed a song not of his own creation:

M-i-c-k-e-y M-o-u-s-e
Mickey Mouse, Mickey Mouse
Forever we will raise our banners
High high high!

He sat down to watch the crowds move from one land to another. Someday, he thought, a thousand years from now, an archeologist will dig up a statue and announce to the world his discovery that the 20th century's god was a rodent with white gloves, red shorts and a happy grin. Obviously he was a friendly, down-to-earth god. Continuing the research, theologians and historians would find that the rodent was indeed the most popular god of all time. They would find that billions of dollars and megawatts of energy were spent recreating the Mouse's likeness in dolls, books, movies and pictures.

They would find that people sang songs to the Mouse, wore watches, necklaces, T-shirts and underwear bearing his happy face, and that generations of children wore hats with mouse ears.

Researchers would find that the Mouse Religion brought more joy and happiness to people than all the other world's religions. No one fought wars over him. No one conquered others and forced the fallen to worship Him. The Mouse demanded nothing of his flock except that they laugh at his antics, gasp at his adventures and sing his happy song.

He started making notes when he was interrupted by the popping of pistol shots. Women's screams and scuffling chaos told him the gunfire wasn't part of any act. He followed the crowd to the buildings containing the various specialty shows.

"What's going on?" He asked.

"Somebody shot Abraham Lincoln," a man said, shaking his head in disbelief. Mendel looked up at the sign that advertised President Abraham Lincoln giving the Gettysburg Address. He had heard others talking about the Lincoln robot that stood on stage and talked and was so lifelike it was hard to believe he wasn't real.

"Hell, this Lincoln's more more alive than any of the past three living presidents," one man joked, "and more interesting."

A jagged space opened as the crowd made way for security police who hauled out a struggling, screaming man. "I shot him! I shot Lincoln! He deserved it!" As he disappeared, the large block began moving, disintegrating into individuals who particled from the crowd body like ants off a cookie. Soon only a few moving crumbs were left.

Mendel stepped into the arcade where men, women and children stood scattered in the dimly lit hall. They stared like zombies as grimly efficient Disney employees swept up the hundreds of bits of hair, clothing, fleshy plastic and pieces of circuitry and wiring. Off to the right, an arm twitched and smoked. Cameras flashed until three security men appeared saying, "No pictures. No pictures please." Some people took pictures of the security men. The Disney employees picked up the body and walked slowly off stage.

"Jesus, what a shame," someone said quietly.

A sudden feeling of unreality, of not being able to distinguish the fantastic in the real world from the intrusion of reality in a fantasy world, swept over Mendel. He staggered back into the poster sunlight to regain some balance.

On his way out of the park, he passed a young, pretty blonde newswoman speaking grimly to a camera.

"A man with a 'Saturday Night Special' today tried to repeat history and shot the likeness of President Lincoln in front of scores of witnesses." Mendel heard the confusion in her voice.

By the time Mendel was across the parking lot, the stage was clean and a new Lincoln waited for the next performance. A new crowd gathered, ignorant of the violence a half an hour before. Lincoln stood in the spotlight and with sad eyes looked down at the reverent crowd. He began to speak: "Four score and seven years ago, our forefathers brought for on this continent a new nation conceived in liberty…."

At 2 p.m., J.W. Beasely stepped up to the microphone covered podium. He wore a Navy blue suit to add a formal air and height to his five foot five frame. He carefully surveyed the room full of journalists who would, following the news conference, spread his words across most of the civilized world. Whether he would be believed or not was another matter. But whether or not the press or the public believed him, the record sales would skyrocket in the wake of the publicity.

He cleared his throat. "Good afternoon and thank you for coming." He looked out at the print and broadcast reporters. "Most of you have been pestering me for years for a certain name." The journalists laughed quietly, some nodding. "I'm going to give that to you today. I am also going to give you one of the strangest success stories of this century. I will give you all the facts I have and answer any questions I can. Beyond that, all I can say is that often truth is stranger than fiction."

Beasely reached behind the podium and pulled up the Soaring album cover. "The man who gave us this, one of the best selling albums of all time…the man's name is Mendel. M-e-n-d-e-l." He waited a moment. "Pronounced *Men*-del. He paused again. No need to rush.

"That was the easy part. Of the more than two hundred million people in the United States, no more than ten know Mendel personally—to my knowledge. Many have met him briefly because he travels by foot across the country to gather material for his art, an art that has touched, in varying degrees of intensity, more people than any other composer in the history of music."

He looked about the crowd again, seeing what he expected—a few puzzled faces, some cynical, some nodding, waiting for more. But not even the most hardened journalists looked bored. Truth or fiction, they knew this was one hell of a story. They also knew it was just the first chapter.

"It is ironic and probably hard to believe that I have not met the man who, frankly, has made Beasely Inc. what it is today. Maybe I'm being too candid, but the reason I never released his name before was that I didn't know it myself until recently. Check and see if that isn't a first in a business relationship." Mild laughter rippled through the room.

"I'm thankful that we have had the good fortune to obtain the material and to share it with the world." He glanced first to the left, then to the right, sharing his attention with everyone in the audience. He was informal but businesslike. He showed no signs of nervousness. Beasely was a pro and the journalists knew it.

"I can't tell you how we get the material. But I can show you what Mendel looks like, based on eyewitness descriptions." He waved his hand and the large curtain behind him parted revealing two ten-foot pen-and-ink drawings—one full face, and one profile.

Beasely's artists, with the help of Poul's descriptions and corrections, had captured a close physical likeness of Mendel with his long, graying beard, the proud nose, and gentle haunting and haunted eyes. More importantly, they had captured the spirit, the restless, tireless energy that infused lines of wear in the intense, gaunt face. Driven artists had captured Mendel's drive, his ability to peer into other dimensions and his will to pursue that vision at all costs.

Perhaps as Poul described Mendel, the artists saw themselves in his image and the pen drew the lines that connect all men who strive to transcribe to others the messages of the spirit . Beasely recognized this and approved the drawings at once, insisting that no alterations be made.

Beasely held up his hand when the clicking of cameras commenced. "There's no need to take photographs. When you leave, you will be given packets containing all the information that currently exists about Mendel, and glossy prints of the art that you now see. In addition, there is a reproduction of the man's only known signature. You now have, ladies and gentlemen, all that I have." A low buzz of voices in the crowd increased, like a growing fly.

He held up his hand and the buzzing faded. "I also admit that I cannot supply any absolute 'proof' that a physical being named Mendel exists." He looked around at the faces of people who were used to people trying to bluff them. "I ask you to simply take my word for it. I have worked hard to earn a reputation for honesty and integrity. I want, today, to simply share with you the knowledge I have and share with the world the man the world loves." He paused, then added quietly. "I want you to know that I stake my name on these last five minutes."

He bowed his head slightly, then lifted it, signaling another pronouncement. "To show my sincerity, I add this: If anyone can prove that I have given any false information, I will not only welcome it, I will relinquish all future profits from the Mendel albums to the charity designated by the party with that proof."

There was a large, unified gasp. He could almost see the headlines forming themselves in balloons above the reporters' heads. His PR staff had told him not to take this last step, but his instincts told him otherwise. To leave the media with such a thin story would get headlines for a week or so. To give the world this challenge would guarantee stories, controversies, eyewitness accounts, accusations, speculation and opinionated observations for weeks, maybe months. A good news story, he knew, feeds on itself.

A myth is timeless.

So long as the public was hungry for information on this mysterious man, there would be new stories. So long as there was information in the media, the public, knowing it was important *because* it was in the media, would want more. This circle was the basis of the whole game, and so long as the game was played, the records would sell.

Beasely nodded. "Thank you." The room broke into a half-controlled cacophony of feet, hands and high-pitched voices as the reporters rushed for the door, grabbed the packets and sped to their offices.

Back in his own office, Beasely had only two thoughts. One was that the press conference was a success. The second was: "Poul, damn your skinny ass, you'd better have told me the truth about every detail."

He stared at the framed drawing of Mendel that set on his desk. Nobody would be more written about or sought after in the next few weeks than Mendel. And nobody would be more closely scrutinized than J.W. Beasely.

❀   ❀   ❀

He had gathered just about the last of them, he was sure. It was a ragged batch. Some pages were marred by gouges and tears. Some songs, obvious to even Poul's trained eye, were unfinished. What the hell, he just picked them up.

"Don't know why in hell old people want to move to Arizona. Goddamn heat's enough to cook you down to the size of a bean." He kicked a small rock to the side and plucked a paper it had been clutching. "There. Done! I'm take a frigging vacation after this. Haven't had one since I started this job. Millions of dollars rotting while I'm frying. Damn sand…."

That night he pulled out a scrap of paper with one line scribbled hastily. He read it over and over. Finally he folded it and tucked it in his billfold. He would keep this one and ponder on its message.

❀   ❀   ❀

Before he had left for Arizona, Poul once again made Beasely promise that he would in no way mention Poul in any publicity. Anonymity was a wise choice. The day after Beasely's conference, Mendel's face was on the pages of every paper in the free world. It was the lead story for the broadcast media which ran and re-ran clips of the conference. The Internet exploded with Mendel chat rooms, blogger sites and fan pages. Young people became obsessed, creating maps of his travels and speculations on his location.

Within a few days the media mushroomed with print and broadcast stories of places where Mendel might have been—a scene always located in the local station's viewing area . "He could have written 'Squirrel Song' here in this very forest," said a pretty reporter into a microphone at the edge of the woods in Kentucky. "Squirrel Song is now scampering to the top of the charts and Mendel remains a mystery."

A New Yorker writer sniffed at the whole affair:

It is patently ridiculous that a man named Mendel even exists. Why would he work so assiduously on something he seems to care about, only to cast it away? How are these songs so mysteriously and systematically 'found?' The American public, again, is being duped. People have no one to blame but themselves. But if it gives them pleasure, then J.W. Beasely continues to laugh his way to the proverbial bank.

Beasely's employees were questioned, and offered money for information. The few who had any information gave away nothing, knowing there was a healthy incentive plan for silence, and immediate dismissal for talking. Beasely had thought of everything.

Within a week's time there was barely a man, woman or child in the world who did not know of Mendel, the solitary genius. Mad Mendel. Mendel the Unseen. Mendel the Mighty. Mysterious Mendel. Etc.

Synchronicity's invisible seed had grown and blossomed around the world.

One morning Beasely's door crashed open. Poul appeared and flung his bag down with his customary sudden entrance. "Jesus, Beaze! Isn't there a tribe of headhunters in the Amazon you may have missed? Christ, everywhere I turn, the guy's face is staring at me!"

Beasely laid his pen down and smiled. "Good morning, Poul. Coffee?" He buzzed his secretary. "Nice tan. Been out West?" He grinned like a man riding the crest of his dreams.

Poul scowled and bit his lip. I was in a tanning salon in the Bronx."

"What's it been? Two years?"

Poul shrugged. "I lose track of time. You're the time and money man."

Beasely nodded and looked at the bag. If Mark Twain had learned that God had lost a strip poker game to Satan, he couldn't have been more delighted than J.W. Beasely at this moment. He couldn't produce enough albums to keep up with the demand, and now Poul, right on cue, had appeared with more material. God, life was magnificent!

"Beaze, there's a certain location—and believe me, I know about locations—where you can stick that idiot grin." He slumped into what was by silent mutual agreement his leather chair as the coffee and pastries appeared. He idly watched the secretary leave and thought about offering her a thousand dollars for just a kiss. He erased it from his mind by scratching the back of his head.

He'd get cleaned up and find a thousand dollar lady for a whole evening.

He picked up a donut and poured a coffee. "Yeah, I got a tan. And now I'm taking a goddamn vacation to get rid of it." His head jerked about. "Where are the cigarettes? Oh, I see them. Never mind." He took a swallow of coffee and shook his head thoughtfully. He lit a cigarette, inhaled and held it. It was the first one he'd had in months. "If Jesus himself had a promotion team for the Second Coming, he couldn't have made a bigger entrance…or done it with more schlock."

"All I did was repeat to the world what you told me." Beasely flicked a cigar ash from a tan lapel. "And if you didn't tell me the truth, we're both done."

"I did."

"I figured."

Poul took a large bite of donut. "So how much money have I made?" He asked, spraying powdered sugar over the rug.

Beasely shrugged, displaying the dispassion for money that Poul had for the songs.

"Many millions. I can check."

Poul nodded. "Do that, Beaze. I'm curious. Whatever it is, I earned every frigging cent of it. And I'm taking a vacation."

Beasely couldn't take his eyes off the bag. "Okay."

CHAPTER 9

Poul sat in a nearby coffee shop and watched people pass. A blonde woman who could have stepped out of a designer's damp dreams strode down the sunlit street wearing sneakers, faded jeans and a t-shirt bearing the now familiar face. Beneath the beard were the words: "I Believe in Mendel."

Cars and trucks passed her sporting a variety of bumper stickers: "Mendel is God"; "Mendel Sings Truth," and of course, "Mendelites Do It Better."

There were others, such as "Mendel is Evil," but they were in the minority so far. His image graced bright posters, coffee mugs, buttons, rings and even children's lunch boxes. They were eating out of the psalm of his head.

Poul lit a cigarette, sipped his black coffee and shook his head at the passing Mendel fan club parade. Mendel's popularity just kept growing. Was it really the art, the music? Or was it Beasely's marketing genius? He shrugged to himself. Maybe both. It didn't matter. From each item sold, the royalty buck was passed to Beasely, Inc., and Poul received his cut.

A young man entered the coffee shop dressed in a colorless, seemingly worn shirt, the "Mendel Shirt," and torn, faded jeans. Both had been approved by Poul, and now as he sat here, sipping his coffee, he realized that about every third person he'd seen this past hour, was actively contributing to his wealth. He nodded and thought, keep buying those CD's. Keep wearing those clothes. Slap those bumper stickers on your cars. Send me money.

Beasely prepared the fourth album, "Song From Earth," based on the Midwestern material. It would be released at the height of Mendel Mania, a phenomenon so named by the media which helped create it.

Beasely had never been happier, working seven days a week, often 16 hours a day, steering his company upward. Soon he would slow down, he told himself, but inside he knew he wouldn't. He loved the business and the more successful it grew, the more driven he became. He was like a dog chasing an old bone attached by a string to the back of a bicycle. As soon as he neared the bone, it transformed into a t-bone attached to a car. Once he neared and sniffed the t-bone, it miraculously assumed the form of a fresh sirloin hooked up to an Indy 500 champion racer. Private sport gave way to a long-run exercise toward suicide with thousands of spectators watching in bemused silence.

Poul, on the other hand, took his success in a more rhythmical stride. He moved to a larger apartment, ate in fine restaurants, made a quick trip to Paris in the company of two female consultants, and spent his spare evenings with a new hobby—mystery stories. He enjoyed pitting his wits against the leading writers. He also saw himself—the only man who had the ability to track the mysterious Mendel around the country—as a colleague of Holmes, Poirot, Spade and the rest.

He chortled with scorn at some writers' attempts at clues. "Ha! You never look at a broken twig as a clue to somebody's direction. To hell with the minor stuff. You get to know the hunted, the length of his stride, his endurance, his mental workings. You learn to goddamn *breathe* like he does. Then he'll never escape." Actually, there were only two areas you needed to know about any man to own him, Poul knew—his dreams and fears. A man's life, and therefore his every movement, is created by his desires and his fears. Nothing else matters.

He had a good idea what Mendel's dreams and fears were. And he knew his own. His desire was money and he had it. He was a millionaire many times over. His fear was losing it.

And that fear made him itchy whenever he was at home too long. There were more papers to be gathered. As Mendel had written in one of his rejected notes: "Man seems capable of nearly everything but extended happiness." After a few weeks the apartment felt confining. Poul gained weight again and felt slow and heavy. With the exception of a few intimate moments with one of his consultants, Poul carried Mendel with him constantly, like a spiritual wart.

A lovely young blonde emerged from the bathroom. "Poul, honey, you've been moping for days."

He shrugged. "Guess I'm bored...or something."

She smiled and came up behind him. She reached down and caressed him but nothing happened. "I don't appeal to you anymore?" She whispered in his ear. Ah, at one time a woman's warm, intimate breath, the perfume, the caress, would have him tearing her clothes off.

"I'm just out of sorts."

"I heard you used to have a different woman every night. You couldn't get enough."

He sniffed. "I'll be leaving on a business trip soon. Why don't you just take care of the apartment while I'm gone." He was embarrassed to realize he couldn't remember her name.

Outside Poul's apartment, Mendel's face popped maddeningly from books, newspapers, subway walls, billboards and the material covering people's bodies. Only the blind were safe from his image. And only the deaf and blind were safe from Mendel overdose.

Inside Poul's mind, Mendel took up all the available space. The composer had become the entirety of years of Poul's life. At every moment he wondered where Mendel was and if new songs were being written and blown away before he arrived to retrieve them. The manic side of him wondered if Mendel had met with sickness or injury or even death. He wondered if Mendel had quit writing. He was forced to remember with each bite of filet mignon, with every sip of wine, that Mendel was solely responsible for Poul's wealth.

With all the publicity now, it was only a matter of time before someone else began finding the papers if Poul wasn't mindful. As greedy as humans are, Poul thought, they'd be damned quick to cash in on Poul's territory.

He packed his bag, mumbling curses, knowing it was his lousy fate to follow the artist until no more songs came forth. "Ah, Mendel. Before you I had no life. Now I have one and it's not mine."

At the same time, a tingle of excitement brought his fattened body alive. No matter how he hated foot travel and raw earth, it was an adventure.

He hailed a taxi. On the way to the airport he idly looked out the window at the men and women in business suits rushing, talking on cell phones, looking at their watches. He looked at the gangs and the homeless, elderly people who shuffled and coughed. The air smelled dirty.

Poul landed in Tuscon and took a taxi to the end of town. He then walked, readjusting himself to the silence, the vast silence, the dust and the sense of stillness. Nothing moved in the hot, dry air.

Who in America had adventures like Poul? What wide-assed executive wouldn't trade his entire retirement pension to be in Poul's shoes? Who else in the world had claim to Mendel? What some people wouldn't give for just a glimpse of Mendel…Beasely included. But he realized none of that was important to him. Mendel was, to him, still a raggedy, crazy artist.

Beasely had made him a desirable image, a wanted commodity. It was the songs that mattered. They had to be gathered. Money had to be made.

No. The songs had to be gathered. He didn't need more money. It didn't matter.

They had to be gathered. Before anyone else touched them, he had to gather them.

❧   ❧   ❧

There was a handful of people in the country who didn't read newspapers, watch TV or listen to the radio, who didn't know about Mendel.

Mendel was one of them.

He sat on a deserted beach between Los Angeles and San Diego, at the end of the country, looking outward, listening to the song of ocean breath. In…out…in…out…He studied the sibilant music of salt water slapping and slurping on hard-packed sand as he listened to the nearly inaudible inhale of the ocean, rushing back into itself in a long smooth gasp. With a guttural roar, it spat itself forth again, offering, taking away, in a smooth, unending cycle of lovemaking between water and earth. He wrote a song in minors, with rich, thick chords and gliding notes that filtered themselves out into the sky, and inward beyond time and reason.

He worked for weeks trying to capture the haunting, velvety sounds of liquid timelessness. One of the few humans in this isolated stretch was a middle-aged beachcomber who made his rounds each morning, shuffling along the water's edge, seemingly without a care or deadline in the world. When he came upon some sea-washed article, he picked it up, studied it quickly and either tossed it into his bag or back onto the sand. Each afternoon he made the rounds again. Soon Mendel looked forward to seeing this coastal nomad who lived off the ocean's droppings.

One day the beachcomber veered off his regular path and sauntered over to Mendel.

"Howya doin' there, friend?"

Mendel nodded, his head bent nearly straight back to take in the six-foot-two inch frame capped by a huge head of wind-swept silver hair flecked with diehard red strands.

"Fine, thanks. You?"

"Ha! Good as a gold tooth in a rich whore's mouth!" He had a deep laugh that rose from the soul. He sat down with a bearish thud. His mouth was shaped in a natural smirk, and his blue eyes radiated devilish vitality. Nothing bothered this man and Mendel felt good just sitting beside him, "Seen you sittin' here the last few weeks and wondered if you mighta got yer ass stuck in the sand."

Mendel laughed self-consciously. He had had almost no human contact for years, let alone a conversation with such an imposing and boisterous individual.

"Uh, no. I've been writing."

"Writing. Mmmm." He nodded. "Hmmm. Writing." He shrugged. "My name's Harry." He stuck out a large calloused hand that resembled a hickory stump.

"I'm Mendel."

"Glad ta meet ya."

Uneven rows of broken yellow teeth, like old cornstalk stumps popped through his grin. "So what'r ya writin', Handel?"

Mendel ignored the mistake and cleared his throat, slightly intimidated by the man's directness.

"Songs. I'm, a songwriter...or a kind of songwriter, I guess."

Harry stared at his new acquaintance, thumbing the corner of his lip. "Seems like I heard yer name around somewheres. You from around here?"

"No."

"Hmmm. You ain't done nothin' to git yer name on the radio or nothin? Robbed a bank or raped a goat? Hmm. Musta been somebody else." He shrugged and squinted up at the sun. "Time fer lunch. How about joinin' me, Handel?"

Harry didn't look like he had anymore than Mendel, but before Mendel could shake his head and politely decline, Harry slapped the sand. "Aah! You ain't gonna tell me no. No way! Here, I got lunch right here." He plunged his arm like a harpoon into his bag and pulled it back with two fingers hooked into a six pack of beer. "Here." He yanked off a can tab and shoved it at Mendel.

"Thanks." It had been years since Mendel had had a beer. It was cold and lively, like a million happy insects filling his mouth and stomach. Harry snapped the top off his can and in one swoop lifted it, turned his head upward and drained the contents. Mendel stared in awe.

"Close your mouth, friend!" Harry laughed. "You'll git it full a sand." He popped open a second can. "Mix sand and this rotgut horse piss and yer stomach'll turn into an oyster!" He sat back and laughed so hard the gulls fluttered away in disgust.

Mendel laughed quietly and drank the beer in small sips. He hadn't eaten since yesterday and his heart quickly pumped his booze-infused blood to his brain which welcomed this mandated mellowness. His mind had been over-worked for too long, and now, given a furlough, everything felt fine.

"Have another, friend." Harry had drunk four and reached for the last one.

"No," Mendel said quickly. One is fine." He shook his head to clear it. "You drink it."

"Take it," Harry demanded. "I'll git more." He jumped up, his massive body creating a shadow the size of a cloud. "It's all over the place, free as the salt water! Ha ha haa!" He lumbered off like a big bear. A few minutes later he was back and settled in beside Mendel with another six pack. Mendel didn't recall any store around the beach. "Where zyou get those?" His face reddened slightly as he realized his tongue was acting up on one and a half beers.

"Those nice folks over there." Harry smiled and aimed his can toward two young men and two women who lay on a large towel staring at Harry and Mendel. Harry waved and nodded his thanks.

"Friends of yours?" Mendel asked.

"Never saw 'em before." He chugged the contents of a new can. "But I ain't the purtiest creature in the world. When I ask someone real polite for a couple of beers, most of the time they don't refuse. I ain't never robbed nobody or sto-len nothin' but once in awhile I ask folks to share a beer or a samwinch." He shrugged. "That's just bein' neighborly. We've lost the spirit of sharin', ya know? I'm tryin' ta git it revived."

Harry's explanation was so natural and unassuming that Mendel simply smiled and nodded. His whole brain seemed to be smiling right now. He hadn't felt so good in years.

"So what kinda songs d'ya write?"

Mendel thought lazily about this. "Just songs. Whatever comes."

"Ya sound like a collector." Harry finished the can and crumpled it with two fingers as he continued his unbroken scan of the beach. "Like me. I pick up whatever comes t' me." Mendel nodded. His eyes were half closed and a simple grin was pasted beneath his beard. His mind was empty of all but Harry's words as they blew from the large man's mouth to his ears. "It's all about the same, I guess."

Harry swallowed the rest of his beer and crushed the last empty can. He shook his head so that his silver mane, like an old worn broom, waved around his ears. "Well, pal, it's time you took a vacation. C'mon with me." Mendel started to protest but Harry stood up and brought Mendel up with him. "I told ya, friend, it ain't healthy to argue with an ol' crazy ass like Harry." He laughed as they picked up their bags and walked down the beach.

A natural talker whose words flowed as smoothly—and as incessantly—as the ocean waves, Harry told Mendel how he had worked as a sideshow strong man, "Harry the Caveman," for 25 years, snarling, bending steel bars and leering at the women. "Funny thing was, the men loved me droolin' all over their women as much as the ladies liked it. Funnier though, was that both pretended t' hate me and be offended! Ha!" Mendel could barely picture this freewheeling friendly bruin acting crazy and vicious.

"Lotta women discovered theirselves after payin' a quarter t' look at me," Harry continued, pushing a muscular thumb against his chest. "Come night time there'd be a dozen or so little ladies around my trailer. I was the closest thing to a wild man they'd ever witnessed and they wanted a first-hand crack at the whole beast!" His laugh was infiltrated with nostalgia.

"Some of 'em was housewives, some college girls, some single wimmin—ah hell, it was all kinds, you know? They was lonely and…shit, I don't know, all tight and bound up from livin' in a closed-in world with too many rules. They told me a lotta things late at night—when they found out I could talk like a normal man. The girls knew they had t' grow up 'n find a decent man with a good job. Heh heh. The housewives found their men and felt a little cheated. Cheated, yeah! That young girl's dream wasn't all it cracked up to be. Hah!" He shrugged. "Turns out decent men with jobs are borin'. I don't know. I ain' never been one. Neither've you, I 'spect. The single women, some homely as a ass-kicked hound dog, some crippled, they was the saddest. They didn't even have a chance to get their dreams mashed with a decent man." He shook his head sadly, then brightened. "But I treated all of 'em with respect, 'n they appreciated that…a lot."

He looked over at Mendel as they walked. "And you know what? Once they hopped inta the sack they was all the fiercest little wildcats that ever clawed up a man—all of 'em! Wild Man Harry didn't have no rules or expectations. He didn't have no pretty language to take away from a simple act that's as old as an animal. What's all this wine and song and manner shit when ya got a down-and-simple need? Ha! Nothing, that's what! Wild Man Harry didn't waste valuable time talkin'. He just growled and gripped 'em and let 'em know he wanted 'em—really wanted 'em, wanted their bodies, their selves, whatever they were and no matter who they were. And they wanted the body and energy of a raving wild man. It was the pleasantest barter ever invented."

His sigh was like a wind current. "Damn! Those were the days. I freed a lot of ladies, Handel. Gave 'em a moment of some kinda dream. And they did the same fer me. A little moment that didn't cost nobody nothin' and made for some memories they'll have when they're gramma's! Ha ha!" They walked on in silence.

"So why did you finally give it up?" Mendel asked. "The carnival, I mean."

Harry shrugged again. "Cause one day I got up and had t' grunt just a little harder to bend that damned steel bar. And then a little harder yet. Ain't nothin' more humiliatin' than a wild man gettin' tamed by age. So I knocked around a little and landed here. The beach is my family. He chuckled again with the easy sound contentment. "I ain' got no complaints, just like you prob'ly don't—no legitimate ones at least."

Mendel nodded. It was true.

That night by a fire, Mendel told Harry of his travels across the country, the songs he had written and thrown away. "I keep finding that every song I write is just a piece of a greater song," he said, staring into the flames. "Every living thing has its own song and that's what keeps it alive and makes it what it is. When the song stops…so does life. Just like your footsteps. You always have to be one step short of where you're going and one step ahead of where you've been. If you're not, you're dead."

Harry burped and nodded. "Ain't that the truth." He raised the stolen half gallon jug of wine to his lips and drank.

"I keep trying to capture the individual songs and I keep finding that within each is a greater one, a melody that runs throughout every being and gives it the—I don't know—the tones and notes, to create its own songs." Mendel threw a stick into the fire and ran his hands through his long hair in frustration. "But no matter how far I reach, I can't get hold of the greater song." He stopped with a look of mild surprise on his face. "This is the first time I've ever said these things out loud and they sound…crazy."

Harry laughed and scratched at his massive stomach. "Ah, yer tryin' too hard. You git so involved in tryin' t' git where you wanna be that you don't appreciate what you got where you are." He took another long plug at the wine and sighed philosophically. "We each got our own ways, I guess."

Mendel nodded as he stared into the black spaces between the orange flames.

Harry studied the now motionless Mendel and felt a chill run up his spine. It was the same kind of chill that Harry had sent into countless spectators during his carnival years—a tingling sensation one gets when one confronts the unknown in one's self. There ain't anything those eyes don't see, he thought. He don't look at things. He looks *into* 'em."

He pulled his blanket over him and laid down. "Sleep, friend. Tomorrow I got just the ticket for ya. Yes sir." His hair splashed in silver streamers over his collection bag that he used for a pillow. "Heh heh. Ol' Harry'll help ya out. Life ain't just for writin' songs."

Mendel broke from his spell and smiled at Harry. "You're probably right." He waited for Harry's rhythmic snoring, then pulled out his pencil and paper.

A trio of shiny switchblades poked at Poul's chest. The concrete wall at his back wouldn't budge. "Come on, dude, you know the routine. Hand over the wallet. Slow."

Poul pulled his wallet out and handed it to the teenager on his left. There were five of them altogether. "Anything else in the pockets?"

He shook his head, like they were waiting for him to do something so they could use their knives. "Let's carve him up," one said.

The leader looked at the others then rammed a fist into Poul's stomach. Poul fell, unable to breathe. Someone kicked him in the head. As he lost consciousness, Poul pictured Mendel. "You're gonna be the death of me yet, damn you." He didn't know how lucky he was in these Western streets not to have any of Mendel's songs with him. They were a possession that in a future synchronistic moment would prove fatal.

A few couples danced while others sat in the dim bluish haze around tables in the country bar. The lean, slightly drunk rhythm guitarist in the five-piece country band was singing "I'm So Lonesome I Could Cry." Mendel, sitting in a shadowy corner, nodded at the beautiful simplicity of the three-quarter beat and the surreal-earthy mixture of the lyrics.

Of course no one ever saw a robin weep, but somehow Hank Williams, a simple, uneducated country boy, took the elements, the very atoms of the emotion, and built a feeling that goes beyond the consciousness into something so solid no one argues its reality or beauty.

He thought about the silence of a falling star lighting up a purple sky and knew he had to return to the country. No one will ever find the perfect song, let alone true love and beauty, in the urban areas, he thought.

Harry leaned back like a king in his palace and grasped the bottle of beer like a burnished bronze scepter. "Drink up, friend! This is life!" He turned the bottle upward, emptying the bubbly gold into his gullet.

Harry ordered three more, two for himself and one for Mendel. "This is where yer song is, friend. Fellas lookin' fer a girl fer the night, girls lookin' fer fellas, everybody's gittin' t'gether fer a little romp and be on their way. A little pleasure while we're here. Heh heh."

The band moved into "Proud Mary," a country-rock tune, and the floor filled like imploding buckshot with couples who swayed and bounced to the sliding hum of the bass guitar and the guitar's banshee whine.

"Look at the babe in the tight blouse over there," Harry yelled into his friend's ear. "Hoooeeee! A prowlin' bobcat if I ever saw one!"

Mendel smiled as he watched the girl, hypnotized by the writhing hips veneered with achingly thin pants and the soft, controlled bob of breasts unhampered by a bra. Her dark hair swayed heavily, in slow motion, around her gracefully muscular shoulders.

As the music continued, her image changed. She floated in the clouds, dressed in a flowing white robe, then fell, descending with graceful swiftness into a chasm where she lured lost men with a lonely song of sensual beauty. She withered into a yellow-toothed hag who has defied death too many times, then burst this disguise to become a sexless, kindly fairy queen overlooking all men. Mendel's chest tightened with conflicting feelings of repulsion, ecstasy and fright. He held tightly to the table to resist the temptation to rush to her arms, or to hurl his bottle, like a poisoned dart, at her breast.

Harry sighed when the music stopped. "Ah, boy! I didn't realize how long it's been since I stuck my plow inta some fertile ground. Hoooo!"

He ordered another beer. "Don't worry about the tab. Sam keeps track a my drinks and I clean the place and do a little wood butcher work fer him. Works out real nice. Don't have all the fuss and bother of money."

He rubbed his chin and stared thoughtfully at Mendel. "What d'you suppose I'd look like with a beard? Somethin' like yers?"

"Like a large wild man!" Mendel laughed. "But a distinguished one."

A hard hand clamped Harry's shoulder and stopped their easy laughter.

"Me and my friends don't appreciate being embarrassed like what you did to us yesterday." Two men behind the young man speaking nodded in agreement.

Harry chuckled easily. "Sorry about that. Just me and my friend was outa beer. Let me buy ya one now."

The young man backed up, and glanced back at his two friends. "It's going to cost you more than that, gramps."

Harry shook his head. "Save your strength, boys. If it's yer girls yer worried about, I'll go over and apologize, tell them ya scared the shit outa me and made me realize my evil ways."

One of the men threw the contents of his beer glass into Harry's face. "We ain't worried about nobody, asshole, except you and your geeky friend here." Harry sniffed and, with a weary expression of an actor recalling an overworked scene, knocked over the table and his chair as he rose like a great whale from a stormy ocean. Mendel grabbed his drink as it slid down the falling table.

The young men's stiff, defiant glances loosened somewhat as the glue of their team courage melted slightly. "Cute move, gramps, but it's past your bedtime," the first one said.

Harry nodded. In the slow wafting stratas of tobacco haze, Mendel watched Harry grow even larger. The sinews in his massive arms tightened and his eyes took on the tight, distant expression of one who has seen dying. "Son, I've killed three men twice yer size, and I've crippled a bunch more. Git back to yer girls while ya still got usable equipment."

"You cocky old fart!" The first man hissed. A knife suddenly glimmered dully in the heavy air. With a speed and grace incongruent with his bulk, Harry grabbed the man's wrist and twisted. The man screamed as the knife flew upward and then clunked to the floor. The two behind him rushed at Harry, only to find themselves dangling in the air. He pulled the one in his left hand toward him and bit the man's nose so hard Mendel was sure he was going to tear it right off. Now it was this man's turn to scream.

Harry looked at the third member who had tears of terror in his eyes. He held his hands up. "Calm down! Back off! I'm sorry!"

Harry nodded, still holding the two men. He clunked their heads together like a musician crashing a couple cymbals, and dropped them to the floor. Mendel was thinking about Darwin's ideas when he spun to the crash of a bottle and saw the first man start toward Harry gripping the neck whose jagged ends dripped with bloated white foam. Harry's eyes were frighteningly cold. "Touch me 'n yer a dead man." Perhaps it was the solid way Harry stood, or maybe the young man was just not a gambler. Perhaps a guardian angel jumped from its rocking chair in the personal unconscious and sent the young man a quick message: "This big guy is crazy and never tells lies. Don't be an asshole. He'll really kill you." The man slowly lowered the bottle neck and dropped it as the other two men stood up slowly, groaning. Without a word, the three men hobbled toward the door.

"Just a minute!" The bellow silenced the place and froze the men . Harry picked up the table and set it upright. "Ol' Harry don't want nobody's night spoiled, 'specially mine. You guys sit down here. The next couple rounds is on me 'n we'll fergit everything."

He motioned them. "Come on, now, don't be strangers."

The baffled men traded shocked stares. "Come on," Harry urged. "I kinda blame myself fer startin' all this. Here, git a chair. No time t' be bashful. Heh heh. Right. Ginny! Bring a bunch of 'em here! Tell Sam I'll fix that roof he's been pesterin' me about! Now, where you boys from?"

It took about half an hour of Harry's carnival stories, bawdy jokes and laughter to put everyone at ease, especially the man with the teeth marks in his nose, but by closing time they all parted shaking hands and laughing. Friends for life.

"I don't believe it," Mendel muttered as they staggered back to Harry's campsite. Those guys tried to kill you and you wound up great friends."

"Just havin' a good time while we're all here," Harry said, finishing off a bottle and tossing it into a nearby can. We ain' built to last that long. Ha! Put that in a song. "Nothin's built to last that long, so Mendel catches it for a song!" His deep laugh fought with the ocean breeze.

And won.

CHAPTER 10

Mendel bent down to pick up a small onyx-colored shell as they made Harry's morning run. "And what if you knew you'd die tomorrow. What would your life have been?"

Harry shrugged as his eyes stayed on the sand for treasures. "Don't know. I guess I'd jus' say I rode high on life, fell down a few times and got back up again." He walked on. "To hell with what it meant." He bent down to pick up a piece of driftwood. "Look at that. Ain' no finer sculptor than nature. Takes her time and never makes a failure that's noticeable."

When Mendel laughed, Harry came out of his reverie, puzzled. Then he understood. "You've thought the same thing. Ha! Maybe I'm a poet!" They both laughed. Yes, Mendel thought, Harry was a true poet.

Amidst the early sun bathers and athletes, a skinny bald man in torn jeans and a battered jacket watched the two figures along the shoreline like a hungry wolf watches a sheep walking beside a koala bear. One he recognizes as his prey; the other is strange and foreign and the wolf is disoriented into immobility. He was not programmed for this new being. It perverted the very laws of nature and therefore his own instinctive movements. Hmmm.

Poul spent nearly a year locating Mendel. LA was full of false leads, to say nothing of his stay in the hospital for the concussion from the muggers, then trying to explain his way out of the homeless shelter where the hospital had sent him.

The first sheet he found was "Assassination Song," which, he concluded, was a bunch of crap filled with gibberish and a sign that Mendel might be losing his sanity. "Assassinating Lincoln! Jesus. He's just a few years late." He found a few other bits and pieces which at first glance he also felt were useless. But parts were missing and probably gone for good. Nothing is sacred in Los Angeles, he thought. Especially art.

He headed south where he finally picked up the trail with a batch of papers in a little alley used by prostitutes and drug addicts.

Now he stood in shock at the sight of Mendel actually walking around with another person. It was out of character, though Poul realized it was to Mendel's advantage in this populated and pop-crazed area to be with someone else. The growing legions of Mendel Hunters were looking for a solitary individual. No one gave this pair of ragged bums a second glance, and no one was going to approach that walking bull with the stubbly face. God, he was big. No, everyone knew Mendel walked alone. Fortunately Mendel's face had not yet made its appearance on beach towels.

Even though Mendel was better off with this big guy, Poul felt a twinge of jealousy.

He wanted to tell that hulking beach bum that Mendel was his friend and that he, Poul had suffered some goddamn hardships over the years, following Mendel, picking up after him, and making him an international star.

Instead he walked to a nearby stand and bought a coffee and a hot dog with some change he had panhandled. "Crazy artists." He bit furiously into the hot dog and took a large gulp of the tepid coffee. "No damned appreciation. All I've done for him."

❧   ❧   ❧

"Uncle Harry!" The children ran toward the two men, howling with joy.

A little blonde girl, maybe seven, Mendel guessed, leaped upwards, entirely confident that Harry would catch her.

Harry laughed and bounced the girl on one arm. "Hey, you kids! It's Saturday already?" He reached down the gentleness of a Buddha after a weight lifting program and picked up two more children with the other arm.

"Hoooeeee! Time do fly, don't it?" He wiggled his large broken nose and stuck out his bottom teeth. The kids laughed. "Hey! This is my friend, Handel."

Mendel flushed with embarrassment.

"I saw you in a store," a red-haired girl said.

"I don't go shopping much" Mendel laughed.

"No, on a picture or something, a book or something, there was you. I *saw* you there."

Mendel shook his head. "No, it must have been somebody else."

"He had long hair and a big beard," the girl persisted.

"Uncle Harry's got a scratchy face," another said, rubbing his hand over Harry's stubble.

"My winter beard!" Harry laughed.

"Did you find anything good?" Another asked.

Harry brought his eyebrows together in exaggerated thought. Then his eyes brightened. "I almost did! You betcha! I found a pearl the size of a frisbee! If we coulda took it to a store we coulda traded it for enough money to buy a million suckers and eleventy thousand milkshakes." The children's eyes were wide, some with amusement, some with suspense. "I had t' wrassle a shark mosta Tuesday night t' git it outa his mouth, he liked that pearl so much. But I got it, I did, and just as I was swimmin' inta the shore, almost dead from bein' tired cause it's hard work wrasslin' a shark—ain't it?" He looked around and each child nodded in solemn agreement that it was hard work wrestling with a shark.

"Jus' as I was comin' in, the biggest ocypuss you ever saw in yer life reached up and caught me by the throat." He grabbed his throat and squeezed to show the struggle. The children stood silent, listening to the gasping sounds coming from his mouth and watching his face turn red. Even Mendel found himself picturing what Harry might have looked like being strangled by an ocypuss.

"Wal, kids, the only way I could git loose was t' stop strugglin'. But when I stopped, I knew I was gonna drown, cause you can't breathe underwater 'less yer a fish or a mermaid. So I thought it over and I figgered out a solution." He leaned slowly down to the kids. "And d' ya know what that was?" They shook their heads as he leaned closer. "I reached out, real real slow...and..." he raised his hands..."and tickled his armpits!" He grabbed a boy and tickled him, then reached for another. "All his armpits!" Harry yelled, reaching for another kid. They screamed and laughed and clustered in to make sure they received their share of joyful torture. "And that's how I lost the pearl," he panted as they finished.

Later, Harry passed out trinkets he'd found during the week and had tossed into his bag for the kids. At lunch, the children went home, making him promise he'd be there to see them next Saturday.

Mendel spent several more days with Harry, learning as much as he could about the man, soaking in his sense of life and happy energy. If God ever incarnated to have a good time on earth, he would pick a body and brain like Harry's, Mendel thought. No, not someone like him. He would pick Harry.

"So sing me some a them songs I been hearin' about," Harry said one night by the fire.

"I don't really have too many," Mendel apologized. "I throw most of them away." He wished now he had saved a few whole songs rather than just parts here and there.

Harry studied Mendel in the firelight. "I thought you was just kiddin' about that. Why, for God's sakes?" It was against Harry's nature to throw *anything* away.

Mendel shrugged. "I wasn't happy with them,"

Harry shook his head, as if wondering what to do with a problem child. "How 'bout sellin' 'em?"

Mendel stroked his beard and stared at his bag. "I don't want to, even if I could. "I'm looking for the perfect song. When I find it, I'll be happy, and if I'm happy, I won't need to sell anything."

Harry scratched thoughtfully at his growing beard. "Handel, at one time I had a mind to be an artist. Never did no art, but I did a lotta readin', y' know. From what I understand, the good artists worked a damn long time 'fore they whipped out a masterpiece here 'n there. And the thing is, all those little drawings and paintings leadin' up t' the big one, they're valuable too. They're good by themselves, but they're also little pieces leadin' up to the Big Picture…"

He struggled for the right words. "They're…little souls in theirselves. Yer gonna find yer song, but you could be sellin' some right now. Yer starvin' cause you want to."

Mendel took a deep breath, finding himself angry with his friend who pretended not to understand, when in fact he did. Hell, Harry lived the same existence as Mendel, except that Harry's purpose was freedom. But the lure of money bends people, turns their heads, twists them from—or maybe toward—their true selves with that wicked promise of an easy life, or power, or whatever it was that made people love the idea of money. Now even Harry was falling for its temptations. Sure, he was playing a game, but how long before it stopped being a game?

"I'm not starving and I'm not doing it for money," Mendel said quietly. "You, of all people know that."

Harry looked at his friend and wondered why he was so angry. He laughed. "Yeah, I know that. Don't take things so serious. You'll git a heart attack 'fore you find that song a yers."

Later they opened a bottle of cheap whiskey Harry copped from Sam's. They swapped the bottle and drank in silence, listening to the waves. "I'm goin' down t' Mexico for a few months and work the coast there," Harry said quietly. "Like t' have some company." He took a slug and stared at the ocean. "Whaddya say?"

Mendel's stomach tightened. He felt weary. Earlier in the day he'd seen a lone gull soaring over the water. He had shielded his eyes with his hands so that all he could see was the brilliant white feathers against the royal blue sky. The gull was an angelic speck in a vast, infinite breath, hanging weightless, without direction, between the blue depths of the sky and ocean. There was no beginning and no end.

He looked into the ancient security of the little fire before them. "I can't." The little flames licked outward at the night's blackness and the ocean's roar. The darkness and the ceaseless, pounding waves filled the void in their conversation. The fire flickered inward toward its death, as if the blackness were eating away at it, swallowing all in the world but the constant, ominous sound beyond them

"Didn't think ya would," Harry said nonchalantly. He took a swallow and burped. "Where ya headed next?"

Mendel made up his mind he would never make any more friends. It was too hard to part. "I don't know. Somewhere."

Harry grunted and finished off the whiskey. "It don't matter." He laid down. "You got the song yer lookin' for. Someday when it's ready, it'll come leakin' out like a new spring creek. Yer pen won't be able t'move fast enough t' catch it all. You'll scribble yerself right inta full blown frenzy and back out again!" His laughed rippled outward, cheering up the night, and Mendel laughed too.

The search for Mendel was growing. A website dedicated to Mendel found new speculations to his location every day. "Based on the location of the songs and the direction he seems to be taking, it's fair to speculate that Mendel is now somewhere in the Southwest. LA? Utah? All indications are that the elusive composer is indeed on the west side of the United States and continuing to write his songs."

The pale, lean young man with long black hair sat in a battered chair of his single room apartment staring at his laptop screen. When the song on his CD player ended, the young man hit the back button, and played the passage over and over. A song about all life being under construction, holding the seeds of its own destruction, but even after being destroyed, life seeds itself to begin again.

The young man listened to the passage into the night, until he understood, until the lines and Mendel were part of him. Then he walked over to the large black and white poster of Mendel on the wall. He absorbed the image—the large eyes that saw through him even though they were paper; the sensitive, sad mouth nearly hidden beneath the gray beard.

The young man nodded as if in a trance and with a serrated kitchen knife slashed the poster to shreds. Then he sat down at his computer to continue his own private quest. He was sure he was getting close.

❦   ❦   ❦

Mendel sat on the beach, reliving moments of the recent past, trying to write and feeling nothing. He caught himself envying the young people in the distance swimming, playing frisbee and tanning their lean bodies. He shrugged off the feeling, though, glad they could live this fleeting moment in life. To live simply and continue his quest was all he cared about. Somehow everything else fell into place. The most complex problem was to remain simple and natural.

Maybe Harry was right; Mendel was trying too hard. The soul can't be pushed. It moves and grows and finds answers at its own pace. He tossed away dozens of scribbled sheets, closed his notebook and shut his eyes, letting the sea roar fill him with its heavy salt rhythm.

As his mind relaxed, it gave him the image of an old man he once saw sitting on a nursing home bench in numb loneliness, waiting for death because there was no one else. The image was followed by a Fourth of July parade, full of high-stepping baton twirlers, high school band members and a Neanderthal float holding a snarling, chest thumping wild man. Men in the crowd chuckled and pointed, women smiled nervously. The wild man captured everyone's attention. His mind skipped back to the dying old man and he knew with quiet certitude that Harry would not live to be old.

Tired, he pulled out his pencil again.

CHAPTER 11

"In his songs, Mendel espouses and at times meticulously describes nature with a sensuality that echoes the celebrations of heathens. He has written songs that promote paganism and violence!"

The minister looked out over his congregation. "This man stands in the path of all that Christ worked and *died* for. He is slowly, in the alluring guise of art, destroying the minds of young and old alike. Our young people cannot be held responsible for their actions, for they have not yet, perhaps, seen and felt Christ in all his glory! But you, the parents, the working Christians, you who *have* felt Christ, and perhaps even have seen Satan in his shifty machinations, you *can* and *will* be held responsible!"

The man at the pulpit held up his Bible in a hand quivering with passion. "Mendel is an agent of Satan and must be fought with all the powers Christ has given us!"

Mendel watched the sun set in the haze of the cloudless horizon and followed the full moon in its slow ascent through the glowing mist. He closed his eyes and looked down at the ocean from the moon's perspective. For an instant he understood his human consciousness in a world of nature. He was a speck beside an all-consuming ocean, a speck that could be crushed and swallowed by a small wave.

Yet his mind contained all that the ocean did, and more, didn't it? The feeling of being a god came and went, leaving him with the knowledge that he had the power to create a sand castle and destroy a seashell. He could create the ocean in his mind, and then erase it. Even greater, he had the power to gather nature's spirit and create a song—and destroy it....

Once more he felt despair. He had created and destroyed equally, leaving nothing in the world but forsaken half lives. As he stood up, he gathered a handful of sand. He studied it, then let it flow through his fingers, watching the rough palm full of seemingly solid mass scatter into a million parts to become one again with the ground.

A grain, a handful, a beach. A cell, a man, a universe. The scabbed, skinny prisoner locked unjustly in dark confinement and seeing the speck of light through a pinhole crack would have understood the black, uncontrollable rage that suddenly filled Mendel. He felt as if he could explode, and in his violence take the world with him. He kicked the sand, feeling a minute joy in the blasting disruption of the grains so neatly packed and designed by the wind and water. If he could only lift the whole beach and heave it into the heavens! If he could grab the moon this instant, crush it into blobby silver shapelessness and drop it among the withered starfish!

He pulled out his pencil to capture his feelings, but stood paralyzed. He snapped the pencil and threw it at the star-cluttered sky. "Damn it. *Damn it!*"

He was powerless in this rage that tightened every muscle in his body. The stars twinkled at him mockingly. "I damn you!" His body shook as images of exploding planets and shrieking souls warred in his mind. If it were in his power this instant, he would set fire to the waters, drown the stars, create chaos, then sit back and laugh from the core of his demented soul! He would bring such disorder to the universe that synchronicity's mainspring would snap and even Satan, angel of chaos, would weep with jealous rage!

But he couldn't destroy the universe. All he could destroy was his pencil, and his songs. "I can't take anymore," he mumbled. The mumble welled into a scream. "Strike me dead, you Divine Bastard! Hell will give me more peace than this life!" Panting with rage and exhaustion, Mendel walked to the ocean's edge and waited. The fringes of the waves lapped and swirled about his feet, washing the sand from them. As he stood shivering, he realized he was composing a song and damned himself for it. He fought to erase it and concentrate on dying, but lines and melodies floated through his overtaxed brain.

Feeling mildly like a fool, but primarily concentrating on the song at hand, Mendel slowly returned to his bag, knowing he was little better off than a toy soldier whose owner insists upon playing with it again and again until its arms and legs fall off with wear.

When he finished writing, he lay down beside his bag and closed his eyes. Images wandered through his brain as casually as Sunday visitors through a rickety old museum: a man with a noose around his neck smiling tranquilly; a woman in a field in the pain of birth; another woman offering fruit to a shadow; a man shouldering a fold-up plastic cross; a child running, falling down, standing up, running, falling,standing, over and over. He forced himself up and began writing again: "We are all immortal, for the moment never ends. There is no death for the moment never dies."

He pictured a human figure as a moment, expanding outward and wrote what he saw—the grace the fall, the glory of the rise. . He saw the countless moments in eternity and eternity in the moment. "The most beautiful song to be sung is singing now," he wrote. "Forever."

In the coming weeks the songs poured forth faster than he could write them. Maybe Harry was right, he thought. Like an overflowing spring, they poured from him.

He wrote a tribute to Harry the Beachcomber, stealer of beer, pacifier of violent men, lover of men, of women, of children, the natural artist who seeks and saves nature's lovely castoffs. He wrote of Harry-with-no-last name, the only free man he'd ever known.

Abruptly the songs ceased. Mendel looked them over, saved a few and left the rest. He headed East again without looking back. The roar of the ocean faded with each step until finally it was gone, and his footsteps once again became his rhythm.

"Ah, Jesus, come down and kick my ass for staying here. I don't need this." Poul's back hurt. His legs ached. The new sunburn on his bare head drove fiery needles into his brain, though he had tried to soothe it with lotion, then with salve. He even tried cold hamburger grease, but it turned rancid and drew flies. One day he found a cowboy hat rendered shapeless with wear and weather. "Fate!" He exclaimed, grabbing it and easing it onto his head. "This hat's gonna be as permanent as a goddamned *roof*!"

He was now in his sixth month of searching. As nearly as he could tell, he had only two pages to go. He had no way of knowing that Harry had happened across one of Mendel's early castoffs and jammed the page into his bag, happy to have the souvenir from his friend.

"Two lousy pages," he kept mumbling, scratching his beard and keeping his eyes on the beach, waste cans, and picking up everything from hot dog wrappers to love notes. One day, just before breaking for lunch, he spotted a crumpled sheet floating about twenty feet from shore, like some fragile, lost boat forlornly heading out to sea. Years of experience and a now finely developed instinct told him it was a Mendel page.

"Stay where you are!" He yelled, splashing with gangly legs toward the paper, holding his bag with one hand and his hat on his head with the other. He was about ten feet from the paper when a gull—a greedy, piggish, narrow-minded species of bird he'd learned to hate above all others—swooped down, snatched the paper and soared in an upward arch toward the beach.

"You bastard!" Poul made a quick, clumsy turn and fought the heavy water as he stumbled back to shore. He ran across the sand as fast as his aging legs would take him, keeping his eyes on the gull above. "Land, you brainless parasite! And don't eat it!" The bird seemed to know it was the object of aggression and stayed airborne. As Poul ran, he pictured himself clutching this useless white bag of feathers and shaking it by the neck.

His lungs burned, his legs weakened and he was soon puffing too hard to curse. The gull glided to the sand about thirty yards ahead. Strengthened by hope, Poul sped up, planning to descend upon the nasty little wretch and terrify it into dropping the page.

Someone yelled: "Watch out!"

Poul looked down just in time to catch the blur of two children diving out of his way an instant before he stormed through the center of an intricate sand castle. He tripped and landed face down in the sand. When he regained his breath, he slowly hoisted himself to his knees and blew the sand from his nose. The children were crying.

"You broke it. You broke our castle, you big asshole!" Before he could pull his hat from his eyes, Poul was jerked to his feet by what felt like flesh-covered vice grips.

"What's the idea, buddy?" Against his will and better judgment, Poul looked up to find himself matching pupils with a man who, with no visible exertion, was able to hold him up in the air. He felt sick.

"He broke our castle, daddy. Smashed it to pieces!"

"I know, baby." The man appeared to Poul to be a TV wrestler or someone who kills elephants with his bare hands. "What's the big idea, buddy?" He also appeared to have not more than a token vocabulary.

Poul spoke in gasps caused by a fairly equal mixture of exhaustion and fright. "Sorry…was chasing…seagull….stole my paper…I'm a poet." The man dropped Poul with disgust. Poul untangled his arms and legs and got to his feet. He reached into his pocket. "Here, buy them an ice cream or something." He handed the man a twenty and turned to the children. "Sorry kids."

"Idiot," one mumbled as they began working on a new castle. Poul counted his blessings to have wired Beasely for more money. As he walked away he heard the man say, "Crazy pervert poet." He also saw the man stick the money in his wallet and knew the children would never see the ice cream.

Poul found the paper where the bird had landed. It was indeed a Mendel sheet. Knowing he couldn't take anymore, he decided to return with what he had and tell Beasely to work without the missing page. Chances were, he told himself, that if it hadn't been picked up and thrown away, some drug-crazed teenager had probably smoked it.

He wondered how many years he'd been gone. It was impossible to guess with this year-around sunshine.

"I'm going to devote the rest of my life to discouraging young artists," he told himself, heading east. "I'll give them grants to practice carpentry or shepherding, have them do anything but be weird artists. Even religion. Hell, if they want to be creative, I'll give them money for a pulpit.

"Goddamn Mendel, thinks he can just gallivant around the country and run my ass off. I'm going to show him one of these days. Somehow…."

A few weeks later Poul stood at the edge of the city. He no longer kissed the sidewalk. Instead he just stood, letting his body and mind adjust to the shock of noise, rushing, and the massive sense of self-importance swirling through the air.

"Keep moving, pal. Keep it moving," a passing cop said. Poul nodded and headed into Manhattan.

There seems to be no question that whoever Mendel is, the man is real. The songs, while varied, are consistent, and they, like the man, continue to grow in substance as the writer travels, seeks inward and outward, and shatters boundaries. His record sales are now at an astounding 500 million. Just as Elvis ush-

ered in a new lifestyle, as the Beatles created a new music, fashion and way of life, Mendel has waved a magic wand over society. The magic wand of music.

Beasely tossed the Rolling Stone article on his desk and rolled his cigar between his thumb and index finger. "There's never been anything like it in the history of music! He just keeps breaking records—no pun intended." Despite himself, Beasely chuckled at the pun. "Anyway, Poul, I'm glad you're back. Let me fill you in on what's been happening."

Poul sat back with his coffee and cigarettes while Beasely paced around the office, waving his cigar intermittently to make a point. "And we're picking up a whole new audience generation. I don't understand it." He shook his head, then stopped and grinned like a little boy, "But I love it!"

Poul removed his shapeless hat and scratched his head. "You mean kids are picking up on that Midwestern stuff?"

Beasely nodded and stopped to pour a drink. "Yeah! We divided the material into two CD's. Part Two was released 11 months ago. Next month the spooky stuff goes on the racks.

Poul stubbed out a cigarette. "Spooky stuff?"

Beasely nodded. "That mystical material. From the west."

"The Arizona songs." Poul shuddered at the thought of that barren, hot, dead land full of cactus and mean tempered snakes.

Beasely waved his cigar and nodded. "Yeah, the 14 to 25 market will get into that. Once the critics get hold of it, there'll be stories of Mendel on drugs and all that crap, I'm sure."

Poul nodded absently, reflecting on Mendel's simple life and how he never touched anything stronger than mint tea when he found the leaves—except this past year with that big guy who drank like a whole *school* of fish. Mendel knocked down a few beers. But other than that—externally at least—the composer led a boring life, just walking and writing, with time off for occasional tantrums.

"The drug stories wouldn't be right," Poul said. "It's not true."

Beasely studied Poul a moment and shrugged. "Ok, so we'll deny them."

Poul exhaled a stream of smoke and didn't argue. Marketing, promotion, publicity. He looked at Beasely who had grown grayer and paunchy. Lines sank deeply into his forehead and around his pale blue eyes. "You've been working pretty hard, Beaze."

Beasely studied his cigar and nodded.

"Yeah, I guess," he said quietly. "Beasely Publishing is the number one house in the world. In the *world*." He sat down and swiveled around to stare out the window. Poul looked at the publisher's desk whose three corners were stacked neatly with correspondence, plans and other paperwork. In the remaining corner stood a gleaming gold lighter in the image of Mendel. Poul shook his head. What do you buy the Mendel Publisher who has everything? A solid gold Mendel icon, of course. Suitable for every cigar smoking, Mendel-crazed billionaire.

Beasely was still gazing out the window at the Manhattan skyline. His hair was thinning too, Poul noticed with satisfaction. "Yeah, I thought if and when I hit the top, I'd be content," Beasely said. "But now I'm working my ass off to stay there…." He swiveled back around to face Poul. "But what the hell, I love it." He stood up and poured another drink. He was uneasy. Something was going on, Poul thought. He could feel it. "Drink?" Beasely held up the bottle. Poul shook his head. He lit another cigarette. . Years of tracking Mendel had forced upon him subtle levels of perception and his intuition told him something big was happening.

"What's up, Beaze?"

The publisher looked at him, trying to mask his uneasiness. "What do you mean, Poul?" His voice was quiet, caressing.

"I'm not a patient man and neither are you," Poul answered. "Forget the con and tell me what's up your sleeve this time."

"Mm." Beasely cleared his throat and put on his business smile. "TV series," he said nearly under his breath.

Poul sat forward. "A what?"

Beasely pulled at his tie. "Uh, we've been thinking of a, uh, TV series about Mendel. It can't lose. In fact it has the potential to be one of the biggest—"

"How the hell can you do a TV series?" Poul fought to control his voice. "You don't know a damned thing about Mendel except what I tell you, and I don't know that much. Jesus Christ, I don't believe—"

"What could be simpler?" Beasely had regained his composure and began selling. "Man in search of something great, something almost godlike as he travels across the greatest free country in the world. He travels alone, suffers, has adventures, pursuing something out there. Meanwhile he writes some of the greatest art of the century. Doesn't take much imagination, Poul. It's all there. And we'll have approximately 100 million viewers counting the days or hours until each show."

Poul shook his head. "Where in the hell did you get such an insane idea?"

"From the Mendel comics," Beasely said very quietly, quickly sipping his drink.

Poul felt dizzy. His face drained of color. "The *what*?" His voice was reduced to a squeak.

Beasely had regained his confidence and nodded matter-of-factly. "The comic book. 'Mendel The Wanderer.' It's the biggest selling thing on the stands. Kids love him, and it's huge on college campuses. We're in negotiations now to start a syndicated strip for the Sunday papers. That's why the TV series—"

"But what the hell do they write about?" Beyond shock now, Poul wasn't sure if he was outraged or just dead weary. A thousand questions arrowed through frantic, confused mind.

"Adventures. Like I said, the guy travels, writes great songs, throws them away. They're picked up by an equally mysterious man—

Poul groaned and fell back into his chair. It was over. The whole show. The fat lady's coming out to sing. She's really fat and has a huge voice. Poul makes his farewell bow. "I'm done. Beasely, you silly, selfish, no-good son-of-a-bitch. You've got pig's knuckles for a brain."

Beasely waved his hands. "No, no! We've changed the name and your looks. I know the dangers involved. God, give me some credit. I told the artists you're shorter, well-built and good looking. Full head of blonde hair and piercing blue eyes. The Nordic look. Balances with Mendel's dark features."

"Mendel is *gray*!"

Beasely nodded. "We'll age him as we go."

Poul rolled his head back and forth against the leather chair. It was all too much to comprehend—and all coming at a time when he wanted to quit thinking. He felt overcome with shock, outrage, and…hurt.

Beasely seemed to read his mind. "I'm sorry, Poul. It's a lot to take in. But as far as the comics, you know how it has to be. The characters have to be gorgeous: Handsome, virile men; sexy women. And it's of utmost importance that you're not recognized."

"Me! What about him? I don't know you anymore, Beasely! I thought you, of all people, had some, some ethics!"

"You're getting your 10 percent royalties," Beasely interrupted indignantly.

"It's not the money! The guy's out there killing himself writing songs. And that's what he wants to do. And millions of people buy his songs. And that's what *they* want to do. All the rest of this is a lie!"

Beasely squeezed his cigar between his back molars until brown juice from its saliva-soaked butt gathered at the corner of his mouth. Christ, every time

Poul returned, they wound up arguing like a couple of aging fags. He was doing what was right for the company. It was growing and so was Poul's bank account. Damned prima donna.

He walked around to the front of his desk and faced Poul. "Listen. Artists, good ones, live like shit. I know that because I've worked with them all my life. You know it because you've been living with one, in a sense. If the artist is truly in quest of great art, he sacrifices almost everything. He lives like a dog while he works to create. His life is outwardly bland and inwardly a living hell." Poul nodded, mildly surprised at Beasely's insight.

"That's right, so leave him alone."

Beasely shook his head and waved impatiently. "Let me finish. The writer sweats, shits and bleeds his art. Does the public believe this?" He paused, as if he were in a lecture hall.

"No. The housewife who changes dirty diapers, the guy who works eight hours a day at something he probably hates, the old people who have no more dreams, the kids who have dreams they're sure will come true—they're not going to believe the artist lives like them, that he's a regular flawed mortal like they are. They're getting from that artist something greater than what they have at the moment. He's giving them the visions they don't have the guts to pursue by themselves. And they want some kind of glamour to surround this person bearing these incredible gifts. Even if it's the glamour of poverty and suffering. At least he's living his life for a cause. In Mendel's case, it's the perfect song. He's a horseless, ragged Galahad searching for the grail, a wonderful, divine, but impossible quest."

Poul rubbed his eyes and sighed.

"People want and need a realistic illusion to accompany the art, which is also an illusion," Beasely concluded. "It's my job to give it to them."

Poul gave no reaction. He was weary, beaten and confused. Mendel drove him crazy, and Beasely aggravated the insanity. Beasely's argument was nice but there was a bottom line. Always the bottom line. He stood up. "I've got to go, Beasely. I'm tired. I've been on the road for years."

Beasely took the lack of argument for tacit agreement. Now, strengthened by his lecture and loosened with drinks, he held up his hand. "There's one more thing before you go." He cleared his throat. "A couple of people in the industry want to put together a concert of Mendel music in honor of his second generation of fans."

Poul nodded. "Fine, honor your asses off."

"They'd like Mendel to make an appearance."

Poul froze. His nervous system couldn't take it.

Beasely rushed on. "All he'd have to do is be here, say a few words of appreciation, then poof! back into the woodwork. No pun intended. Uh, at first I rejected it." He rubbed his chin. "Then I thought, hell, with the promotion we would give that, it could make TV history." He rolled his cigar between his thumb and finger thoughtfully.

"Granted, it might be a shock to Mendel when he learns of his popularity, but he's seasoned enough to handle it. I think. I'd let you handle that part. Afterward, he could return to the hills and keep writing." Beasely's blue eyes sparkled with excitement. "A perfect climax to a distinguished career not half over."

Poul's face was blank. Beasely was unbalanced. He'd become distorted. Pulling Mendel in would be like throwing an eagle into an airtight cage. If the bird somehow survived the ordeal, it would never manage freedom again. He looked at the man before him and wanted to spit in his face.

"No." He put his hand on the doorknob. "Don't ever mention it again."

Beasely nodded and blew a thin stream of smoke from his pursed lips. He smiled politely. "I thought you'd say that. But think it over. The whole world wants to see Mendel, to hear his voice, watch him breathe and move. They want—just for a moment—to see the man behind the art."

"On a TV screen?"

Beasely nodded. "That's today's reality. Poul, the public has made you a rich man. You owe them something. Think about it."

Poul leaned against the door and scratched his thigh. He was beyond thinking.

With unsteady legs, he walked over to the cigarette box and lit another. "What about your cute little philosophy about the artist remaining exotic and larger than life?"

Beasely shook his head, causing the sagging jowls to wobble like pudding in a little earthquake. "He'll remain larger than life. We're just establishing him as truly real."

Poul bit his lip and held himself from taking Beasely's throat. "Your power and greed have gone to your little brain, Beaze. Never happy with what you have. You always want more. You said it yourself. Forget it."

"You've been alone too long," Beasely said, his voice taking on a steely edge. "The rest of us are in the real world, and millions of real people want to see Mendel…including me."

"You just want to stay number one," Poul hissed. His small eyes glittered like an angry ferret. "You want to display him like a freak in an international side show and add award plaques to your walls." He crushed the cigarette. "You're sick, Beaze. And I'm sick of you." He grabbed the bag of songs and started again for the door.

"I was afraid you'd say that too," Beasely said almost too casually in this mental poker game.

"Well, pat yourself on the ass. You were right. Buy yourself a Mendel doll. See you—"

"That's why I've created a Search Force to begin hunting for Mendel."

Poul froze. His very guts felt like ice. He forced a deep breath into his lungs to break the arctic paralysis. He saw himself killing Beasely. Surely a judge would understand. A man had grown so powerful that he could set up men to track down a fellow human like a hunter stalks a rare animal. Instead of putting the trophy on the wall, he places it on a stage for all the world.

"You fool. You rotten, greedy, egotistic fool." He had no desire to mask his hatred.

On Beasely's round, innocent face, even evil smiles appeared as mischievous grins on an aging imp. "Maybe, Poul. But I've had a team of young computer geeks doing studies, following the path of the songs, feeding the information into a specially developed software program and extracting some general information on a pattern. Fascinating program. It's all based on a linear progression of his material. From that we extract the essence of various aspects of his personality and project what he might be searching for next—and where. In a few weeks, we should be able to come within, oh, 50 feet or so of his location."

He sipped his drink and smiled as Poul seemed to shrink. Beasely hated to put his friend down this way, but it really was time to bring the artist forth and herald his years of achievement with a good send-off into the future. And he himself wanted to meet this wonderful man whose songs never failed to score with the public and the critics. It was ridiculous that a company president was not allowed to meet his star client. He smiled at Poul's sagging, defeated features.

Poul nodded, as if in a trance, as he set the bag down. He opened it and reached in with what appeared to be the slow action of a man handing the spoils to the victor. With the precise mechanical movements of a primitive robot, he pulled out two sheets and walked stiffly over to Beasely's desk. He picked up the gold Mendel lighter. Despite Poul's obvious intentions, Beasely, slowed, by shock and dulled brain cells, didn't react in time.

Poul held the papers in front of the motionless publisher. "I wish to note that I have no idea what two papers these are," he said in a monotone. "They are possibly central to a song, possibly a whole song. Maybe they are crucial passages to one of the most important songs he has yet written. We'll never know." A flame shot from Mendel's little golden mouth and set the corner of the paper ablaze.

"No!" Beasely hurled his drink at the fire, missed, and drenched Poul's beard. "Fool! Stop!" His eyes bulged in terror and Poul wondered if he might have a heart attack. "Poul! Put it out!"

Poul dropped the paper before the flame reached his fingers and ground the warm ashes into the carpet. "Would you like to see it again? It's a simple trick." He held up the second paper.

"No! You're crazy! Don't!" Beasely's usually round face was lopsided with horror and disbelief.

"Sit down." Poul's voice was calm and authoritative. He did not itch himself. Beasely obeyed. "That's what will happen to the songs—these and the ones in my apartment. Then there the songs I've hidden for insurance. And after that there are all the songs that I will gather and burn. And after that there are all the songs that will never be written if you bring Mendel in, although I doubt if a force of a thousand computer geeks could find him because you are all mindless barbarians. You are all—even the ones out there hunting him now—greedy animals. You are not men."

He looked squarely at his partner. "But if you did find him, you would interrupt his purpose. You'd unbalance him and ruin him and you'd never see another song—not a damned one. You'd not only lose your shirt, Beaze, you'd be known as the fool of all fools. You would be remembered as the narrow-minded power monger who ruined the man who made the music. That's a hell of a legacy."

Beasely swallowed and Poul could see he was sobering up at a considerably faster than normal pace. There was no sound in the office except the click of the lighter as Poul lit a new cigarette. He studied the little figure, noting that the nose was too small and the features too full and rounded. All that resembled the real Mendel was the hair and beard. And these bumbling idiots think they can find Mendel, he thought.

"He's a human, Beaze. A man with a purpose, and it would be worse than murder for anyone to break his search—worse because millions of people take energy from him and they would be deprived, too." Beasely swallowed again, appearing each moment smaller and more frail. "Touch him and it's the end—for everybody."

Beasely took a long, deep breath, exhaled and closed his eyes as he leaned back in his chair. Poul waited for him to say something, but the small man appeared to be unconscious.

Still numb with anger, Poul picked up the bag once more. "I don't like you tonight, Beaze. You make me sick. Sleep on it and see if you're any different tomorrow."

The publisher remained motionless long after Poul slammed his office door. The single, small tear that idled on his eyelid could have been an excretion from a newly dead man.

❧   ❧   ❧

Mendel moves in silence...hmm. Interesting. He shrugged and kicked a stone. True, too. Mendel walks in silence...no. Mendel floats in...no. The first is best.

Mendel moves in silence to the music of the years. Hell, I'm getting poetry. Me, a goddamn layman. Ha, who needs you, Mendel? I'll be a writer myself!

Mendel moves in silence
To the music of the years
Through winds of golden laughter
And storms of silver tears.

Poul laughed again. At the same time he was deeply moved. It was the first time he had ever thought of poetry. It had come to him, just come to him, almost naturally or something. For the first time in his Mendel career, he pulled out a pen and pad which he usually used to note direction or chalk up pieces of collected paper. He wrote down the first stanza, then added:

Mountains rumble inward
Lizards swiftly fly
Mendel searches, earthbound
Reaching toward the sky.
A god in ragged clothing
Avoiding noisy throngs

Not knowing he is worshipped
As a song-creating song.

He shrugged at the absurdity of his writing poetry—especially stuff that actually rhymes, he thought. He pocketed the lyrics and continued on. It had been weeks and he had not picked up any clues. The feeling of some sort of impending doom gnawed at his stomach. "Where in the hell is he?"

There was no sign of Mendel in Colorado. No trace in Wyoming. He found a song in Nebraska. "One song. One damned song! What's he doing?" He studied the area and concluded the song had drifted southward, so he turned north. Near autumn he came upon a campsite. It was not much more than a couple weeks old. "Either my radar's fading or he's getting haphazard as hell," he mumbled.

He quickly turned east, forgetting food and sleep, wanting only to find the writer so he could gather whatever he could and get back to New York.

There are times when even synchronicity can seem a little out of synch. Poul felt like an unbalanced pinball chasing a more unbalanced and faster pinball in a tilted machine placed on a fault line.

He finally breathed a sigh of relief when he found Mendel in Illinois. He sat down for a leisurely supper and opened the can of Spam he'd been saving for this special occasion.

The nomadic shadow life was having its effect on him. His back was bowed from constantly stooping to pick up songs over the years. His eyes were sunken and watery from keeping a constant watch before and behind him. He moved now with the slightly hunched stealth of a hunted animal, though he was the hunter.

Or was he? He lived continually on the lookout for Mendel so the composer wouldn't spot him, and he felt a real need to hide from other eyes. He'd been questioned too many times, mistaken for an escaped robber, murderer, rapist—any man whose picture in the post offices resembled him.

Many did.

The years had worn on him and given him a shifty, seedy, hardened appearance, hardly the look of a man with millions in the bank and investments around the world.

Though it meant he had to watch his every move now, Poul felt a great relief, almost at home now that he had Mendel in his sight. He lay down after supper for his first decent night's sleep since the last time he was with Mendel. It was peaceful but not comfortable. He lay his head on the nearly empty Mendel bag and tried not to think about his aching back. He wished he had a bottle of wine. A variety of bugs persistently explored his skin, even though one or two of their comrades were slapped to death. But at least Mendel was near.

As he relaxed, his mind wandered to the soil. "Damn. I wonder if I have enough money to cover up all this dirt? Strikes me as a fine project. Move all the farmers to the Midwest, fence it off and macadam the rest of the country." He made a note to ask Beasely about funding when he returned. He ran it over and over in his mind, trying to bulldoze the dirty, black feeling in his gut that something unpleasant was lurking in the future.

It was huge, dark, and unstoppable.

CHAPTER 12

After twenty-five years, Mendel music was now an integral part of the culture and when anything new infiltrates a society already crowded with symbols, slogans, and confused individuals longing for sameness, there are stirrings of discontent. For every thousand persons longing for the security and anonymity of the unchanging familiar, there is one who would give anything for disruption and fame, or notoriety.

Mendel, the most popular unknown man in the world, had long been a threat to many. An increasing number of religious groups seized upon his images of dancing ghosts, his ideas about the soul leaving the body to mingle with higher, purer realms, and Heaven being nothing more than what each man makes it, now and after death. They used these song extracts to show that Mendel was a tireless agent of evil. The Anti-Mendel Movement (whose members became known as Anti-M's) stood as a wall against the Pro-M's, whose members defended Mendel with a fervor equal to the Anti-M's. The Pro-M's believed that Mendel was more likely God's messenger than Satan's. In fact, several of the more progressive churches used extracts from his works to exemplify man's search for truth, which ultimately leads to God.

A few people on the outer reaches postulated that the lone figure was Christ himself.

"After all," one critic wrote half-seriously, "Christ spread the word through poetry and parables because they were the easiest methods of making people understand and remember the teachings. If he were to return today, in what way would he choose to spread his messages? Through the art form that reaches the most people—music."

The tabloids fueled the feelings of a growing national cult that Christ was indeed due to return around the beginning of the millennium. And by God, this man just might be Christ. A National Enquirer story summed it up:

> Both the Anti-M's (media-dubbed AM's) and the Pro-M's (PMs) are convinced they are right. A showdown is coming and it may not be pretty. The PMs have always been the large majority, but the AM forces are growing and sources say that there may be violence. Morley Shiffer, a professor of psychology at Georgetown University said, 'Mendel's music has washed itself into society. The PMs feel his messages are leading society to something higher. The AMs feel just as strongly that his music is brainwashing people. It's an emotional issue, not an intellectual one. There could be big problems.

A prominent music critic at the New York Times said:

> Music certainly can be intellectual, but its power, whether it's Bach or Elvis, is emotional. Music, if it's good, creates emotion. If it's really good, like any good art, it creates love, or hate. It creates a passion.

Beneath both sides, crawling like deadly cockroaches, were the solitary individuals, as quiet and anonymous as the composer himself, searching for Mendel, hoping to find him and in one violent instant, kill the man and ride his ragged shirt tails to worldwide attention and everlasting recognition. What are a few years in prison when you are assured immortality in the history books beside the famous man you assassinated?

For all these reasons, the world was shocked, but not surprised when TV shows and radio programs one evening were interrupted with the announcement: "Mendel, considered the 20th century's greatest composer, has been murdered. Police are holding a lone gunman who claims he shot the writer to rid the world of evil. Stay tuned for information as we receive it...."

The next day, newspapers internationally ran banner headlines:

"Mendel is Murdered...King of Composers Dead by Bullet....Crazed Man Ends Era...MENDEL IS DEAD." With sorrow, morbid curiosity and a strange excitement, people watched television, bought newspapers and racked up millions of Website hits to imprint into themselves a photo of the man who had been on their minds for so many years. The photo had been taken after death and showed the grizzled man with long grayish hair, beard and an innocuous dime-size spot above his right eye.

Most of the world's people collectively stopped a breath. Some said prayers of thanks, but most wept, held moments of prayer for his soul, lit candles in his memory and demanded the death of the killer.

Most people were *not* ready for Mendel to die.

❧   ❧   ❧

Poul, on his way back to New York, missed the news. He had left the crazy writer on a hillside, convinced he had the man's direction down pat his time. He was now ready for his vacation. He would return in a year and collect the goods. All he wanted to do now was enjoy the fruits of his paper-picking labors. "Maybe a trip to the islands with Barbara. I think that's her name. Betsy, maybe. Ah, what the hell. I'll take both. Why not? I own the islands. They can be my island managers."

He felt better than he had in years. The black feeling had left him a couple nights ago. He would find himself some wine, women and concrete, although he was finding it increasingly harder to stomach the polluted air in and around cities.

He had reconciled himself to the fact that Mendel was almost like a shadow brother, a half-real figure who always strode before him, searching and creating, and in the midst of this act, giving meaning to Poul's existence. Mendel was his life. He was trapped in it, as was Mendel himself no doubt a prisoner of his own independence. Well, it was clear that Mendel could live within those parameters, so Poul made up his mind he could, too.

He also promised himself that if Mendel had not burned out in due time, say another five years, then he, Poul, would simply retire like any other businessman. Come 55 or so and that was it. Kiss the Big M bye-bye and lead the good life. He was attached but not married to the guy. The world would probably be sick of Mendel soon anyway; if not from the songs, then from Beasely overkill.

Ah hell, the sad fact was that he *was* just about married to the crazy bastard. Somehow, he'd find a way to retire, though. One way or another.

He got a bus at the edge of the city and watched with growing sadness and anger the shattered apartment windows and dull glares of people as they passed through Harlem on the way to Beasely's gleaming Land of Oz.

✿ ✿ ✿

Police escorted a man in his mid 20s out of the police station. The TV cameras showed a muscular man with short hair and drooping brown eyes.

"You've confessed that you murdered Mendel?" A reporter asked, sticking the microphone in the man's face.

"Yes. I killed him." The man's lawyer was trying to push the reporters away.

"Are you an Anti-M?"

"Yes! Death to Mendel! I rid the world of the evil force destroying mankind!"

Millions of people watched as the man spit at the reporter. "All of you are destroying mankind!" He was hustled into the police car with an officer holding the man's head to make sure he didn't bump it on the door frame.

✿ ✿ ✿

He was thinking about his islands when he entered Beasely's building.

Maybe he'd invite that Harry character. The beach bum could give Poul some neat insights into Mendel, and he'd be right at home on an island. He could walk his ass off around and around the edges, never hit a beginning or end. Maybe Poul would even buy Harry a junkyard so he'd never run out of things to pick up. Hmm.

His musings, like his body, stopped in mid-thought at the sight of the publisher who had aged a decade in the year or so Poul had been gone.

"Where have you been?" Beasely's voice had the weak, trembling quality of an old man.

"Where I usually am. Out beyond the neon. Why?" His stomach tightened and he felt a need to itch in several spots at ones. "You look sick as hell, Beaze."

Beasely took a deep breath and closed his eyes. Broke. He's gone bankrupt, Poul thought, seeing his islands fade into collection courts. Beasely rubbed his face and pulled a file of clippings from a drawer. "Then you haven't heard." He shoved the file across the desk.

Poul opened it and stared at the newspaper clips, his face fading to white as he skimmed the headlines. His hands quivered and he shook his head as he backed up, slowly, to get away from the news, from this sick unreal feeling, from this planet. No. He rubbed his wrist. No. How could it have happened so fast? It couldn't. It wasn't possible. It was a mistake.

He only left Mendel a week ago. That long? Yes, maybe a little more. He had left him happy healthy and alone…and alive.

"No. It's not true, Beaze. It's not true." His small eyes were those of an animal cornered, bright with terror.

"I'm sorry, Poul. Believe me." He spoke quietly and took a drink. Beasely's face sagged like tired clay and his eyes were cloudy with lack of sleep. "I thought you knew."

Poul shook his head and stared at nothing. Everything in his mind said it was not true, that it was impossible. His instincts were too great, his closeness to Mendel too strong. If Mendel were dead, he goddamn would have *felt* it somehow. He would have *known*. He wouldn't be standing here now. He'd be dead himself.

"It's not true, god damn it!"

"It happened three days ago," Beasely said, staring at the clippings. "In San Diego."

Poul's head jerked upward, a marionette cranium on an invisible string attached to a joyful cosmic hand. Beasely continued in a quiet monotone. "They found one of his songs, or a page of one, in the murderer's pocket. The guy took it from Mendel's bag. The man had been searching for Mendel for years. Jumped him in an alley and…put a bullet through his head." His voice trailed off.

When Beasely finally gathered the courage to look up from his glass, a wave of cold electricity jolted sobriety into him with a mainline shot. That crazy ass Poul was smiling! Beaming! Beasely was suddenly frightened, here in the presence of a madman, of a person so shocked by the loss of a loved one that he snaps and is capable of doing anything.

Poul whooped and clapped his hands. "Ha Haaaaa! Beaze, baby, it's not him! Ha ha haaaa! I *knew* it! Mendel's alive! God damn it, I knew it!" Poul was indeed mad with joy. His life had been ripped from his very heart and then thrown back, and he felt more alive than he'd ever felt in his life. He was in love with life!

"Mendel is alive, Beaze. He's alive!" Poul danced around the office and kissed Beasely's pale head. "Rejoice, buddy! The man's still with us!"

"Poul, calm down." Beasely spoke in a soft, fear-tinged tone. "Take it easy. It's okay."

Poul laughed and scratched his chest with the exuberance of a man who has just leaped from an exhilarating shower.

"Beaze, you don't understand. I just left Mendel a few days ago in the mountains in, um, very far from San Diego. There is no way he could have made it back to California. He wouldn't have anyway. He was about to turn south. Don't ask me how I know. I just do. I know him. I love him. I know Mendel as well as I know myself and he's alive and all right. He's—". He stopped suddenly and fell into sudden sullen silence. He looked at Beasely in shock and sadness. "I know who it was," he said quietly. He stared at the silent Beasely. "The dead man. I know."

The publisher looked puzzled, feeling the stirring of hope that Mendel might indeed be alive, and wondering how Poul could know all this. Wondering if Poul were even in his right mind. Beasely felt his heart flutter as it had so often these past few months, and didn't know how much more stress he could take.

"Is there a picture? Of the dead man! Is there a picture?" Beasely dug through the clippings and handed over an Enquirer photo. Poul swallowed, nodded slowly and sat down. It was Harry, the man who loved life so much, whom Mendel called the freest man alive. It was Harry whose joy of life was obliterated by a bullet. Hadn't Poul overheard Harry ask Mendel to go to Mexico with him, saying he was stopping along the way to see some friends? The friends were in San Diego. And, yes, of course! The page that Poul couldn't find! Harry, the sentimental old pack rat had picked it up, recognized it as his friend's and saved it as a souvenir. Maybe he even knew of Mendel's fame and never said anything to Mendel. Yes, he must have known, and knew, too, that Mendel must not be told for his own good.

Maybe not. Maybe that was assuming too much. It didn't matter. Poul shuddered and fought back tears for this good person whom he'd envied and who was now dead.

A voice boomed into his head from a distance, bringing him suddenly back to the plush office. "Who was it, for Christ's sakes?" Poul looked blankly at Beasely who was taking a deep drag on a cigarette, waiting anxiously.

"When did you start smoking cigarettes?"

"When Mendel died."

"He didn't die, you damned ghoul!"

"Well then who did? It's a simple frigging question!" Beasely was screaming. He closed his eyes, took a deep breath, and another drag. "I'm sorry, Poul. My nerves are...when I heard…. Poul, please, who the hell was killed?"

Poul stared at the photo again and shook his head. "Harry."

Beasely was near tears with exhaustion and frustration. He struggled to control himself. "Harry *who*?"

Poul shrugged. "I don't know his last name. A beach bum."

His fingers trembling, his face the color of a birch tree in a rainstorm, Beasely, in a very quiet voice, said, "Poul, I'm not a well man. I'm near a nervous breakdown. My stomach hurts and my blood pressure is as high as my office. Tell me the whole goddamn lousy story before I lose control and rip your face right off your skull."

To Beasely's immense relief, Poul told him the story, from the long walks Mendel and Harry took, to the beer cadging and the children who loved Harry.

When Poul finished the story a relieved and fascinated Beasely said, "I thought Mendel never had contact with anyone."

Poul ran his hand over his face and shook his head. "I don't know how they got together. I wish now he'd never run into Harry."

They were quiet for awhile. "You're sure Mendel's okay?"

Poul scratched his ear. "I'm not sure of anything anymore. He was when I left him."

Later, after supper, the two men discussed course of action. Poul, wolfed down an elk burger smothered in fried onions and peppers with a side order of baby mushrooms steamed in soy sauce. He wanted to leave Mendel dead.

He noticed that Beasely's hands shook continuously these days. If they weren't fidgeting with a cigarette or cigar or glass of scotch, they simply shook, like fragile, weakening elm leaves in an autumn breeze. At first Poul thought it was the shock of Mendel's "death," but the shaking had been coming on for some time, like the sick color of Beasely's skin and the drawn, haggard features that ate into his once pleasant baby face. The publisher shook his head. "No. We can't do that."

Poul leaned across the table. "Yes, we can! Let them bury Harry and Mendel goes too. He can live in peace." They stared at each other. "Beaze, if we announce the truth, all hell will break loose. Every God damned maniac in the country will be after him. It will be a new challenge. Mendel will be killed for sure."

Beasely looked away and shook his head. "I can't. If he's still writing and we're still producing, then he's alive. Songs don't come from a dead man."

"Bring him back to life and he will be dead."

"I'm sorry. I can't. I've got faults, but I've never lied and I won't lie to the public about this. Besides, if he's dead, where does that leave you, Poul? You're just going to wipe him out of your mind? Leave him alone? Sit back with your wealth and relax?"

Poul leaned back and sighed. Both of them already knew the answer. He couldn't wipe out Mendel, just as Beasely couldn't. The damned guy was the definition of their lives.

The thought took him back to the present. What if they said nothing and left Mendel dead? That wasn't to say that some fanatic wouldn't recognize him one day and kill him. What if one of those organizations—the AM's—saw him and spread the word that Mendel had risen from the dead?

Christ, there would be chaos.

"Raised from the dead. Exactly." Beasely smiled.

Poul started. His partner was now reading his mind. "What?"

"You just mumbled something about being raised from the dead. Good idea." Poul shook his head, wondering if he was losing his mind. He could have sworn he was just thinking.

Beasely signaled for more drinks and brought his chair around beside Poul. He leaned in close and talked low. "Listen, let me run this by you. We'll throw some flair into this next promotion...." He just couldn't help himself, Poul thought.

The plan called for Poul to identify Harry, claiming to be the man's cousin. He could quietly bury the man and retrieve the missing page. The announcement that the wrong man had been killed would bring a new flood of publicity, mass speculation about Mendel's location and, hopefully, a joyous celebration of his being alive. The carefully controlled theme would be, simply: "Mendel Lives!"

"It's beautiful," Beasely said softly, tears of sentimental joy in his slightly inebriated eyes. "Just beautiful. God."

"Subtlety is not your strong card, Beaze." He was mildly disgusted, but by now was used to Beasely's genius, coarse as it was, for publicity.

"But you'll go along, right?"

Poul studied his glass of wine. He had long ago given up the illusion that he had any control in this whole matter. Mendel's life was locked up in a fate that seemed to be running quite smoothly without any interference. It was operating despite a whole world *attempting* to interfere.

Both Poul and Beasely were little more than poor players in a game staged by an unseen director who seemed to write the script in little stages, one step ahead of them.

"Whatever you say, Beaze."

The publisher smiled and pulled out a cigar. "The California beach material we're calling 'The Children's Songs,' kind of like Blake's 'Songs of Innocence.' A new beginning. A new life. Right after we announce that he's alive, we'll bring out his latest—and best—album. Perfect!"

Poul nodded. Everything was perfect. He sat back, sipped the tepid liquid and felt the brevity of man's life in the continually shifting universe of his dreams. He went home, opened a new bottle of wine and drank until he reached that part of the night where there are no hours.

Then he passed out.

Not even the constant police and fire sirens, which bothered him more each time he returned, could stir him.

CHAPTER 13

Dust plugged every pore of his body. It matted his hair and beard and tan clouds poofed in puffball explosions when he patted his clothes. He couldn't remember ever being so parched. "Keep going," he thought. "The perfect song is at hand." He laughed silently, feeling, as he always did when he seemed as far down as he could be, that a miracle was about to happen. It always did, no matter how small. It always came when it was supposed to and he was provided for. Gentle swirls of dust trailed his feet over this dirt road.

He wasn't surprised to come upon a house about a mile later. It was old and small, sagging in the middle, too weary and old to beg for paint. Clumps of goldenrod and ragweed ate at its crumbling foundation. Under his feet the porch boards creaked in resigned pain. Though his knock was gentle, the door rattled convulsively. He was about to turn and leave when a slim young woman with long black hair and wide brown eyes opened the door.

"Can I help you?" Her voice was soft and confident. If she was shocked at the man's dirty, ragged countenance, she didn't show it.

"I'd like—". The back of his tongue pasted itself to his throat and his voice creaked to a halt. He felt his face redden and quickly pointed to his throat. The woman laughed knowingly and motioned him in with a grace he'd seen only in mountain lions running, deer leaping or mature swans gliding in still summer ponds.

He bowed his head in thanks and stepped inside. The woman stepped over to a chipped, gray porcelain sink and drew a glass of water from the faucet. He nodded in thanks as she handed it to him, then emptied the glass in a few gulps.

"Ahh." He tested his voice. It worked. "Thanks. I was…very dry."

"So I heard," she said, smiling. Her large, dark eyes looked at Mendel without a hint of self-consciousness, as she were studying a flower or a picture that she liked. "My name is Mara."

Her quiet directness was as natural as a stream.

"Hello. I'm Mendel." He was about to ask for another glass of water when she smiled and motioned him to the kitchen chair.

"You're tired. Would you like some coffee, Mendel?"

Uh, yes. And maybe another glass of water."

She was already busy at the stove. "Help yourself. I've got a deep well. The dry weather never seems to affect the supply." He noticed that although there were light bulbs in the ceiling, there were no outlets in this ancient Appalachian shanty. There were no clocks, no radios, no calendars. The kitchen cupboards held only the barest necessities: a few chipped dishes, some pots and pans, a few glasses. In the center of the kitchen was an old table and three chairs.

"You look like you've been traveling a long, long time."

He filled his glass, a little giddy from the fresh scent of her hair. "Yes, it seems that way."

He pulled out a chair and sat, feeling at once comfortable, and, in a stimulating way, mildly intimidated by this woman who had none of the small, nervous feminine gestures of patting her hair, smoothing her skirt or giggling. She was quiet and sure of herself. Each movement was graceful and direct to her purpose. She placed some rolls on the table and sat down across from him. As she poured the coffee, Mendel studied the long, thick black hair streaked almost imperceptibly with strands of silver, as if she had combed her hair with the delicate spider webs that gleamed in the morning sun outside her door. He saw sadness in the round eyes, eyes like a fawn with knowledge. But the bouquet-shaped laugh lines that traced lightly around the corners told him that she overcame any unhappiness with humor. The graceful hands that held the pot were muscular from work both in and outside the house.

"Do you live alone?" He took a large bite of a roll and immediately wondered if it was too large to be polite, and realizing the question was none of his business.

"Yes, I do." She sipped her coffee and smiled easily, as if waiting for another question.

"Aren't you afraid?" Inwardly he cursed his awkwardness. It was a stupid question since she lived alone and seemed not to be afraid of anything. He tried to correct his error. "I mean, I come knocking at your door. I'm a total stranger. Yet you invited me in."

Her quiet laugh was both gentle and hearty. "If you were a criminal or whatever, you'd still be a man who was tired and thirsty." She tilted her head slightly so that her hair fell over her shoulder. "But you're not a criminal. You're a writer." Mendel felt a prickle shoot up his back. "You have also been traveling a lot of years looking for something. You find a little bit here and a little there and then you move on." She smiled at his stunned expression, then sighed. "And you're not finished."

Still holding his roll, Mendel sat immobilized before Mara's gaze that seemed to have the ability to enter his soul and read his very life. Fascinated, he asked quietly, "How did you know all that?"

A child-like but alluring smile traced across her lips as she held her cup with both hands. "Well, criminals don't walk much through these parts. It's pretty slim pickings around here." Mendel nodded in agreement. She continued. "You have a pencil sticking out a hole in your pocket." Without thinking, Mendel reached up and pushed it back into his pocket, embarrassed for some reason. "Your bag lies open on the floor and there's nothing in it but papers. You're pretty obvious, Mendel."

There was a moment of silence and they laughed together, as if she had reached the punch line of a shared private joke that brought them together in a sudden intimacy felt by both but understood by neither. Then Mendel cleared his throat and leaned over to close his bag. He had never felt so exposed and vulnerable as he did with this incredible woman.

When he regained his composure, Mendel sipped his coffee and said, "Alright, you are a lady Holmes who throws out all but the facts. But you say I'm not finished searching. I don't know of any physical clue that would bring you to that conclusion." He had her on that one, he thought, feeling like a child who has begun to master a new and exciting game.

She was silent, as if carefully constructing the coming words. "You have intelligent eyes that have seen and studied many things," she said. He held her stare and their eyes were like two armies studying each other before declaring peace. "Your eyes have much wisdom, but they're still searching. They aren't at…rest. Whatever they look at they pierce too deeply—like they are doing to me right now."

She smiled and it was Mendel who dropped his gaze to the coffee cup and tried to fathom the soul that seemed too large and old for her young body.

"I—I'm sorry. I'm terribly rude."

"And finally," she said raising her finger in a mock announcement. "You haven't had many dealings with people. For all the traveling you seem to have done, you are a very shy man."

Now Mendel laughed. He wanted to hug her for being so natural and putting him at ease. "You're right, Mara. I've spent too much time with myself. It's a bad habit." Subtle sensations sang through his body and he stared in wonder at nothing.

Mara smiled and motioned to the coffee pot. Mendel nodded. "How long have you been traveling?" She asked as she filled his cup.

He thought and shook his head. "I don't know. Decades, I guess."

She looked at him and smiled thoughtfully. They finished the coffee in easy silence. When he stood to go, she stopped him again with one of her surprisingly direct questions. "What do you write?"

He smiled again, reminded of Harry's directness. "Songs."

"Do you sell them?"

"No. I throw most of them away."

She looked into his eyes and he felt warm. "Why do you work and suffer to write a song just to throw it away?"

She was lovely and he fought to gain control of this new, warm sensation that sang throughout him. "You already know that," he said. She nodded, waiting. "I'm searching."

"Searching for what?" She asked innocently. "I don't know that."

He felt lightheaded, staring into those large eyes that seemed to question…and yet know. He broke his gaze and looked out the open door at the bluish rolling mountains. "I'm searching for the most expressive song in the world, Mara. I want to write the song of all the world. There is so much of life—the earth, air, water, nature, people, joy, sadness, growth, decay. I want to create the song that contains the universe…the perfect song."

He stopped suddenly, realizing that he had told her, a total stranger whom he'd met less than an hour before, more than he'd ever told anyone except Harry. Saying it out loud always made it sound ridiculous. He waited for her laughter as a condemned man waits for the guillotine blade to drop.

Instead, Mara nodded with an understanding smile. He felt the strange warm sensation again and understood why a few lucky, happily married men considered themselves kings, and why other men would give their very lives for that moment of a woman's unselfish understanding. It gave a man a faith that no god ever could.

He picked up his bag. "I should be going. Thank you, Mara. If there's any way I can pay you—"

"There is."

They studied each other—he looking beyond the dark hair and peaceful face into the lonely, powerful soul; she past the graying hair and beard and into the energetic, determined, yet oddly timorous eyes.

The armies had made peace and were fraternizing. Soldiers walked among each other, stiffly shaking hands, introducing themselves and sizing up their former opponents. Then they talked of their families back home and how they missed their wives and children and then told jokes until the two armies melded into one large community that hated war.

"I'd like you to play some of your songs for me," she said simply. Mendel lowered his eyes. Confused, he shrugged and started to repeat that he had only bits and pieces. "I have an old guitar," she said. "My...someone I knew played it." She went into another room and returned with an old acoustic. "It still has all the strings." She handed it to him gently and he took it gently. "It needs tuning."

He felt awkward, self-conscious, warm, excited. "It's been a long time since I've played," he said.

"It's been a long time since I've heard music."

As the sun set fiery red into the silhouetted mountains, the little house came to life with fragments of happy tunes Mendel had written in the New York State forests as a youth, the earthy song parts of the Midwest, and the wacky California numbers. When he played one of the haunting Arizona songs, he was shocked to look up and find her quietly crying.

He laid his fingers over the guitar strings, hushing into silence the last minor chord. "I'm sorry. Is something wrong?"

Mara shook her head and brushed away the tears with the tips of her fingers. "No. It's beautiful...almost too lovely to listen to." She stared at the flames in the fireplace. "It brings out memories of things...things we remember, and things we never thought we knew...and maybe some we don't want to know." She moved closer to him, as if his warmth assured her of their aliveness in a dark night on a darker earth.

"Finish it, please." He continued and when the song was done, he returned to the lighter song parts and Mara clapped her hands and tapped her foot in time with the music and applauded at the end of each song. She laughed as if she'd never known tears, as if she were a golden goddess who banished darkness to the lower bowels of hell to be cremated in its own eternal fires.

Mendel played an instrumental piece about rushing water, giving him time to think. Mara's eyes had the capacity to become worlds. When they wept they were enormous dark clouds that encompassed feminine sadness for the earth and its tragedies. When she laughed, the pupils became tawny, lightened by an inner glow. It was good to hear his songs played and to have someone respond to them. That's what music is made for, he thought.

He'd forgotten that. Music is to be heard and shared and felt. Only then does a song truly come to life. He cursed himself for throwing away so many songs. He could spend the rest of his life playing his songs for Mara.

It didn't matter, he thought happily. He would write new ones. He stopped to rest. "They'd sound better if I practiced the guitar a little." He rubbed his burning fingertips.

She smiled and pulled her hair back, leaning against the couch arm like a contented panther. Her powers were great, he thought, realizing that he would have much time to practice.

As he strummed the guitar searching for the subtle sixth and augmented chords, Mara fixed coffee and sandwiches. They talked. He told her of his travels and she told him of her daily life around the house but nothing of her past. She opened a bottle of wine she had made in the spring from dandelions.

Later, as Mendel had shared his songs with her, Mara shared herself with him. As she eased out of her clothes, Mendel confronted a song he'd often heard but never played. She taught him the melody, slowly and gently, accompanied by the soprano voices of a thousand crickets and peepers and the bass chorus of the invisible frogs in the nearby pond. The willows and pines, like a section of whispering cellos, backed the voices with peaceful sympathy.

After a time that sped by too quickly, there came a moment when Mendel didn't hear the music or notice the darkness. He felt only himself rush out of control, pouring what felt to be his very self into the flowing subterranean depths of a feminine refrain. Then he heard the short song of two sighs after a moment that transcended even the sound of the rich, expansive E minor.

For a time his wandering stopped. Never in his whole life had he come so close to happiness. He told himself that he had reached the end of his search, knowing that their happiness would last forever.

Mara only wished it could.

CHAPTER 14

Mendel Is Alive!

In a bizarre turn of events, it seems that the world's most reclusive writer, Mendel, is alive. The information was revealed yesterday when a man who gave his name as Paul Smith identified the recently murdered man thought to be Mendel as Harry Smith, a beachcomber and first cousin to Paul.

J.W. Beasely of Beasely Publishing which handles Mendel's material made the announcement yesterday during a press conference. Beasely said the beachcomber had apparently spent time with the elusive artist and came into possession of one of Mendel's papers.

Beasely said Mendel is alive, working and unaware of the attempt on his life. Meanwhile, millions of fans who mourned the "death" of the man who has become one the 21st century's most puzzling legends, are rejoicing over what has been termed a "miraculous discovery of mistaken identity."

It is expected that the cry for a public appearance by the invisible artist will become even stronger. However, if the past is any indication, those cries will be in vain.

Beasely laid the paper down and chuckled. He flicked a cigar ash from his beige suit. "A stroke of genius, Poul. A stroke of genius."

Poul stared out the office window, wondering where Mendel was. "Yeah. Genius. You're a real stroke, Beaze." His arm was raw from scratching. The windows were gray with smog.

Beasely ignored Poul's remark. A large spark dove headlong onto his lapel. He jumped from his chair and brushed it off. "Damn it! I go through more suits…." He inspected the spot and, satisfied that there was no char mark, sat down again. He took a puff and held his cigar out cautiously. "We'll ride this publicity for a good year. We release 'Children's Songs' next week, dedicated to Harry Smith, the man who died for Mendel"

Poul groaned. "That's a little much, Beaze."

Beasely shook his head. "When the public is involved, it's real hard to go too far." He took a puff and held the cigar away from him before another ash attack. "Then we give them 'Ocean Depths/Soul's Heights.' Double platinum time, friend." He leaned back dreamily, trying to ignore Poul's sullen scratching. He idly vowed to buy the man a flea collar.

Ah, life was good. That little killing and subsequent publicity was Heaven sent. Of course he felt badly for the dead man, this Harry guy, but, what the hell, that was out of his hands. He didn't control fate; he just made the most of what fate handed out.

"Beaze." Poul turned from the window, ran his hand over his tired face and looked at his partner with a blank expression that fought hints of disgust, anger and fatigue. "Harry was a human being."

Beasely wondered how two men who fought so much could damn near read each other's minds. Hmm. Well, leave it to Poul to make such a startling observation. He nodded, wearing the expression of shallow somberness one sees on the faces of distant relatives at an old man's funeral. "I know, Poul."

"He's dead."

"I know." He studied his cigar, wondering what Poul was getting at.

"Mendel's a human."

Poul's voice was the same monotone he had used that time he burned the song. Sensing he was being led into a trap, Beasely's eyes became distant. "Get to the point, friend. From all you've told me, he's a human." He wished they didn't have to bicker all the time.

Poul bit his lip and stopped scratching. He had done that, too, before he burned the song, Beasely recalled. He was feeling like a mouse who senses there's a starving cat lurking in the shadows. He wanted a drink.

"I guess that's it right there." Poul's voice was low, almost a growl, mismatched with the thin body. "You don't care that he's a living human. Yeah, you give me little Beasely platitudes on how he's a regular guy who eats supper and pees in the bushes, but you don't give a damn, really. You've made a pen-and-ink sketch, a batch of albums and a ton of icons. You've made a god of him…and you control the god." Poul took a deep breath. "He isn't a goddamned god and neither are you."

Beasely's face flushed. He was used to Poul's whimpering, but the guy had hit a nerve again. He poured the drink he needed and took a large swallow. He let the pleasant lava burn into his stomach, then turned to Poul. "Okay. He's not a god and I do care. Okay, Poul?"

"Sure. A man's dead and Mendel could be—probably will be—because of us. You don't give a rat's ass!" His arms swung outward in his building rage. The publicity, excitement and suspense had worn on him. For God's sakes, he had to lie to get Harry's body and "correct" the situation.

For the rest of his life he would not be able to shake the sight of the gray still face whose forehead wrinkles were broken by a bluish bullet hole. Beasely sat in his office, basking in triumph while he made a different kind of killing.

And if Poul lived for a century, he would never get used to the rushing, the plottings, the daily readings of the Divine Song Charts, the Mendel polls, the marketing and psychology of keeping Mendel before the public. And now the exploitation of another man's violent death.

Beasely correctly pointed out that Mendel had become of everyone's life when headlines began appearing in the weekly tabloids:

Mendel is an Alien Bringing in New World Order!
Mendel is Reincarnated from Atlantis Poet!
I'm Having Mendel's Baby!
I Was Part of Wild Mendel Mountain Orgy!

It was too much. Beasely had created a world and everyone within the vast Mendel industry lived his life for Mendel via Beasely. Beasely was Oz, a ruler whose power came from a fabrication that he'd fashioned into myth.

Industry employees fought for control of their turfs and to move upward. They judged their status by how soon they heard the latest Mendel story that Poul told Beasely and by some process of oral precipitation drizzled downward. People earned promotions and ulcers from Beasely. They staked their career goals on how well Mendel might do in the coming years. They would do anything to make sure he did well because Mendel's future was their future.

And no one, not even Beasely, truly *knew* if Mendel existed. That was the kicker. Poul smiled.

Beasely, studying him, frowned.

Poul's smile faded. No, it wasn't the kicker. The truth was that it didn't matter if Mendel existed or not. So long as the songs kept coming in, the people would continue creating him. Whether or not Mendel was real was beside the point.

For one nightmarish moment, Poul wondered if Mendel did exist. Or was he, Poul, one of the century's most adroit dual personalities who had thought he had been following a composer genius, but all the while writing the songs himself? Or maybe all this was a dream in some laudanum-laden Coleridge creation. Or maybe, as in Poe's poem, he was trapped in a dream within a dream, unable to ascertain if he were dreaming his life, living a dream, or dreaming a dream about life which itself is a dream…the vision passed.

The real kicker was none of the above. He took a deep breath and found a cigarette. He scratched himself to reaffirm his reality. The kicker was that none of this idiotic industry had to exist at all. Mendel would sell now and forever because his art was real and true.

The songs were important. Everything else, all this plastic and paper propaganda served one purpose—earnings.

He was tired.

All money does is create a demand for more.

Same with power.

He was tired. He sniffed and took a drag on the cigarette. "Sorry, Beaze. I guess I need to rest."

Seeing an opening, Beasely smiled as if to a wayward son who has admitted his erring ways. "There's been a lot of pressure the past few days."

"Not just the past few days!" Poul shot back like a weary gunman. "I'm tired of the whole thing. This entire industry. It works for nothing but profits and control." He closed his eyes. "That's all I have to say."

Beasely stared at his desk, refusing to let his nerves get the best of him. "Just remember it was you who brought in the songs and it was you whose prime concern was the money to be gained for yourself," he said. "It was I who took a gamble on it and built the industry we have today. Don't start the bleeding heart shit with me. I'm doing exactly what I am supposed to do in my business. You got what you wanted, and from all you tell me, Mendel is doing what he wants." He sighed and his voiced softened. "Go and get some rest."

Poul sat in his leather chair, closed his eyes and said, almost kindly, "Beasely, sometimes I hate you." He paused. "I hate me. I hate the things we're doing to ourselves. I hate everything that's happening."

The sound of a siren rose upward from the streets far below. Poul stood up with effort and moved to the window where he looked down on where people were speeding, eating, arguing, crying, dying, being born. In Times Square they rushed through their lives beneath the gigantic billboard bearing Mendel's image, a promotion for the latest album.

Poul shook his head. "If people would just take what he gives them and not make a damned religion of it." Two fire trucks weaved their way through the traffic, sirens blaring and louds horns honky angrily. "I was wrong about you making a god of him. They do. You just help organize the worship."

He lit another cigarette. "I'm sick of it all. Someday, not too long from now, we're all going to be dead." He shrugged. "Just dead." He looked over at Beasely, whose pasty face and unhealthy tone was emphasized in the fluorescent light of his office lamp. "What will it have meant then?"

Beasely grunted himself forward and poured a fresh drink. "We'll be forgotten, but the songs will stay as long as there are people." He sipped the drink and fingered the Mendel lighter. "The songs will live and we'll die. But while I'm here, I'll gather all I can and play it for all it's worth. I'm too crass for you, but that's the way I am. My father—." His voice trailed off. "I've always been what I am and I won't apologize." He shrugged and sat back. "So, someday we die."

Poul blew on the end of his cigarette and stared at the red tip. "Yeah."

Everything was working just the way it was supposed to. Poul had his wealth. Beasely had his kingdom. And Mendel walked in freedom.

Who was the happiest of this little trio? Mendel suffered daily with hunger, homelessness and frustration. Poul had so much money it meant nothing to him anymore, and he was caught up in two men's games. Mendel's quest was so simple and powerful Poul couldn't break from it. Beasely's was so complicated Poul was like a fly in a spider's web, entangling himself more with each vain flail.

Beasely was easily the happiest of the trio, playing the game he created and controlled. A game which he continually won.

Ah, Christ, he was tired. The next day he was on the road.

All games would come to a halt if certain groups had their ways. When the media announced that Mendel still walked among the living, religious and parent groups denounced the artist with more fervor than ever.

In his office, Beasely turned on the TV to catch a press conference by a prominent minister. There were enough print, broadcast and Web reporters to assure international coverage. He waved the newspaper headline about Mendel's "return to life."

"This is living proof that Mendel is Satan's agent!" he cried out. "He could not be destroyed by mere bullets. Indeed, in classic Mephistophelean fashion, Mendel *projected* his image onto another man and let that man *die* for him!" The preacher's face was hard with practiced outrage. "He deluded a hapless man into thinking a beach bum was Mendel. Mendel is evil! There is no other explanation."

"This hapless man had a gun," a reporter said.

Without missing a beat, the minister nodded. "And he killed the wrong man. Mendel is an agent of *Satan!*"

Beasely shook his head. "What people are capable of! He turned back to his computer. "Well, they're doing all my PR work for me."

The next night a university professor representing the Pro-M group, gave a rebuttal. "Of course Mendel isn't Satan. He isn't the Christ, either. But at this moment in time, he may be as close to a Christ as we'll get. Through music, he's entertaining people, as Christ did with parables. Through his music, he's showing people ways back to themselves, as all the great teachers have done."

"Why won't he reveal himself?" A reporter asked.

The professor paused and looked directly into the camera. "Would you?"

Beasely nodded. "Good answer, man."

A few minutes later his secretary brought in the paper. "You should see this," she said, pointing to the headline "AM-PM Forces Clash Around Country." Beasely read the first paragraph.

> *(AP) Like boils on an ailing body, Pro-M and Anti-M forces clashed in Washington, D.C., Chicago, New York and Dallas. Hundreds were injured in this battle of beliefs. A 53-year-old man died of an apparent heart attack while arguing with police. A woman in Dallas threw herself into the path of an oncoming truck. A five-year-old girl in Chicago was killed instantly from a gunshot wound to the head during a gun battle between the two groups. Police are investigating to find out if it was bullet from an AM or PM believer.*

He put the paper down sadly and turned to his secretary. His fingers were suddenly cold. "Sharon, find out who the little girl is and her family. Make arrangements to pay for the funeral and set up a trust fund in her name. And keep it anonymous." Sharon nodded without a word and left.

Despite the violent feelings of the more radically inclined, the vast majority of people accepted Mendel as just a part of their lives along with nuclear waste, terrorism, the greenhouse effect, reality TV, cancer research and increasing population.

Critics were given a new lease on life with Mendel's resurrection. A writer for Atlantic Monthly used the Arizona songs as a basis to review the artist's works to date:

> *...if a critic is honest, he admits that criticism of an excellent work, or of an excellent artist, is doomed to failure, for a critic cannot adequately translate or criticize the raw power or eternal beauty that springs to life in a particular work or set of works. Mendel, if that is indeed his name, brings us, compacts for us and hands us the mystical beauty and terror of a life fully lived each moment. If we listen closely we hear what he says over and over in varying degrees of subtlety: that the dawn of life was this morning's dawn and it will be followed by another and another. Between are countless discoveries, joys, and horrors.*
>
> *Mendel describes states of emotion, discoveries and memories of man with equal intensity. He offers us music from a realm where reality is more real than what most of us see, or have the courage to face. All states of existence seem to be within Mendel's reach. He has reached out so far and with such grace, that even what might seem to him to be failures, are to us breakthroughs into the light of a new consciousness, new discoveries in the moments of mortal existence and the eternality of the universe. Mendel, so far as we mortals can see, seems truly in touch with the immortal.*

Critics with a more New Age bent felt the songs were manufactured by a top secret Bill Gates operation that had programmed and synthesized music and poetry of the last 20 centuries, combined it with the latest studies of neural maps and synaptic wish lists and created a stream of music to, very simply, control everybody.

In the end, the opinions were little more than time-passing games by people who made money indulging in such games. The bottom line was that Mendel had become a crucial part of the collective consciousness, the collective heart-beat, and the world economy.

❧   ❧   ❧

It was dusk, the time when three-dimensional things take on the quality of shadow. Poul had developed and nurtured a sense for danger, but he was not ready for the slight rustle, and the feel of a knife that suddenly and silently pushed against his throat. He could tell the knife was razor sharp. The steel was cold. He didn't want to die.

"Don't move. Just don't move." The serrated points were like needles in his skin. He didn't move. A hand enveloped his forehead. "Get on your knees."

Poul slowly lowered himself. The young man behind him, lean, pale, with long black hair, was sweating. "I been tracking you on the computer for years. Now I found you. You need to know that I'm going to kill you." The knife remained fixed. So did Poul.

He swallowed carefully. "Why?"

"Mendel is bad. *Bad*! You're keeping him alive. If I kill you, I kill Mendel!"

Poul swallowed again, slowly. There was a long silence. A small wind sighed through the pines, a song of sadness.

"Are you one of those AM's?"

"No way! They're idiots. I'm an independent, and I'm good."

Poul was speaking in the darkness with a man ready to slice his throat. "Why do you want to kill Mendel?" He asked with a quiet sincerity.

The man snorted as if Poul were an idiot. "He sings of construction and destruction. We all carry the seeds of construction and destruction!" The knife bit into Poul's throat. He wondered how long it took to die by throat slashing. Do you die of lack of oxygen or loss of blood?

"Want the truth?" He asked quietly.

Instantly the knife bit deeper. He felt something warm trickling down his neck. He knew what it was.

"And what's the truth?" The young man asked with derision.

Poul said a quiet prayer. His mouth was dry. He swallowed again and said gently but with conviction: "If you're a man, take the knife away and face me. I won't fight and I won't run. I'll tell you the truth."

It seemed like forever but the hand released the pressure. The knife came away. The young man kept his hand on Poul's forehead as he made his way around to the front of Poul.

Drugs, Poul thought. The cold, clammy skin. The gauntness of the hand. The desperate feeling of the man. What the hell did Mendel *do* to people?

"The truth!" The young man hissed.

"The truth is Mendel is a lie," Poul said gently. Without thinking he reached up and wiped the blood from his neck.

The young man shook his head nervously. "No. He's real. I know it. I can feel it. His songs are real. He's *real*."

"He's made up."

The young man stood up and looked down at Poul. "You're lying." There was a wildness, an unpredictability in the young man's voice and movements. Poul shook his head. "Then why are you out here?" The young man asked. "You're tracking him! You're the man who gathers the songs!"

God, help me say the right things, Poul prayed. You'd better be here helping me. "I'm the man who *makes* the tracks," Poul said. "J.W. Beasely is the man who creates the illusion. It's all illusion for the sake of art…and commerce."

The young man looked shocked, then hurt, then deadly. "You're *lying*!" He screamed. Small animals scurried in fear through the trees and brush.

Poul closed his eyes and took a deep breath. "No. It's all about art, money and power. Simple as that. I'm sorry."

In the dark he couldn't see the kick coming. It knocked the wind out of him. He couldn't breathe. The man's mouth was suddenly next to his ear. "I'll find out! I'll find out and if you're lying I'll track you down again and you die! You and Mendel *die*! I know everything about you, Poul. Everything! If you're lying I'll find you and kill you!"

The young man disappeared silently into the trees. Poul worked patiently to get his breath back. He crawled into some nearby bushes, curled into a fetal position and after a long time, fell into a frightened, exhausted sleep.

The next morning, cold and aching, Poul realized what he had done. "Oh, my God," he groaned, sitting up. He forced himself to his feet and headed back as fast as he could.

❦   ❦   ❦

The young man with long, black hair entered the office. "I want to see J.W. Beasely."

"I'm sorry, he's tied up," Sharon, the secretary said. The man was pale and lean. There was something unsettling about him.

"No, he's not." The man strode forward. Sharon rushed from the desk to stop him. He punched her and she fell. He kicked opened Beasely's door and strode into the office.

Beasely jumped up from his desk, surprised, frightened. "Who are you?"

"My mission is to kill Mendel." Beasely stared, dumbfounded. "But Poul says he's not real. He's made up."

"Where's Poul?" Beasely asked, suddenly short of breath. "What did you do—"

"I left him alive. He'd better not be lying. Is Mendel made up?"

Beasely shook his head. "I've never met him. I don't know." He was scared, stalling for time.

The man pulled his serrated knife from inside his jacket. "Not a good enough answer." He stepped forward.

Beasely stood up from his chair. "Hey, take it easy. Let's, let's talk about this. You don't need that." He felt himself sweating. One moment was perfectly normal and the next moment he was facing death.

The young man waved the knife. "Take your tie off."

Beasely looked at him puzzled. "What?"

"Take your tie off! Then your shirt! Hurry up." Beasely obeyed the desperate command. His fingers shook and he couldn't push the buttons through the holes. Finally he had the shirt off and held it.

The young man stared at Beasley, quiet and deadly. "Is he made up?"

Beasely slowly nodded. He had never felt so helpless and naked. "We created—"

The young man's eyes flashed with a wildness Beasely had never seen in a man. "The creators must be destroyed! In creation there is destruction and in destruction the seeds of creation! *Destroy the creator!*" He pulled the knife back to slash Beasely's throat just as the room exploded with gunshots from two security guards. The man lurched forward and the knife came down on Beasely.

Blood from two men filled the office.

❧   ❧   ❧

Poul limped into the city. The attack had taken a lot out of him, but he had to get to Beasely. Manhattan seemed lethargic. It was unnatural, but then, Manhattan was unnatural.

He knew as soon as he entered Beasely's building that he was too late. There were more security guards and checkpoints than he'd ever seen. They let him through when he said he was here for a family emergency. When he reached Beasely's suite, there was a woman he'd never seen where Sharon, the secretary usually sat. "Where's Beasely?" He demanded. "Where is he?"

"Mr. Beasely is dead," she said quietly. "He was attacked by a man with a knife two days ago."

Poul stared at her, feeling weak and unable to think. He stumbled backward against the wall, then made his way back to the street. "I killed him. Christ forgive me, I killed Beasely!"

❦   ❦   ❦

He made his way to his apartment and tried to sleep. He couldn't. He tried to eat, but he couldn't swallow the food. He read the accounts of Beasely's murder. The stories related the stabbing and how the security guards had shot the perpetrator and killed him instantly. Somehow, he managed to kill J.W. Beasely in the last instant before his death.

Realizing he had no other life, Poul left the city. Weeks later, he found Mendel pulling weeds in the garden outside the little house. There was no sign of any songs. He sighed, relieved to be back with Mendel and to know he was alright. The guy is traveling less and taking longer rests, he thought approvingly.

Poul squatted in the bushes, wondering how Mendel had become so rooted. He never expected Mendel to stay in one spot long enough to raise a garden. A few minutes later, when the stately dark-haired woman emerged from the house, he nearly fell back in awe.

"Jesus, ever-loving Christ," he whispered. She was one of the most striking women he'd ever seen—not beautiful in the bland Hollywood or Fifth Avenue sense—but possibly, yes, definitely in the classical sense.

Wearing a simple dress, she walked with a fluidity that defied the earth's hardness. He couldn't estimate her age. It didn't matter. Her essence rendered Earth time meaningless. Her being flowed outward and entered his body like a sweet fantasy and dark nightmare. She was all presence. One didn't live with her; one lived within her. "Jesus Christ," he kept muttering.

When the woman knelt beside Mendel to pull the weeds that were gently trying choke the struggling tomatoes, no words were spoken. It was as if they were one, that they had always been together and always would. They were so complete as a couple that Poul wondered how Mendel had existed before her. For the first time since he discovered Mendel, Poul saw peace in the man's actions. Perhaps he had found what he had been searching for. Perhaps this was the end of the journey...and the end of the songs.

Beasely was dead and Mendel was at peace with himself.

That night, shivering in the trees behind the house, Poul listened to the music that drifted from the open window, pure songs of love that were simple, uncluttered and lovely in their clarity. Aside from the Children material, they were the first Mendel songs Poul understood.

Their power was such that he had to fight the urge to enter the warmth of the house and let the presence of these two loving beings cleanse the city filth from him. He closed his eyes and let himself be carried by the songs, away from the world and his hatred of all that he had become.

The next morning he headed back, confused, not knowing how long Mendel might stay in this little house. Probably forever. He hoped so. "Yes," he told himself, "maybe he'll get a little saner now that he has a woman. He was heading for a fall, the rate he was going. He'd better appreciate what he's got." Poul felt like a man without a destination, suddenly devoid of a plan in life. Maybe he would just hang it up and buy his island and cover it with concrete; plant a few tastefully placed trees. They would be something that didn't drop leaves or shed. Maybe a cactus or two—shaved, of course.

The songs he'd heard were the most beautiful Mendel had ever written. Hell, if a song could affect Poul, it had to be pretty special, he thought. The world could stand a few real love songs. But it looked like Mendel was not about to throw them away.

Somehow, it didn't matter anymore. Beasely was dead. Poul wondered who was in charge of the company now. He shook his head, knowing he would carry the guilt of Beasely's death for the rest of his life.

❈   ❈   ❈

The pencil that had only known a life of music was now drawn across a two-by-four. Mendel laid the board across the workhorses he had built and Mara held it as he sawed.

When the end of the board fell, Mara admired the evenness of the end. "You're good."

Mendel wiped the sweat from his forehead and nodded. "I'm getting better."

Mara laughed. "Five years of practice does a lot for a guy who had never used a saw."

"Or a hammer, or a screwdriver," he added. He laid the saw down and held her. "I had never known love, either."

Later they staked tomatoes in the garden. "Here, get it close to the plant," Mara said, pushing it into the soft earth. "Here." She handed him a strip she had cut from a stocking. "Tie the stalk to the stake. Leave it loose enough that it doesn't choke the plant."

"Where did you learn so much about gardening?" Mendel asked, his hair now cut short and his beard gone.

She pulled some weeds around the tomatoes. "I grew up in the country. We raised a lot of vegetables." He waited.

"And what else?"

She looked at him and he saw an entire lifetime of experience, joy and sadness. She kissed him gently. "Let's think about the present. Isn't that really all there is?"

He nodded. "I just don't understand why you don't want to share your past with me."

She studied the tomato plant, then looked at Mendel. "What we have is what we create now. And in this moment I have never been happier. I don't want this moment to end." They finished staking the tomatoes, had lunch and made love in the early afternoon.

Mendel thought about all the spring times he had written about. Now he truly *felt* them.

The days went by, then the seasons, and yet another year.

      ❦   ❦   ❦

Not knowing what to do, Poul did the only thing he was good at. He wandered. Everything he had known was gone. Mendel was settled and happy. Beasely was…. Some days Poul walked south. Other days he walked east or west. It didn't matter. Nothing mattered anymore. Even the money didn't matter.

Poul hadn't asked but he was pretty sure he was a billionaire. What a joke. He had more money than he could imagine, but nothing to buy. With the investments Beasely's folks made for him, Poul was making money doing nothing. Hell, the very act of breathing was making him profits.

Sometimes, suddenly feeling weak, he would fall to his knees and cry. None of it mattered anymore. Nothing mattered.

Months went by. He wasn't even sure what state he was in. Maybe North Carolina judging by the accent. He wandered into a small town with one street and on a whim took a job as a cook in the Dew Drop Inn, a little bar on the edge of town where mechanics, truckers, farmers and the jobless hung out. The owner, Auntie Lou, a small, round woman with short white hair and a no nonsense attitude, showed him how to fry burgers and mix drinks.

"Mixed drink," she said quickly. "Pour the drink up to here, width of yer thumb. Fill the ice up t' here. She pointed to two thirds of the glass. "When they want a second, don't dump the ice out. Ice holds the flavor so you don't need to pour as much liquor in the second time. Little things. They add up to profit."

Poul got to know the regulars in just few nights. Little John, a six foot two Vietnam veteran who weighed two hundred and forty pounds, introduced himself to Poul. "Name's John. Call me Little John. Where you from, Yank?"

Poul looked up. "Uh, New York...well, mainly from New York."

"You don't look like no New Yorker."

"What do they look like?"

"They look like arrogant robots with sticks up their asses."

The others around him laughed, though Poul could see they didn't know what a New Yorker looked like. It was just good to laugh at city people.

"Thanks, Little John. What'll it be?"

The big man eased himself onto the stool. "Bud and a shot of Ol' Grandad. Straight up."

"Big John don't take no ice," Freddy Smith said. Freddy was a logger with three missing fingers and a big gap in his mouth where an errant log knocked out eight teeth and flattened his nose."

Skinny, a man with an unhealthy brown color to his sagging skin, shook his head. "No sir, he don't. That's why you got a job there, Paul. Auntie Lou, she teaches the bartenders t' skimp on liquor. Last one did his job, alright. Little John drunk down a whole herd of Wild Turkeys and the bartender he was startin' t' cheat a little. Little John hauled him out over the bar and hurled him. The man looked like an arrow shootin' through the air. He's ailin' with a kincusshun and two broken arms."

Poul nodded thoughtfully and knew he was not going to be blind in his loyalty to Aunty Lew.

Poul became friends with the gang. They were a big family. They looked out for each other. If one got sick and couldn't make it, a volunteer would deliver beer to his house. If one broke up with his woman, the rest would console him by getting him so drunk he passed out. Then they'd drag him out back and make him as comfortable as possible.

One afternoon a dark-skinned man of about fifty strolled in and ordered a beer. He sipped the drink in silence for about five minutes. "You're not from around here," he finally said, looking Poul over with a professional scan. He reminded Poul of a smooth carnie.

"No, I'm not," Poul said, wiping the bar, keeping his gaze down.

The man sipped his beer and lit a battered briar pipe. "You look lonely."

"Bartenders are supposed to be lonely."

The man's large brown eyes looked beyond Poul at the shelf behind him. Poul felt uncomfortable, as if the man were somehow reading him. He had a kind face, though. The skin had fine lines at the edges from a lifetime of squinting in the sun and smiling.

"You look like a man who has lost everything, including his way."

Poul picked a glass from the sink and began wiping it, a chore he found that kept him from itching himself. "You're the first person who's said anything like that."

"I'm the only person to take the time and look."

Poul looked from the glass and towel. "What do you want?"

The man smoothed his black mustache with a bemused expression. "Can you afford a couple bottles of wine?"

Confused, Poul looked down at his glass, polishing a little harder. "What do you mean?"

"My sister helps people who have lost their direction. She's a…seer."

"Who said I lost my direction?"

The man laughed softly. "You wouldn't be here if you knew where you were supposed to be."

Poul shrugged. "I've found that I'm always pretty much where I'm supposed to be."

The man laughed, again that soft laugh. Confident, reassuring. "Very true." He drank his beer. "Well, if you decide to—if for nothing else than a little diversion, we're five miles down the road. There's a group of us. You will be more than welcome. My name is…John.

Poul listened to his instincts. He always had. His instincts told him nothing, but his loneliness told him to go. He asked Auntie Lew if he could leave a couple hours early.

She considered it. "Well, you ain't missed a night yet. Fact I'm tired of lookin' at ya. Git outa here. See you tomorra night."

Poul arrived at the camp an hour later. Pick up trucks and vans made a protective semicircle in the field. Several campfires lit the faces of young and old people huddled around talking in low voices. He caught the faint odor of marijuana. Beside a rusting camper, musicians with a mandolin, fiddle and guitar were playing a gypsy version of one of Mendel's joyful Midwestern songs. It was a strange, exotic scene, but he immediately felt at home.

John seemed to materialize out of the darkness, a trick of the flickering fires, Poul decided. "Ah, Paul, welcome! I am so glad you could join us. You are a man without direction and without friends. For the time we are here, we will be your friends. Poul nodded and handed John the wine. "Thank you. That is very gracious. Come, let me introduce you."

John took Poul around the campfires and introduced him. Each person smiled and said welcome and meant it. He settled by the fire with the musicians. A young man with long dark hair and very white teeth said, "What would you like to hear, new friend Paul?"

Poul shrugged. "The one you just played. I only caught the tail end."

"Ah, Joy of Sunrise," the fiddle player said. "One of Mendel's most joyously inspiring songs." They played it again, each taking a turn at the lead while the other's drove the rhythm. When they finished Poul and John applauded.

"What few people realize is that Mendel is a musician's musician," John said. "He understands that music and life are one, that the very act of breathing is music."

"He speaks from a place where there is no time," said the guitar player who ran through a series of chords from the Ocean CD. "He speaks from the soul and in the soul there is no time." He stopped playing and they all stared at the fire in silence.

Then a sound, high and desperately lonely, grew in the night. Poul sat paralyzed, the hair on his neck and arms standing straight up until he realized that this sound of pure loneliness, came from the fiddle. The note wailed, softly, lovely, and forever into the darkness and Poul felt tears filling his eyes, overflowing, followed by more. The note was like a Siren gently reaching into his heart and turning some valve that let his emotions finally flow. His longing for Mendel, his guilt about Beasely's death, his despair when he realized he had nothing and no one in life. He had no reason to live.

"What Mendel song does that come from?" He asked when he was able to speak. The fiddler, a robust old man with a big white mustache sadly shook his head. "It's a note that he has not used yet," the man said.

John stood up. "Come, meet my sister, Paul. She's inside waiting for you."

"How did she know I was here?"

John smiled, his black mustache rising like wings. "My sister sees things." He shrugged. "It's a gift."

They stepped up inside the camper. Poul was overwhelmed by the sweet incense. The lights were soft and reddish. A woman, around forty, Poul guessed, stood up and extended her hand. "Good evening. I'm so glad you came."

"Thank you."

"My name is Nadeen. Please sit down, Paul."

Poul turned to John and saw nothing but the wall. He didn't understand it. John had been a few inches from him. There hadn't been time for him to turn and go and if he had the trailer would have moved with his weight.

Poul felt strange—not frightened exactly—but into a state of dis-ease, as if he'd stepped into an alternate reality. Nadeen sensed his uneasiness and spoke in reassuring tones. "Please sit down, Paul. Relax. You need to relax."

She opened the small refrigerator and took out the bottle of wine he had brought. She poured two glasses. She was a thin woman with dark hair. She had seen a life of travel and hardship and had dealt with it with grace and dignity. Poul liked her. More importantly, he trusted her. He didn't know women at all. That nasty Miss White had colored his views of women. His wife had hated him. The rest of the women in his life were beautiful, nameless toys.

In the dim red light he couldn't see the color of Nadeen's eyes, but he saw the life of pain, joy and drudgery she had led, and the dignity. It was something he didn't see in many people.

They made small talk for awhile. Poul scratched at his wrist without realizing it. "Paul, look at me," she said with gentle authority. Surprised, he obeyed and felt her eyes, her gaze, move into him and fill him. "You stepped off your path because you had to. You will step back onto it. Of this you can be sure." She spoke in sort of a rhythmical, timeless incantation.

"I don't think so, Nadeen."

She shook her head once, signaling him not to interrupt the flow of information that was coming to her. "You have led a life of adventure, but few surprises. You think you have given up, but you are just resting. Your adventures are not finished."

There was a long silence. "You don't understand, Nadeen."

She smiled. Her eyes were closed and she spoke from eons away. "I *do* understand...*Paul*..." She smiled. "I do understand. Your friends are very special. In this dimension, leaving and returning are often confused. And why not? Sometimes they are one and the same." She stared into the dark distance behind Poul's head. "You will be faced with some major decisions." She paused again and smiled. "And you will always do the right thing."

Poul waited, then asked. "How do you know?"

Nadeen, eyes still closed, smiled and nodded. "Because we all do the right thing...*because all things are perfect.*"

A cool numbness flowed through Poul's body. Christ, she knew. She really knew! When the shock subsided he realized that someone else knew and he wasn't alone and he wanted to lean forward and tell her everything, everything about his life and his frustrations and his hopes and fears and guilt, but she knew this, too, and held up her hand.

"No one thing or one person is more important than another. I don't want names, or events or emotions. I am here to reassure you that your life is good. Every individual life is important. You have many responsibilities ahead. They won't be easy. They never have been. But you are one of the fortunate few who have seen the results of your labors. You are not finished. You will endure pain. You will have joy. You are not finished."

He waited for a few moments. "Nadeen, in all respect, you could say that to anyone.

She opened her eyes. Her laugh held girlish innocence and the eons of Hera. "Exactly, Poul. Exactly." Then she smiled and leaned forward. She looked into his eyes. "Just remember the words that you carry in your billfold and everything will be fine."

Poul felt prickles throughout his body which led to the feeling of being frozen. He was sure his heart stopped. Nadeen's eyes seemed to grow larger until they were two vast liquid brown oceans pulling him in, washing over him, knowing every moment of his life and every cell in his body. "How..." his voice was gone.

She smiled warmly. "Never ask how. Just be in the moment, fully. Your friend understands that." He felt himself nod. She led him outside. They each smoked a cigarette, listening to the music fill the air.

They shook hands warmly and he left, feeling awed by her powers, and humbled by her perspective. That night in his room he took out the piece of paper in his wallet and looked at it again, studying the handwriting, the words, the feeling.

❧   ❧   ❧

Poul spent the next few days thinking about the gypsies, their freedoms and their chains, and their total acceptance of life in the moment. He thought about Nadeen's words and told Auntie Lou he'd be moving on.

She sniffed and scratched her butt. She wiped her hands on her greasy t-shirt, went behind the bar and pulled out a cigar. She swiped a wooden match across her jeans and lit it.

"I didn't know you smoked," Poul said, feeling suddenly sad with the odor that he associated with Beasely. He fought back tears.

"I don't smoke. Cigars ain't smokin'. Cigarettes is smokin'. Cigars is relaxin'."

She pursed her lips and sent out a stream of heavy gray smoke. "You been here, what? Three months?"

He nodded.

"Month longer'n I expected. When you headin' out?"

"When you can find a replacement."

She let out a cackle. "Honey, I been runnin' this place thirty-six years, and I've seen a hundred of guys like you come through. Don't worry about me. Take off when you need to." She went to a little closet and pulled out the broom. She handed it to him. "Right now, earn yer keep."

That night the regulars drifted in, watched some sports on the TV above the bar, then turned to CNN. "There's trouble brewin' in a few cities with them AM's and PM's," Little John said. "Gittin' more tense each night."

Poul joined the others to watch the crowds of people in different cities. On one side of a park were thousands waving anti-Mendel signs. On the other side were equally fervent people holding signs proclaiming that Mendel is Good, Mendel is A Savior, Mendel Is Music."

"Don't understand it," Skinny said, shaking his head slowly and taking a chug from his bottle.

"Ain't no music worth getting' that excited about," added Freddy, fingering his lip with his two remaining fingers.

Little John said nothing. Finally, he nodded to Poul. "Double Wild Turkey." Poul nodded and reached for the bottle. "On the rocks."

Poul stopped, confused. "You drink it straight up."

"Not tonight." Was there an ominous tone to his quiet declaration or was it just Poul's frayed nerves?

He scooped ice into the glass and poured the double. Little John nodded once as Poul placed it before him.

"If I was in one of those cities," Skinny said, "I'd have me a hick'ry limb and I'd bop and AM's and the PM's in the noggin. Knock some goddamn sense inta their heads."

"Cops'd shoot ya down," Freddy said, snapping the thumb and index finger of his chopped up hand.

They were cut off by the harsh thud of a glass. "Another," Little John ordered. Poul nodded. He picked up the glass and started to pour the whiskey, then stopped. Auntie Lou said to leave the ice. He pictured himself sailing through the air like an arrow and decided he'd had enough physical hardship without actually inviting it. He looked over at the three men who studied the TV a little too intently. Poul nodded to himself. It was a test. He dumped the ice, rinsed the glass and made a fresh drink.

Little John nodded. All three men were silent as they worked on their drinks. Finally Little John stood up and went to the men's room. "Well, Paul, you didn't pass or fail," Skinny said.

"The hell I didn't," Poul said. "If I'd done what Auntie Lou wanted, I'd be in a broken heap out on the sidewalk."

The two men laughed. "Little John ain't laid a hand on a man since the war. He's a peaceful as a mushroom."

"Then what's the story about him flinging men around?"

"Just fun," Skinny said. "Little John's one of them software programmers. Certified genius from what I hear. Used t' live in New York, fly all over. Lives on royalties—you know, money from his inventions."

"Patents," Freddy said helpfully.

"Don't never have to work another day in his life."

"Then what was all the tall-tale bullshit?" Poul asked, a little angry.

The two men shrugged. "Just passin' time," Freddy said. "Havin' a little fun."

Little John lumbered back to the bar and sat down. He looked at Poul with eyes that held bemusement and a wildness fraying out from tumultuous inner worlds. "Life's but a walking shadow, a poor player who struts and frets his hour upon the stage, to be heard no more…."

He picked up his glass and gestured to Poul. "Wild Turkey, straight up."

❦   ❦   ❦

A few weeks later Poul trudged into Philadelphia. He had some money from his bar job, and ate dinner at Wendy's. Then he found a park where he could get a good night's sleep behind some bushes.

But around 8 p.m. people began walking in from all sides. People with signs. "Mendel is Evil!" "Mendel is The Force!"

"Ah, Christ," he moaned softly. "Can't the world just give it a rest?"

He watched as the crowds on each side grew, swelling cells clustering, larger and larger, until they took on a huge alien life of their own. Groups within each body chanted. Individuals yelled. The ones on the front edges screamed threats to the opposite line.

Poul grew uneasy, then frightened. He'd never experienced anything so huge, so powerful, so out-of-hand. Before he could run, the two groups came together, colliding in a screaming, yelling battle, swinging signs made of cardboard attached to two-by-two boards. Warm liquid splattered on his face. He wiped it quickly and saw that it was someone's blood. He tried to run but couldn't move through the battling bodies.

Cops suddenly were everywhere. There were gunshots. Poul pushed. He knocked down a young woman and tried to help her up but someone's foot kicked her in the head. A large man, pushed by someone else, hit Poul and knocked him into another man who grabbed him by the throat. The man was suddenly yanked backward. The din of thousands of people yelling and screaming was deafening. Pushed one way, then another, Poul lost all sense of direction. He was inside a tornado of human bodies and helpless.

More gunshots. He turned, then turned again, realizing he was more afraid than he'd ever been. He was a speck inside a riot of two crowds with opposing beliefs. Mendel the savior! Mendel the destroyer!

A body falling backward hit him from behind and pushed him into a young woman. Both of them fell and he landed on top of her. She screamed and began clawing at his eyes. Then something hard hit him in the head. He rolled with a groan and with blurred vision saw a cop standing above him.

He was led, then dragged to a car.

❧   ❧   ❧

"What's your name?"

"Poul," he said in a daze. Police were all over the place. The biggest one stood over him as he waited in a chair by a desk. People sat at computers. He realized he was in a police station. How he made it there was foggy. Everything was foggy.

"Poul what?"

"Paul. My name is Paul."

"You said your name is Poul."

"Somebody hit me in the head. I'm not at my best right now."

"So it's Paul."

"Yes."

"Paul what?"

"Paul Smith."

"Right and I'm Paul Newman."

"Nice to meet you."

"Smart ass. Let's see some ID."

Poul thought a moment and reached to his back pocket. He shrugged. It hurt to shrug. He wouldn't do that again. "My wallet's gone. Somebody must have stolen it. Never trust people in a riot."

"Don't get funny."

"I hurt too much to be funny."

"We need ID."

"I'm sorry, officer. I'm ID-impaired."

"You're gonna be charged with attempted rape."

Poul lifted his throbbing head. "Rape! I was pushed into that woman and she tried to claw my eyes out." He pointed to the scratches on his face.

"That's what they all say."

A few minutes later he found himself in a cell. He felt almost grateful. It seemed safe and fairly quiet. Mendel created all this, he thought. He lay, with slow care, on the bed. No, Poul thought. *He* helped create it. Beasely had a hand in it. All three of them were responsible. Now Mendel was domesticated and Beasely was dead. And all these stupid people were rioting because they had different thoughts on the music of a particular artist. Music that the artist himself rejected!

Poul tried to turn on his side, but it hurt too much. Hell, what's the big surprise. People have been doing the same thing for thousands of years in the name of a particular religion. People are always looking for reasons to kill each other, he thought. The cell bed didn't match the waterbed in his apartment, but it sure beat the cold ground.

He put a hand over his bruised ribs and saw Beasely. You poor bastard, he thought. A hell of a way to die. He breathed in slowly, then let it out slowly. He discovered a lump on his head and wondered if he had a concussion.

He couldn't get the crowd's size and loudness out of his head. Several thousand people became one huge, out-of-control monster.

Sleep wasn't very restful, but it was a distraction from the pain.

CHAPTER 15

The police let him go when the woman decided not to press charges. Poul took his time returning to New York. He had made up his mind to give his money to charities and spend the rest of his life writing his memoirs. He had nothing now. And he had no desire for anything. He wasn't even sure he desired life.

When he did finally make it back, Manhattan was like a big, noisy cauldron of sounds, smells and colors he didn't like. He went to the Beasely building to see who the new management was and to tell them Mendel had retired.

When he entered the suite, Beasely's longtime secretary, Sharon looked up from her work. An expression of disbelief spread across her face as the blood left it. "Poul?" She whispered as she clutched the collar of her blouse.

Poul shook his head quickly, that Alice-in-Wonderland feeling sweeping over him. "Sharon. You're back...."

She nodded. "We thought you...you were dead.

He shook his head. "No. I was here two days after it happened. You were gone." He looked around the office that suddenly seemed strange. "Someone else.... His voice trailed off in his confusion.

She stared at him until she calmed. "Yes, it was horrible." She looked down, trying to erase the events. "I had to take time off. It was so horrible." She composed herself. "But it's all getting back to normal." She hesitated. "As normal as it can be after something...." She stood up and led him to Beasely's office. "Go on in."

"Yes, I wanted to meet the new—"

The publisher looked up from his computer, then leaped to his feet. "Poul! You're alive!"

The blood left Poul's head. He felt weak and cold. He managed a timorous "Beasely," before he fell in a dead faint.

Sharon hovered over him with cold, wet cloths, dabbing his head and face. He brought his eyes into focus. Beasely towered over him, cigar in hand. He stood up, thanked Sharon and moved to his chair.

Later, over sandwiches and beer, Beasely explained. "It all happened so fast, Poul, and I'm not ashamed to tell you I was never more afraid in my life. I've never seen a more determined man. Even after he was shot—and I'm telling you he was dead on his feet—he brought the knife down, caught me across the arm, sliced an artery, then ripped a gash across my stomach took fifty some stitches. Fifty-four to be exact."

Beasely reached over the desk and picked up a figure of Jesus that now stood beside Mendel. "A higher power saved me. I'm sure of that. And He saved me for a reason. I don't know what it was, but I'll spend the rest of my life searching for the reason and trying to repay the debt I owe for my life." He held the figurine gently, and spoke in almost a whisper. "He saved me for a reason." His hands trembled and there were tears in his eyes.

Still feeling sick, Poul ate slowly. "But why say you were dead?"

Beasely snapped out of his thoughts and looked at Poul. "I guess I was almost dead, I lost so much blood. The rumor got started with one of the TV networks. It took damn near a week to get it straightened out. I had to do a press conference from my hospital bed." He leaned forward. "Poul, I'm sorry for what you went through. I didn't know you came back. In fact, I thought *you* were dead. I thought that kid had killed you."

Poul nodded slowly. "And without meaning to, I sent him to kill you." He shrugged slightly. "We're both alive. I don't know why."

Beasely nodded tentatively. "I'm having a hard time sleeping. I've never been so scared. And it makes me wonder how many more people like that are out there." He shook his head. "I'll never feel safe again. Ever. One minute I'm reading song charts. The next minute I'm lying on the floor bleeding from knife wounds. A complete stranger who tried to kill me is dead on the floor. I'll never feel safe again."

Poul lit a cigarette. "You shouldn't. Something huge has been created." He thought of the riot and watched the smoke swirling in front of his face. "I guess it's good, what the songs have done. But every good thing has its evil side."

Beasely stared at the Jesus figure and was quiet for several minutes. "When I was in the hospital, recovering, realizing someone who hated Mendel nearly killed me." He paused. "I...then I thought of the little girl in Chicago who was...killed." He rubbed the figure's face with his thumb. "A child, an innocent child died." He bit his lip and took a deep breath. "And I *didn't*...." He squeezed the figure in his hand and quietly cried. "All my money and power and I couldn't bring back that child's life." He rubbed the figures with all his fingers and thumb in a desperate attempt to work out energy and find comfort. He stopped and sobbed quietly. "But God gave me my life back." He looked up at Poul, his tear-swollen eyes imploring. "I was so sure of things once."

Poul closed his eyes and took a deep breath. "Keep your eyes on the bigger picture, Beaze."

The publisher looked out the window. "And what is that?"

Poul lit another cigarette. His mouth was dry from smoking. "What you said. Life and death are fleeting. Art is forever."

There was a long silence.

"Is that worth a child's life?"

Poul took a drag on the cigarette. What the hell had led them here? He was so tired. He let the smoke flow from his mouth. "I don't know. I guess there's fate, there's faith...and our hour upon the stage."

❧   ❧   ❧

Poul spent the next several months relaxing. He bought dwarf Japanese junipers in gallon containers and began practicing the art of bonsai, trying to recreate the beautiful forms he found in nature. Bonsai was perfect! You could be with nature, then sit it up on a shelf.

The sense of peace was shallow, though. Long recovered and with no new material, Beasely was in a quiet frenzy. He was a haunted man, with the attempt on his life and the deaths of others because of the music. He had a list of those who were killed or who committed suicide because of Mendel's music. He set up a fund for victims of Mendel music violence.

At the same time he was driven to continue his quest. Poul had brought Beasely a tree he had fashioned but Beasely had never been outside the city limits of New York, LA, London and Paris. Trees were something in paintings, on coffee tables and in movies about people who didn't have the good fortune of being New Yorkers.

It was early afternoon. The sun was burning through the smog outside, and Beasely whipped his cigar before him like a spastic conductor wielding a fiery baton. "Damn it, Poul, they're crying for more! It's been too long! There has to be something!" He jammed the wet end of the cigar between his yellowing teeth and sent out a few weak puffs. His eyes crossed as he tried to focus on the anemic stick. In a weak fit, he yanked it out and threw it across the room. "God-damned excuse for a cigar. Like smoking a paper sack full of dried camel shit."

He turned back to Poul, his voice switching from exclamatory demands to a pleading whine. "Please, Poul. We've used up all the songs—and all the tricks." He held up his hands and a finger leaped to attention with each listing. "We've repackaged old albums, recorded unused originals, put out four 'greatest hits' CDs, and produced four 'Mendel Tributes.' We're out of famous frigging musicians! We're out of greatest hits.

Christ, man, we've got to have some new material or we're dead!"

Poul stood motionless. Beasely stopped and adopted a quiet, friendly tone, unconsciously rubbing his shirt that now hid a giant scar. "Just go see if there's any new stuff. Maybe there are some old songs laying around you might have missed." He paced around to the front of Poul. "Do know how many years it's been?"

It was a rhetorical question. He asked it nearly everyday.

"Eight."

Beasely waved his arms. "Eight years, seven months and 14 days!"

"Time is relative."

Beasely's turned red and he went for his scotch. "Time is—" he stopped himself.

"Money." Poul finished it for him.

Poul sighed and rubbed what was left of his gray hair. He sniffed thoughtfully and nodded. "Ok, I'll see. But don't get your hopes up."

Beasely bowed his head as if in prayer and nodded once. "Thank you."

"Sure. Give me a few days and I'll go." The truth was that Poul was ready to get out. Far from luxuriating in his riches, he found himself, as the years passed, increasingly ensnared, entrapped and entangled by endless hours of attorneys, laws, taxes, charities, loopholes, shelters, annuities, and investments. He struggled with more decisions than Adam had when the order came down to name the animals. His money was giving him nothing while he was giving himself to money. He was one of the richest slaves in America.

Since the incident with the knife man, Poul kept to himself. He didn't go out with Beasely anymore, afraid something would slip about Mendel and his location. It was painfully obvious that some people wanted Mendel dead. These Anti-Mendel fools. Some of the more radical ones organized Mendel hunts. Fortunately they were city people who couldn't last more than a few days out of the city and were totally lost when they left a freeway.

Poul knew the Bible. Miss White made sure of that. He had also read a lot of history in the past few years. From the beginning, man, in his energy, confusion and insecurity, has had a desperate need to create a hero then destroy him. The destruction has to combine violence with a moral statement. All religions boiled down to a religion of reassurance that the right life is the one lived in poverty and suffered in silence. Humans have methodically killed other humans to get this belief across. They had done it for centuries and were still doing it. Mendel, who wandered outside society and spent a life creating, was one of society's most dangerous men. This made him a prime target. By now it didn't matter if you were a frustrated postal worker or a terrorist, Mendel was the grand daddy of big game. Kill Mendel and you get to give your message to the media.

And you become history.

Mendel became an accomplished carpenter and a decent gardener. He split wood for the fireplace and rebuilt the stone fences around the property. He made notes for songs during the spring, summer and fall. During the winter when they were often snowed in, he fleshed out the songs.

Mendel had never known sexual and spiritual love for another person. He now exchanged it freely with Mara. Sometimes, unable to contain his feelings, he wrote hymns to the female body, to the sure grace of a woman's movements and the strength of her being. He wrote of the gentle cyclic coursing of blood that brings new life, of caves one enters in blind lust, where one dies and gives new life; of caverns where new gods are created and emerge whole and alive and divine. He wrote of woman's goodness and power and the feminine magic that gives birth, blesses life and nurtures growth; of woman who gently mourns death with wise acceptance of its part in life.

As he wrote the songs, he sang them to her, strumming the tunes on the worn guitar. "They're beautiful," she would tell him. "Share them with the world."

"I am."

"No, with the world."

"You are."

One night after this banter, she said with almost sad determination: "Someday you will, Mendel. All the world will sing your songs."

"I'll be famous!" He laughed.

"You are a great artist," she said with quiet seriousness. "Listen to your own music, Mendel. Believe in yourself."

He laid the guitar down. "It's our music. You are all I care about."

She studied him silently until he felt uneasy. Something inside him itched like a faintly bowing lilac branch on a cloudy June night. He ignored the dark feeling. "I love you, Mara."

She smiled. "I love you, too. Let's go to bed. We have to fix the fence tomorrow."

His eyes remained open after they went to bed and he sucked in her graceful form lying naked next to him. Even on moonless nights he lay awake and re-created her form so that he could pull her image into him and hold onto it in his dreams.

He knew no man ever loved a woman as much as he, Mendel, former drifter and penniless bum, loved Mara.

❦   ❦   ❦

Poul sipped a coffee in the half empty diner and stared at his unlit cigarette. The city was closing in on him. God, now you couldn't even smoke in a diner. Pollution, laws, people. Poul hated it all and he was ready to go. He was not looking forward to returning. He missed Mendel. He was sure the man was still settled comfortably, but hoped that maybe Mendel had whipped out a few love songs and tossed them out the window.

Poul pulled from his billfold the torn piece of paper he'd found in the Arizona desert. One sentence. Poul never shared it with Beasely. It was a secret Mendel had uncovered and it made more and more sense as time passed. He held the paper gently and nodded at the words.

It was time to go.

It had been years.

❀   ❀   ❀

As he headed south through Virginia, Poul took his time, enjoying the solitude, the freedom from appointments, meetings and TV. Time magically dissipated from hourly engagements to blocks broken only by sunrise and sunset. Nature had a few good qualities, he conceded as he breathed in the clean summer air. He took his time also because he was out of shape and his thicker body had lost touch with the rhythmic demands of the rolling hills.

It did feel good to get away from the city, even if the dirt was still dirty and the forests were still wild and unkempt. At least they were natural. He laughed to himself. "Nothing is dirtier than nature, except man."

He had almost made up his mind, too, that if Mendel were happily settled with the woman and retired from writing, he would tell the artist about his fame and fortune. He would promise Mendel that he wouldn't reveal the couple's location, but in return he would ask that he be able to live near them. They would split the money and just forget the world. If they were discovered, they could hike on down to Mexico or maybe a small hotel outside a rain forest. Hell, buy the rain forest and protect it from developers.

Maybe Mendel would want to build a nice mansion in the mountains and seal it off. It didn't matter. Poul was flexible. He was like an old dog raised by one master. He just wanted to be near Mendel, who was the only man, crazy as he was, who made any sense. Granted, he'd never talked to Mendel, but he knew him. He knew him better than any man alive.

As he neared the vicinity of the house, Poul slowed. The full scope of his fantasies struck him. He was actually going to confront the man he'd been trailing for years. He was going to have to tell Mendel that he had been regularly stealing Mendel's songs, selling them and making Mendel, quite possibly against the latter's will, rich and internationally famous.

He was going to have to explain a half a lifetime of activities, all of which revolved around using Mendel's life.

He wasn't sure if he could do that. He scratched at the beard stubble on his cheek. "Damn." He lit one last cigarette and inhaled deeply. It didn't taste as good out in the open air. Shit, he'd play the whole thing by ear. See what his courage measured when he arrived at the house. Yes, play it by ear, as he had played his whole life. He stopped, scraped away some leaves, and mashed his cigarette into the damp earth.

As he neared the little homestead, he was both shocked and, somehow, relieved to find the property devoid of life. The garden was a chaotic tangle of weeds, broken tomato vines and brown, bug-blistered string bean plants. The once neat lawn shagged up over the little slate slabs that led to the front door standing open like an arm reaching toward something that is gone. All was silent but for the breeze that whispered faintly through the hemlocks and spruce, like the ghost of a lost, mourning child never born.

Death's damp coldness ate into his body. His heart pounded against his chest like a frantic prisoner. Almost inaudibly, as quiet and tenuous as a grain of dust settling on a trembling feather, the word escaped his lips: "Shit."

Time had dissolved from rushing city hours to leisurely days during his walk. Now it melted into nothing. He could have stood there for a moment or a year before he took a breath and walked forward. He stepped inside the door. A few chipped, dust-covered dishes waited in the cupboard like sculptures in a pauper's museum. One plate, spotted with moldy, uneaten food and a few dead ants, rested in the sink bowl.

Poul stepped into the living room but found nothing except two chairs and an old guitar that lay on the floor between them. Though he wanted to go no further, he swallowed and entered the bedroom. He gasped and fell backward with a stifled cry at the dim outline of an old, broken man weeping in the shadowy corner. He shut his eyes and grasped at the doorsill for support. When he opened his eyes, the form had melted, leaving before him the rumpled, unmade bed that had held the pleasant burden of two persons, then one, then none.

Poul had somehow always known that if something tragic happened to Mendel, he would know. He was that close to the man. He shook his head slowly. Something nearly as terrible had happened. Part of Mendel had died, but Poul could not see any further. He waited until his breathing had returned nearly to normal, felt once more the spirits of a pathetic drama, and ran from the house. He ran until his legs buckled and pains shot razor spears through his chest.

He had to find Mendel. Where ever the man was, he was not safe. Not only was he a target of the civilized world, he was probably a threat to himself. Finally, at dusk, Poul dropped, exhausted. In the stillness of the mountains, he sobbed and his tears soaked into the gentle earth.

❦   ❦   ❦

Sharon brought in the *New York Times* and laid it on Beasely's desk. "You need to read this.

The publisher, whose palsy was increasing by subtle degrees, lit a cigar and read story:

> *In a small commune in northern Idaho, a group of 12 people known as the Mendel Millenium Group, were found dead in their small house. A suicide note by leader Corey Mason, said Mendel had shown them the way and that they were now at peace. They had apparently drunk poisoned tea. Forensics experts are now investigating...*

Before the attempt on his life, Beasely would have worried about a lawsuit. Now he laid his cigar in the ashtray, bowed his head and prayed for their souls. He prayed, too, that no more people would die because of Mendel, the music, and Beasely Publishing. It was out of hand, and he, who helped create the situation, felt helpless.

❦   ❦   ❦

Mendel's whole existence had been spent living as truly and deeply and fully as possible. Now he wished only to die as he moved toward the Eastern coastline. He wished with each step that it would be his last, but neither the perfect song, nor death, was in his reach.

They had been as happy as one mortal couple could be. Mendel had wanted nothing but to live with Mara until they were old and left the world naturally and together. He would love every new age line in her face, worship her aging body and youthful soul. Maybe he had known in his heart that it couldn't be, but he had refused to acknowledge it.

Maybe.

Somewhere in the distance he heard his footsteps, slowly plodding forward. Always forward. He felt sick to his stomach, again. He was weak and fell to his knees. Tears, again.

Maybe she knew too and did admit it, because she began changing. Yes, he could see it now as he read the memory of their brief lives together. She had pressed him to describe in minute detail his journeys and experiences as though she wanted not only to live them herself, but to know him as deeply as he knew himself. She had stayed awake longer nights to talk with him and hold him as they lay in bed. Her dark eyes had grown sadder—not much—but enough that Mendel had noticed and had silently wondered what was wrong.

He had wondered, then quickly shut it from thought.

Mendel the visionary, who sought worlds others dared not behold, had blinded himself to his immediate future.

In the final weeks, Mara had bought enough food and supplies in town to allow them the luxury of not leaving each other at all, and they had spent the week talking, making love, holding hands, working together, and singing the songs he had written for her.

At the end of the week Mara had told him to leave. It was as simple as that, and he had stared dumbly, like an animal stunned by a well-aimed arrow. The scene played over and over in his mind: the paralysis of his shock and the flatness of his answer, now standing out in his memory like a harsh rectangular tombstone poking frozen from a dark winter hillside:

"Never."

She had nodded, her eyes full of love and conviction. "You have to Mendel. I'm sorry."

He had swallowed and tried to smother the nausea and weakness. "You have a husband, a lover. He's coming back." She had shaken her head and blinked quickly. "You don't love me anymore."

She had taken a deep breath but stood firm, fighting back tears. "I love you more than I have ever loved anyone. But you have to go. You have to continue your search. It's beyond your control or mine." The tears won and her eyes filled as she stared at him, strong, yet vulnerable and weakening.

He shook his head and wanted to scream. "Never! I'll never write again! I'll never return to something as paltry as a song when I have you to give me life and love and a meaning that's real. Never, Mara! I love you!"

She had taken his arms as if to steady and quiet him. "It's the plan of your life and I was part of it. And you can't see me—." She stopped and looked at the floor. She looked back up at him, bit her lip and continued. "Don't make it harder for us. There's no choice. Let's just be together tonight and love. Please, Mendel. If you love me as truly as you say, then you'll do this for us…and for me."

She had dropped her hands from his arms and stared at him, a helpless, frightened child about to be alone. He had wiped the tears from her eyes. It was then he saw it, faintly, as one sees the traces of dusk just before sunset.

And, as the shadows expand and darkness fills itself heavily and irrevocably into the earth, he felt it.

His head had moved back and forth slowly as he stared. "No." His voice caught. He felt sick and small, wishing he had never been born to feel this sorrow, this wrenching of his life's meaning from him. "No. I won't leave you."

She had turned away. "Return to the songs. The rest must be written." She had said no more. That night he played his love songs, struggling to control his voice and hold back the tears that needed to be shed. They drank wine and talked. Though at first he had trouble, they made love and fell asleep in each other's arms.

When he woke he had only the songs.

Mendel wiped away the tears and stood up, slowly, his hands shaking. He shivered with the cold. Now he walked, seeing only her image, wishing for nothing but to be with her. He would simply walk, he told himself, until he died.

But an artist is not free to pursue mere transitory desires. The truer the artist is, the more entrapped he is in his destiny. He is his own master and slave. Despite his wishes, Mendel found himself alone in the mountains, writing of love, of parting, and the hollowness of the soul when one loses what he has most dearly loved. He wrote of bitterness, of anger, and of a sorrow that runs deeper and longer than tears, of injuries that heal into invisible scars, which, if the man survives, force him to grow. Every note, every word, was written with a pain and love that not even death can destroy.

❦   ❦   ❦

"He's gone."

Beasely studied his partner who resembled a cadaver. "Dead?"

Poul shook his head. "Gone."

Beasely silently counted to ten as his doctor had instructed. His high blood pressure was at the danger level. He must stay calm and maintain a serene outlook on life, or there wouldn't be anymore life to look out on. Relax, see life as an interesting experience, the doctor said. He felt his doctor was full of shit. But all the same, he didn't want to take unnecessary risks. Beasely might lose his perspective once in awhile, but he acknowledged the admonishment that he couldn't take his kingdom with him.

Quietly, he said, "Damn it, Poul, will you just give me a straight answer? Just once in your life, fill out your lousy cryptic statements? Please."

Poul itched the insides of his palms with his middle fingers and blinked. "I went back to the place where he was staying. He's gone. She—I found a few pieces of paper, and his trail, but he's gone." He lit a cigarette. "He's alive."

Beasely looked down and wondered how long ago he'd snapped his cigar in half. He dropped it into the ashtray. Other publishers had hundreds of artists and they seemed to manage all of them well enough. It was all he could do to keep track of one writer whom he'd never even seen. He had to get around to writing his memoirs. He would entitle them: "How I Discovered and Managed The Century's Greatest Artist Without Ever Really Being Sure He Existed." Just once before he died he'd dearly love to meet the man. Someday….

"I'm going to shave, change and leave," Poul said in a monotone. "He's in trouble."

Beasely poured a small drink to calm his nerves and help him see life as an interesting experience. "And then what?"

"I don't know. Make sure he'll be okay, I guess."

Beasely nodded as if they were talking about the weather and pulled out some reports. After a moment of shuffling, he cleared his throat. "I really hate to mention it at a time like this, but…"

Poul's mud brown eyes narrowed, then he nodded. "Songs. I'll see."

Beasely lowered his head, sighed and flicked an ash from the desk. "Sorry."

Poul shrugged. "I understand."

The publisher looked back up at his worn, skinny friend. "Be careful."

Poul nodded again. "I'll be back." He started out the door and stopped, turning back to the desk, remembering the vision in the house and the swiftness with which life runs its course. "Take care of yourself, Beaze. One friend at a time is enough to worry about."

Beasely smiled. "I'll be okay. Thanks."

Poul wasn't so sure. He wasn't sure of anything anymore. Something still didn't feel right.

CHAPTER 16

From a *Wired* Magazine article:

> *Mendel's music has saturated itself so completely into society that everyone knows his songs and his name. Everyone. Everyone alive knows at least one Mendel song, and probably more. No one has ever seen Mendel. Yet he is worshipped by millions and reviled by millions. Is it art that creates this passion? Or is it the collective hopes and fears of a society in a moment of time? Does Mendel really exist? It's almost as if it doesn't matter anymore. Maybe it never did.*

He continued moving, flinging his Mara songs away as soon as he wrote them, ridding himself of pain, draining his emotions through the dull lead tip of a worn pencil and letting nature fill the void of his heart with things that were new. Anything.

His hair was now snow white and shaggy and his beard edged downward once more upon his chest. He found himself on the Northeastern coast and spent a year absorbing the ocean's power into his being. With half numb fingers, he scribbled lines as they entered his head:

":...the dream of ocean fecundity...salt water birth cries fulfill the siren's song...flowing submarine pulses give swell to the gentle waves of death...kind and understanding waves of death..." One night he envisioned himself as the last living thing on earth.

Knowing he would die, he ran, then walked, and finally crawled to the ocean's edge. He prayed with an intensity that sang through the universe, and he knew the power of a speck, the universal energy that man has within him.

With this knowledge, and the power of planetary regeneration, he crawled into the water's womb where his body was gratefully accepted and decomposed into its separate cells. In time, the cells would attract and mate and reproduce. In time, life would return to a barren planet. He would be the forgotten god of all life.

He wondered who the first one was.

He shook himself from the vision and picked up his pencil: "All is creation and destruction. All parts hold the spirit which is never destroyed. The spirit is the life, the joy and sorrow of the universe....All exists and nothing is final."

He put the idea into songs and worked on them for the next several months.

"All the parts, from planets to dust, contain the spirit, and all sing the happiness and terror, the beingness of being."

"Man's works are greater than men; art is greater than the artist."

"Man has the freedom in his destiny to paint it with the colors of his character."

Something was still missing. He grabbed the sheets of paper and read through them again. The pages fluttered in the breeze of the Maine coastline, making the reading nearly impossible. As he fought to concentrate on the lines, the ocean roared louder into his head, creating a maelstrom of raging waters with no outlet. They smashed in turbulent frustration against granite walls of his mind.

What was missing? The harder he worked, the greater the songs, the nearer he seemed to come to the perfect song, the greater the feeling of failure.

He stared out over the beach that lay cold and littered with gutted shells and leprous starfish. A lone gull rose up from behind a rock with a treasure in its beak. As it soared out over the water, it apparently realized the dangling condom was not edible and let it drop like a rubber-tipped bullet into the sea.

Mendel laughed with sudden bitterness. "Yes, we're both fools and starve for seeing what is not. Come back, bird, and let me talk of eternal beauty to a scavenger who lives on garbage! I'll tell you of the glory of love and you tell me about used rubbers!"

His eyes bright with rage, Mendel yanked out his pencil and scribbled some lines on a paper scrap. He wadded it viciously and heaved it. Another gull scooped it up and disappeared into the darkening distance.

"That's right! Take that to your nest! See how long you can live on words!" He laughed maniacally as he turned and the wind blew his gray hair across his eyes. Blinded, he saw Mara again, raised his fist to the sky and wailed.

❦   ❦   ❦

"Poor bastard. He always does it on a beach." Poul scratched the underside of his chin, recalling the California beach where Mendel cussed out God and asked to die. Maybe it was the seagull with the paper that sparked the rage. Poul could relate to that. Damn birds ought to be stuffed and distributed to small town museums.

At least Mendel was alive; that's all that mattered. He was without her and still alive. Poul wanted to run down and throw his arms around the man and tell him it was time to quit all this, that he was not alone and that millions of people loved him for his songs. "The guy has suffered enough," he thought. "I'll just tell him the truth and let him decide if he wants to go back. He can even have my half." He had realized years ago that money no longer mattered. His life in the city was superficial. He felt alive only when he left the concrete. It was time to bring Mendel in and let the chips fall as they may. With an air of authority and determination, Poul sniffed and stood up. No screwing around this time. Just tell Mendel.

Let the chips fall—. Like a flat pebble sinking slowly to rest in a thick summertime pond, his thoughts settled to a halt as Mendel stopped his ranting, picked up his bundles and let them fly with a delirious cackle.

Poul stood motionless, feeling hot, dizzy and more tired than a human should ever have to feel. He had a sudden vision of himself without the use of his legs, bound to a wheelchair, free of having to chase Mendel ever again. He shook his head wearily and fought back tears as the next several years of his life passed before his eyes.

He watched the dozens of sheets bump along the sand, glide into the air and pinwheel inland with the wind's whimsy. The artist walked, head bowed, down the beach.

Poul bit his lip and turned inward to his favorite vision of earlier years. "Mendel, someday I'm going to tell you what a success you are and how people idolize you and live their goddamn lives by your songs. I'm going to drum it into your head that you are one of the greatest artists of this or any century. Then, Mendel, I'm going to kick you ass over whiskers. I swear I'm going to...."

He watched the general direction of the papers, waited for Mendel to disappear, and moseyed down the slope, his aching joints not allowing him to hurry even if he wanted to. He knew full well there was no hurry. Little moments held a few surprises here and there, but the general pattern of his life was set. The papers would be scattered around the kingdom, but they would all be waiting somewhere. And he would find every damned last one of them.

He clutched the bag full of Mara songs he'd found in the Appalachians and began gathering the wild sheets along the beach. "This trip could have been so easy," he grumbled. "I swear the Devil gets into him when I come around. Well, Beasely ought to be happy. I wonder how many thousands of times I've bent over in my life…."

Though he didn't want to fully retire, Poul was getting tired of this glorified rag picking. There had to be some sort of compromise, some advancement in technology of junk picking. Progress was what America was all about. Maybe he would hire an assistant who could pick up the papers and file them as they traveled. At least he would have someone to talk with.

Conversations with himself had become tired reruns. Sometimes he said a few words to the clouds or made a comment to a sympathetic looking tree. Once in awhile, after being alone for too long, he joked with his food, but always stopped himself before it became a dialogue. Cracking a one-liner to a can of bean soup was permissible, but entering into a talk that demanded more than a tin ear could get one tossed into the can. Ha ha…

To help pass the arduous hours, Poul sang tunes from the Children's Songs albums, the only stuff he really understood:

❦   ❦   ❦

Anti-M posters appeared around the country showing Mendel's face distorted into evil features. Beneath it were words calling for his death and the cessation of his ever-spreading hellish influence.

They were balanced by Pro-M posters that depicted Mendel with saintly features. "Live your life on a true note—listen to Mendel."

Over the years his image had been so expanded, distended and distorted that had he walked into a restaurant, no one would probably recognize the real Mendel. It didn't matter. He had become a myth and the periodic rage-venting exercises had entered the realm of therapeutic rituals. Mendel had become more feared, loved and hated than nearly anyone on the planet. Since he was beyond democracy and religion and many steps ahead of the FBI and CIA, people resorted to pagan rhythms of mock killing the king. Leaders of other countries envied the U.S. that it had such a convenient and lasting symbol with which the population could purge itself. It was a gift no national leader could buy or easily create. And many have tried.

Poul awoke to the sound of snuffling and scratching. A black bear was going through his bag looking for food. Poul sat up and unzipped his sleeping bag. "Hey! Get the hell out of there!"

The bear pulled its nose from the bag and looked at him with beady brown eyes that showed curiosity but no fear. Poul studied the bear right back. "I've worked too long and hard to gather those songs. I am *not* going to lose them know. Understand?"

The bear ignored him and went back to the bag. Poul jumped up and took a step forward. "Out of there! Damn it! Go find honey or a picnic basket."

The bear pulled its head out of the bag and sat down, studying this wiry creature dancing around. When it started into the bag again, Poul rushed forward without thinking. "Get out! Out!" He screamed as loud as he could. The bear stood up, raised its front legs and roared in defiance. Christ he was big. Poul didn't care. He picked up a stick and continued toward forward. "Get the hell away from the bag," he said in a low, slow growl.

The bear dropped down on all fours and stared. Finally it turned and lumbered away huffing in exasperation.

Poul watched him, then sat down to get his breath. He fell back on the ground, clutching the bag. "I just attacked a bear." He broke into a sweat and took a slow deep breath. "Jesus Christ, I just attacked a bear." He shook his head in disbelief, knowing he'd do it again if he had to.

A hawk soared in the shimmering blue air above him, circling first wide, then narrowing into a graceful inward spiral. Somewhere below was a mouse. Mendel felt the creature's heart pounding as it sensed the hawk and scuttled through the dead grass that lay like a tangled, tawny death mat. He felt the hawk's dispassionate concentration, a deadly feathered machine following genetic instructions as it carried out its particle of universal programming.

Reaching the center of the spiral, the bird stopped for an instant that held Mendel's own heart suspended. Then it dropped like a black missile toward the three-inch target on the earth. Riding the hawk's back, Mendel heard the air rush past as the bird cut through the atmosphere with increasing velocity. He felt the rodent's numbness as it realized death was in the coming second and he gasped within the red explosion of beak into flesh and the last unfelt scream that escapes with the soul's flight from the body.

Like the crashing of planets he heard the violent music of life leaving one body to feed the flesh of another. He shuddered with the feelings of impact and stillness. The bird pushed back upward, carrying the limp body home where it would rip the warm flesh in an act of being, neither good nor evil.

There is no gentleness or violence, Mendel thought later. There is only the music of existence. He nodded to the images that entered his mind late in the night. The next morning he awoke to a light rain splashing on his cheek. The water washed the spots of blood into the absorbent earth.

He wrote songs of dripping spears, thuds on the earth, groans, death screams, bodies in meaty shreds. The dark copper hue of recently abandoned battlefields filled his pages. In nearly all of them there was hope and peace inherent in the clash of flesh. In the largest sense, in any violence, there is no victim, no victor. There is only continuous existence.

❧   ❧   ❧

Feeling a hundred years old, Poul limped back to the city with the complete Mara collection and the "loss" songs, or whatever they were. Let the marketing people name them. His shirt was tattered and he had a slight scar, a souvenir from a brief battle with a farm dog over a paper. He had about one more trip left in him, and whether his spirit wanted to quit or not, his body was ready to call it a day for good.

Several hundred people with Anti-Mendel signs jammed the sidewalk in front of Beasely's building. On the other side of the street a crowd just as large chanted "More Mendel music! More Mendel music!" A Mendel song blared over the traffic that was slowed to a crawl and honking. Drivers were swearing at both the AMs and PMs.

Poul groaned quietly. "Not again. Just let me through, somehow." He clutched the bag that held the equivalent of several million dollars in songs,

Police hovered around the edges of the block, waiting a few more minutes before they broke up both crowds. In America, people have a right to gather and practice free speech, as long as they don't tie up the traffic.

As Poul shoved his way through the AM crowd, a middle-aged man hollered at him. "Are you an AM or PM?"

Poul had grown to hate crowds and right now he was angry. "What?" He said testily.

Are you for Mendel or against Mendel?"

"Depends on my mood and the day," Poul said, continuing his way through the bodies and signs, praying he made it before getting stuck inside another riot.

As he neared the door guarded by armed security guards, someone yelled. "If you're Anti-Mendel, how can you get in there?"

Poul shook his head and clutched his bag of songs. "Positive thinking."

❧   ❧   ❧

"Hordes of opposing assholes." Poul positioned his body into his leather chair. God, if he could only take it with him on the road. "How long have they been out there?"

Beasely stared down at them from his window. "Couple years. The people in the groups change. People come in from all over the country—hell, all over the *world*—to demonstrate. AMs on one side. PMs on the other. It's quite the phenomenon." He said it quietly, with some sadness. "Sometimes people die."

"I'm familiar with it," Poul said, shivering with the memory of the riot.

Beasely turned from the window and crossed the room. He moved slowly and sat carefully. "The AMs have even filed a suit against Beasely, Inc. for promoting music that incites violence."

"They ever hear of the Beatles?"

Beasely shrugged. "They can't win. It's just one more hassle that takes more of my time...and my nervous system." He rolled his cigar between his fingers. "I have to wear a disguise and have security escort me out the back way to get to my car to go home. Those AMs would kill me if they could get their hands on me." He sighed. Poul noticed how much more subdued Beasely seemed since the attempt on his life, and the death of the girl in the Chicago riot. Beasely broke the silence. "How's Mendel?"

Poul nodded. "Okay. He's been through a lot, poor bastard. But he's alright. Better than me, I think. Christ, I almost got eaten up by a German Shepherd who did basic training with some neo Nazis. Laid claim to a song page. Ha! I saved Mendel's song from going to the dogs....." He lit a cigarette, his weak attempt at humor spent. "Chased a bear in Pennsylvania. Stinking things grow big in those mountains."

Beasely nodded, not knowing whether to smile or look sympathetic. He had put on several pounds since Poul had left, but his palsy didn't seem to be any worse. Maybe there was hope for him, Poul thought.

He did have a habit of rubbing his stomach, tracing the knife scar, Poul noticed. Traumas form eternal imprints.

"I'm not going to stay," Poul said. "I hate the thoughts of going back out there, but he's getting to an age where he shouldn't be wandering around alone. I'd really like to talk him into retiring. He's been searching for the perfect song long enough, it seems." He stared wistfully out the window. "Nice dream, I guess."

Beasely's eyes lost some of their age. "I really would like to meet him, Poul. We could get him a penthouse—"

"No way. He'd be murdered in a week."

"We could keep it a secret."

"We can't even keep him a secret when he's anonymous. I couldn't keep me a secret. I couldn't keep you a secret. You nearly get killed and wind up with more security than the United Nations, for God's sakes."

Beasely thought about it and nodded sadly. It was true. He was too tired to fight, though. All he wanted was to meet Mendel. All the power and money he'd earned and he couldn't accomplish this one small goal.

Poul slid the bag toward his partner. "There's enough here for years."

Beasely surveyed the bags. "Good. Thanks, Poul."

The lines in Poul's narrow face had deepened with the weather and road life. The sharp, angular crevices accentuated a ruddy health and inner weariness. The prospect of going out was depressing. But the idea of staying around here was worse. He was tired and angry with the way life was going. "He's an asshole too," he said suddenly.

Beasely looked up from a packet of song papers. "Who?"

"Mendel. He just doesn't know when to quit." He stood up and limped toward the door. "But then, neither do we." He turned back to his partner and studied him. "Take care of yourself, Beaze." He was quiet a moment. "Next time I come back, I'm going to stay, I hope." He looked at the doorknob, blinking quickly. "We'll talk over old times, or something."

Perhaps taken by the same sentimental feelings, and the reality of the rapidly decreasing number of years left to them, Beasely stood up. He hesitated and walked over and took Poul's hand. "I'll be waiting."

Poul held his hand. He had that dark feeling again. "Yes," he said quietly. "Please be waiting."

❦   ❦   ❦

The raindrops made a padding plop on the leaves. Mendel squeezed the water from his beard. He picked up his bag and left the crumpled, dampened songs of violence all around him. Singing of hell and grandeur of the mind, of the beginning and the end of man, the songs when incorporated with song parts from other periods were edging toward his goal.

Whatever it was, this missing part, it was as small as a bump on the vein of an elderberry leaf, small as a molecule riding bareback on a frisky atom. It was quicker than an eye blink, but as important as the concept of eternity.

He followed little paths, some overgrown and nearly invisible, through West Virginia, Kentucky and Tennessee. He walked through Mississippi and turned toward Louisiana, then made his way through Alabama, Georgia and back north through South Carolina. He was getting closer to the perfect song.

He felt as though he had spent lifetimes on earth. Yet it all seemed so brief. Now, his hair white, his body parts wearing a bit, his clothes nothing but tunic-like shapeless rags, he accepted the fact that his spirit and body would soon part ways.

His determination to find the perfect song had not eased a bit, but he wondered if he would indeed find it before the end of life cancelled the quest. Well, he would search until his breath bade him farewell. He kept moving. Death lays to rest the weary and forlorn, the confused and distracted, the upset and the disappointed.

He pictured death as a kindly, bland-faced doctor who checks out patients from the hospital, gives directions to the lost and rescues millions from the asylums of their minds and the crumbling temples of their bodies.

Maybe death wasn't a doctor at all, but merely a caretaker. At any rate, he was neither grim nor happy. Death was just a businesslike professional with a job to do, making no exceptions, ever. He was imaginative only in the ways he executed the particulars.

CHAPTER 17

Poul kicked a nearby rock and swore. Mendel was not supposed to be writing this much. The guy was on another mad streak, scattering papers all over the countryside. "Six months," he muttered. "If I don't find it all in six months, I'm done. The public and Beasely be damned." He spotted another paper to his right and headed slowly toward it.

"If I had any sense, I'd heave the whole mess and go back and tell everybody it was a joke, a lifelong hoax. And now it's over. There never was any Mendel, but it sure was fun while it lasted. Now, pick up your music and go home, everybody."

Poul was not having a good week. Mendel was obviously still searching for the perfect song which meant God knew how long until they could finally pack up things and retire. He cursed himself for not quitting and just leaving Mendel. He cursed himself for needing Mendel. "The only thing with any sense anymore is the goddamn *wildlife*." He picked up the page and scraped off the dirt.

Poul thought about the note in his billfold and wondered if Mendel believed what he wrote. If he did, why did he continue this search?

Mendel kept moving. It was so simple when he was young. With enough energy and dedication he would simply break through the sloggy chains of mortality, gaze upon the eternal, and write it all down. His youthful mind saw him seizing the moment as Prometheus seized the fire, as Faust seized knowledge, as Beowulf seized Grendel's arm, and tore it off.

But time wears down the hardest rocks and quiets the loudest storms. Mendel once felt knowledge would come to him like a bolt of lightning licking down in a phallic thrust from a rent heaven and inseminate his mind in a melding of celestial passion.

Now he saw it as a billowing cloud. He wrote in his notebook: "It moves along, lumbering with slow grace over its blue track. When it meets another cloud, it doesn't push its new acquaintance aside or declare war and smash it. The two clouds flow into one another and move along to meet others. 'They' become 'it', a thing greater than the sum of their parts. Their shape and texture constantly change, evolve, dissolve, but never disappear.

"So it must be with men. We bumble along, gathering, learning, growing and understanding through acceptance. Each man has a life that is a universe. He lives a million individual moments that no other individual can live. He gives something to the world that no one else can give."

He thought of Mara and savored her image, then turned back to his paper and forced himself to write.

"While we are on our individual paths, none of us is great. We are all bumblers, searchers and gatherers. Even our leaders are living a thousand moments for each mighty statement they make, a million moments for each great action.

"The greatest sin is to shut ourselves from thought and experience, for the universe and eternity are within each individual life. Our eyes must always be on greaterness and our ears tuned to all songs."

"There's more out there, but this is all I had the strength gather," Poul sighed as he entered Beasely's office. Once inside he stopped at a sight he'd never encountered before—Beasely's desk without Beasely.

A new receptionist rushed in from another room. "Can I help you?" She halted when she recognized the hunched, frail-looking man with the bald head and scruffy gray beard. "You're Mr. Poul."

Poul nodded and scratched quickly at his cheek. "Yeah, where's Beasely?" It was more of a demand than a question. Something was wrong and he was old and didn't have time to waste. "Speak up, girl!"

The girl cleared her throat. "Mr. Beasely is at home. He had a stroke six months ago. He told me when I started working that if anything happened to him—"

"Yeah, you're part of my staff and you're sworn to secrecy about my existence."

Slightly hurt and offended, the girl looked at him. "Yes, sir."

Poul felt light-headed, not part of this office or even of this life. His voice belonged to someone else, coming from a hollow room and entering a chamber of nothingness. He looked around at the empty office, realizing this situation was really no surprise. He'd been watching Beasely deteriorate for years. He simply refused to acknowledge it.

"Where is he?"

"Home."

"I know that! You said that. Where does he live?"

She told him and stepped back from this crazy, possibly violent old man. Poul rubbed the back of his neck. "Sorry," he said angrily. "It's been a hard year. Who's in charge of operations?"

"Mr. Phillips, sir."

Poul picked up the song bag and handed it to her. "See that he gets this. I'll be back."

He rushed out. He had never met this Phillips guy, but the man had been with Beasely for two decades and Beasely had talked of him with trust. He took a cab to his friend's house.

Poul stopped dead when he saw the pale, motionless bag of flesh that used to be the solid, cigar-chomping lovable tyrant. The eyes were still clear, but it wasn't hard to see that the man would rather be somewhere else.

"Beaze?" As he leaned over his friend, Poul's face crinkled not only with sorrow, but with the look of a man who has suddenly seen the brevity of life. "Beaze, I'm back." He reached out and touched the cheek. The pale blue eyes looked up in recognition and glistened. Poul blinked quickly and swallowed.

A chunky, motherly nurse entered and said, "Now remember, let's all stay calm. We don't want to excite Mr. Beasely. He has to stay quiet." She looked down at Beasely. "Don't we, dear?"

Hmm, Beaze had been a problem patient, Poul thought. "Can he talk?"

The nurse shook her head. "He's only said one thing in six months. It was 'poll' or something like that. The doctors figured he wanted to know about the latest polls or something on Mendel's albums. So we've been bringing in Billboard and showing him the figures."

Beasely was looking, with frustration in his eyes, at the white ceiling.

After an uneasy silence, the nurse left. Poul shook his head and leaned down toward the head. "Jesus, Beaze, I'd have come back sooner if I'd—"

"Shuu...upp!"

Poul jumped back with a gasp. "You *can* talk! Kind of...."

"Yehhh...." The words emerged with great effort and dragged helplessly.

"Why haven't you talked to the doctors?"

"Asshh...holeshhh." Poul nodded. "This...em...barr...ssingg...po...sishunnn."

Poul agreed. For decades, hundreds of people lived to obey his slightest whim. The irony of it was that people now waited on him to an even greater degree. They even wiped his ass. From a ruler to an infant in one fell stroke.

"Beaze, if there's anything I can do—"

"Izz!" His whole body seemed to concentrate in this mighty effort of sticking words together and forcing them through the paralyzed tissues of his lips. "Wan...meeetuhh...Men...dew..." His head relaxed, and his face showed his exhaustion from the effort to formulate and push out the words.

Poul closed his eyes. He felt sick and tired as their collective lives passed before him. He sat down in the chair by the bed and put his hand on his friend's arm.

"Pleashhh."

Poul took a slow, deep breath. His hands felt cold and numb. He studied Beasely's pale flesh and prayed that what he was about to do was the right thing.

His lips were trembling as he stood up and looked down at his friend. "You have met him," he said quietly.

The blue eyes in the mask like face studied him with surprise, then disbelief, then joy, then relief. "Alwaysshh sus—sus-*pected* it...."

There was silence as Beasely stared at the ceiling, gathering his thoughts and then forcing the thoughts into language. "P-Prooove it."

Poul closed his eyes for a minute, bit his lip and took another deep breath. He took out his wallet and drew out the ragged piece of paper. He unfolded it slowly, his hands no longer trembling. He held it above Beasely who read the note and finally nodded ever so slightly. Beasely's eyes filled with tears that slowly made their way down the sides of his face. He shook his head almost imperceptibly. Poul leaned down to the barely moving lips.

"Thank you," he whispered. He closed his eyes and fell asleep, exhausted with effort and emotion of their moment together.

Poul sat and held his friend's hand as life gently left through one last tired sigh. No one is ever ready for the profound emptiness when a friend dies. Poul sat motionless, holding the cold hand.

In the grand scheme of things, the death of the man who created the Mendel myth meant very little to the world. The Mendel Machine was moving smoothly without him, which is what Beasely wanted.

Poul fell forward on the still body and cried as he had never cried in his life.

❧   ❧   ❧

Clean shaven and in a tailored gray suit, Poul spent the next few weeks working with Phillips, a square-shouldered man with straight gray hair that matched his expression. His almost total lack of emotion was a hard contrast to Beasely's passion, but he knew the business.

"So, Phillips," Poul said one day. "Do you ever smile?"

Phillips looked puzzled and adjusted his glasses. "I guess. If there's a need."

When he was satisfied that everything was in order, Poul prepared to leave. He didn't care if the new music was recorded or just plain forgotten. He didn't care about the business at all now that Beasely was gone. His only concern was that the original manuscripts were stored in his bank vault with the rest of his life's accumulations.

If Mendel didn't have any need for them, Poul would have them to jog his memory about the particulars of their adventures. It would help with his memoirs which were going to start soon. He was going to write the truth and show the world how foolish and gullible people are. He was going to get something out of life besides dirt beds and money he didn't use.

He was going to get the last laugh.

He felt guilty about lying to Beasely, but it was what his friend needed. It also made his passing a more pleasant one.

❧   ❧   ❧

"Call a halt to it, Mendel. We're all getting too old to play anymore. We've already lost one." He crouched stiffly at safe distance. The conflict of needing to be out of the city and near Mendel, and his ambivalent feelings about the hard, lonely life with Mendel was growing more unbearable with age. It was, he knew, coming to a head.

He was perhaps more than ever caught up in Mendel's power, and at the same time he was growing more insistent on breaking away and leading his own life in the decreasing amount of time left.

The tension was driving him closer to the edge than he'd ever been. The dream of living with Mendel in a pure, simple existence clashed with reality. Mendel would never stop until he found the perfect song, and accomplishing that little feat was not looking good. Poul long ago gave up trying to know what was right for himself. He wrung his hands and searched for an answer as he sat in the shadow of Mendel's exploding emotions and persistent search.

One night Mendel danced around his campfire. "Mountains crumble! Heavens fall! The stars revolt and nothing's all! Ha ha haa!" He raised his arms over the campfire. "The greatest creation is the continual creation of the self in time!"

Poul shook his head. "He's going to pop a vessel just like Beasely."

Finally the night came when Mendel did not write or sing, and Poul knew he was done for awhile. The next day Mendel would throw away the songs and depart. Poul made his bed early, relieved that his wait was over and weary at the prospects of what lay ahead. He tried to find a position on the ground that would ease his aching back.

That night Poul dreamed of a faceless man who told him the dream he was having was real. "It's as real as your day life," the man said. "And Mendel's visions are as real as your crusty socks." The man laughed, which amazed Poul who had never seen a man with no face laugh. "Humorous, these limited perspectives you people in 'life' have. I suppose it's necessary, though. Mendel expands and translates for the rest of you who cannot break through the barriers. Know that what he gathers and gives is real and true…mostly!" The man laughed and faded as he brought a cigar to his head.

The next morning Poul woke with the phrase "I suppose it's necessary" ringing in his head. That was all he remembered and wondered what it was that was necessary. He pulled on his shoes, noticing again how ragged and filthy they were.

He ate a can of sardines and set to work picking up the songs Mendel had set free earlier that morning.

Mendel dropped his bag and stared out over the rolling mountains. The air was bright and clear and slow-moving clouds seemed etched with a sharp pencil across the sky. "I'm so close," he told himself. "I can feel it." He pushed his hair back and looked at the bag. He stared at it as the sun burned its way through the clouds, arched upward and then slowly fell. At dusk Mendel lifted the bag and emptied a lifetime of scraps, parts, words and notes.

He dropped to his knees and scoured the pages, recalling where and how each was written: a birth scream; a train whistle's shriek; a rainy morning jet roar; the womb's muted rhythm; the mysterious song of dewdrops; a robin falling to a quiet death in the forest; the odor of love before love and after love; the warm smell of Sunday fried chicken; the coursing of daily blood, monthly blood, streaming blood.

He felt a million years old.

From the opposite hill Poul shook his head and mumbled. "This isn't right. He's never done this. Ever. Jesus." His breathing suddenly came hard and he wondered if he was having a heart attack. "Oh, God, don't let me die here." His mind raced back to Miss White's fiery eyes and the portrait of Christ hanging in church. He saw himself writing 5,000 commandments, spending a lifetime eating sardines on lonely hillsides and finally lying alone, as wolves, then worms nibbled away at his skinny carcass.

When his breath returned, he knew this was the end. It was over. He was going to hurry to Mendel and introduce himself and hug him and talk and reassure himself that they were both real and living and had spent lifetimes doing what they had done and now it was finished. It was time, damn it. He jumped up, but he moved too fast for his age and condition and when he bent down to grab his bag and stood up again, he fainted.

He was considerably more calm when he awoke and realized he had to wait a little longer. There was something profound about Mendel at this moment, like a female giving her whole attention to birthing, or a man concentrating on dying, both needing to experience it fully and do it well. It would be an interruption of one's most private moments for Poul to bother Mendel now.

The first snow flurry came and Mendel was still digging through songs, humming lines, cutting sections and pasting them to others. Others he threw away. Unable to bear the cold and the boredom, Poul returned to the city, dumped his few songs, shaved, and took a long hot bath.

Throughout the coming days, he thought only of Mendel. What in hell was the man doing, anyway?

CHAPTER 18

From The New York Times:

The Mendel Empire has surpassed Elvis Presley. A third generation of listeners has created an even greater demand for Mendel's songs. Like Elvis, Mendel has his own category on Ebay. On the Perfect Song Website, owned and operated by Beasely, Inc. you can buy anything from Mendel underwear to several computer game versions of the Quest for the Perfect Song. A Google search for Mendel resulted in nearly a billion references....

Mendelites worldwide played a complex game in which they searched for their own perfect song. Bookstores had one shelf of critical studies, illustrated lyrics, unauthorized biographies, and personal experiences. TV documentaries traveled to sites mentioned in the songs, trying to re-create the writer's life and movements. Movies "inspired by the life of Mendel" were romances, adventures and quiet introspective studies that always ended with the composer fading into an existential fog.

"Spielberg or Lucas are the only two people who should try to do Mendel," Poul once told Beasely. "They're the only ones who would begin to understand him."

Beasely had nodded. "Or Jackson. The Lord of the Rings guy."

Over the past two decades it had become a hobby to find a real item from the real Mendel. And it became a quest that surpassed even that of the Holy Grail.

Fan clubs, solitary individuals and amateur detectives scoured the U.S. for a piece of paper used by Mendel, a rejected pencil, a thread from his clothes, a lock of hair. Some of the more enterprising entrepreneurs sold jars of water which they claimed had been blessed by Mendel and would insure the imbiber a long and healthy life. Those who drank a cup each day would find their powers of creativity expanded infinitely and sexual powers enhanced beyond anything imaginable. Other salesmen sold strands of hair from his beard which they said gave the holder the power to commune with spirits—both good and evil.

And people bought them.

Had anyone ever found something of Mendel's that they could truly document, that man or woman would have become a multi-millionaire and a celebrity overnight. The truth was, a few dozen people over the years had seen Mendel, some even exchanged a word with him, but thanks to the media's distortions and their own blindness, they never realized it.

By the time Mendel Websites appeared, any facts about the man—which had been created by Poul and Beasely—were lost in the speculations and fantasies of millions of individuals. Each claim, each conjecture, added to the myth which expanded exponentially.

❦   ❦   ❦

Phillips handled the company with knowledge and efficiency, except for one small move.

"I let your name slip," he told Poul in his expressionless tone. "It was unfortunate and I apologize."

"You what?" Poul stared at Phillips with a mixture of disbelief, belief and anger. His chest tightened again. Damn! He strode over to the quiet man. "You let it slip on purpose, you son-of-a-bitch." Phillips said nothing. "Why did you do it?"

Phillips adjusted his glasses. "Another element to boost sales." He leaned over to the computer and hit a few keys, bringing up a chart. "We think we can boost sales fifteen percent immediately by adding you to the marketing mix. We—"

"Who the hell is we?" Poul screamed.

"The marketing staff," Phillips said with a trace of annoyance.

"My life, you idiot, is worth nothing now! Nothing!" There would be phone calls, thousands of interview requests, people asking for autographs, book deals, movie rights, speaking engagements, and the usual attempts on his life.

"Sorry, sir."

"You're not sorry in the least," Poul hissed. Phillips knew neither Mendel nor Poul had much time left and he let Poul's name out to give the world something fresh and exotic to think about. There had always been speculation about some mysterious man who followed Mendel. Now people knew it wasn't Paul Smith, and, compliments of Phillips, they had a fairly accurate sketch of the thin man with the walnut face and small eyes.

"Even Beasely wouldn't stoop that low, you bastard." Phillips just stared at him. He was a new generation machine programmed simply to run a business and increase profits. Poul and Mendel were merely old cogs quickly wearing out.

"There have been innumerable requests for you to appear on talk shows, do a documentary, preside over a popular game show called, in Mendel's honor, 'In Quest of the Perfect Match'—"

"Phillips!" He cut the man off. "Tell them to take every request, no matter how small, and jam up their commercial asses!"

Phillips remained expressionless. "I think you're taking this too personally. It is a business as you know—

"Of course I'm taking it personally. It has been my whole *god... damned...life!*"

Poul reached toward the bowl where he'd plucked smokes for nearly half a century. It was gone. "Where are the cigarettes?"

"We don't smoke, sir, and—"

"I do and I want a goddamned cigarette now!"

"Of course."

"Make it fifty!"

"Certainly, sir." Someone appeared a few minutes later with three packs of cigarettes. Poul lit one and stared out the window through the gray haze that layered the city. Poison. The whole place was poison. Everything was over. There was nothing left now and he worked quickly to piece together a conclusion.

After some thought, he crushed out his cigarette and turned to Phillips who was waiting patiently for the old man to speak.

Phillips was a patient man. Dealing with this crotchety old fart wasn't easy, and he had been warned. But the man was the Grand Master of a two-plus-generation show and had to be humored. He'd be gone soon and the company could get on with the business of revamping Mendel's image to fit the new and younger audience.

Poul rubbed the tip of his nose and stared at the young man. "I want a tally of my holdings," he said matter-of-factly. "I want all assets converted to dollars. Put everything into a bank under a Mendel Trust Fund. Got it?"

"You're giving up your wealth?"

"Life is more important." A few years ago he could not have imagined himself saying that.

Phillips nodded. "I understand, but I don't think it's a wise—."

"Shut up."

"Yes sir."

"When that's done, I want my name erased from the face of everything you ever knew." Phillips nodded again and made a note. Poul continued to rub his nose thoughtfully. "Hold out some for me. You decide. Put that—fix it so when I need money I can call one person and that person can get it to me immediately. Okay, Phillips?" Phillips thought a moment and nodded.

"Anytime, anywhere. Clear?"

Phillips nodded.

Poul nodded in mocking imitation and said with a sneer, "I knew I could count on you."

Phillips caught the sarcasm and looked up at Poul. "Yes, sir, you can."

♣   ♣   ♣

He left the city, the traffic jams, foreign tongues and neon promises. A billboard showing a sleeker, more hip Mendel, promoted the new CD, Songs of Love and Loss. Poul shook his head. He had refused to listen to the CD knowing he couldn't stand the pain that those songs must carry.

He hoped he could find Mendel easily this time. He couldn't get rid of a sense of doom. Something was about to happen.

A few days later he felt better, walking the dirt road and basking in the silence. His stained, crooked teeth poked out through his smile. He had made up his mind.

He was going to show himself to Mendel. Let happen what might happen.

Some men are judged insane when they reject society's accepted version of reality in favor of a self-created one. Others are considered artists. Others are simply lost in the world.

※ ※ ※

Mendel put the last pieces of paper together and sat back to look at the completed work. His whole body hurt. He thought how pleasant a beer would be and wondered where old Harry was. Something whispered on a stone to his left. A huge milk snake poured down over the slate boulder into the dark crack of two smaller chunks of the dull gray stone. A few moments later the snake's head emerged up through the crack, slowly, straining, concentrating all its efforts in rising. As it pushed forward, it glistened like new copper in the bright sunlight.

Mendel hunched forward. In all his years he had never seen this common, miraculous feat. Now fully exposed and shed of its burden, the snake seemed to recognize the presence of another being and shrank into a small coil. From the mass, the triangular head rhythmically rose in a graceful sway, its black-tipped tongue flicking out from the gleaming royal head. The two beings stared at each other, both falling into a mutual sway beyond time, until they merged. Suddenly the snake loomed upward until its head met and became the sun and its body encompassed the earth.

Its glittering black eyes glared into Mendel with dispassionate knowledge. Mendel reached his hand out to the snake who in turn flicked its tongue and waited. He grasped it gently with both hands and held it on his lap, feeling the muscles ripple like tiny volts of electricity beneath the gleaming scales. The snake's history, the serpent's vision, passed into him. Much later it crawled from his motionless hands and disappeared.

The gods have named you rightly, he thought. You are the king of animals, condemned to earth. You hold one of the largest and most difficult, and simplest, secrets of life.

A new song ran through his head, but he didn't write it down:

He crept to his lifelong song that he'd been pasting together and held it up. It was his final song and it was imperfect. He held this new song in his mind but knew he could not release it.

Man is a force bound by the physical, as the serpent is bound by the snake. Perfection is a fragile illusion vanishing upon touch, and revised with each living moment. If man reaches what he defines as perfection, he stagnates within its confines, just as the snake suffocates if it cannot shed its constricting skin.

Man extracts the essence of yesterday's moments before he sheds the bulk of them. Lightened, he runs into the new day.

Mendel saw the small missing detail and understood as he stood over his final song. He closed his eyes and lowered his head to rid himself of the dizziness. Such a small, yet frighteningly large detail.

In the instant of blackness that swept through his reeling brain, Mendel saw how the snake becomes the serpent. He had reached the perfection of himself as nearly as he could, and now he must go on.

Can a life be messy and perfect?

Of course.

When the sun set he built a fire. How fortunate he was, he thought as the blaze grew, that no one else had been witness to his lifetime of fumblings. Only Mara had seen and she would never tell anyone.

Mendel pulled a stick from the fire. He stared at it thoughtfully and smiled, then whirled it in the air until it flared in the dusk. Then he laid it on his final song. As the evening darkened, the flames from the paper pyre crackled and danced in the quiet Appalachian hills.

Poul looked on horrified. "Good God, what in hell is he doing?" He stared in disbelief at the burning song Mendel had worked on over a half century. He shuddered almost convulsively as his own dreams, shrouded in smoke, floated toward the skies.

Mendel stood up before the fire and chanted in an almost inhumanly loud voice: "Woman and earth open your gentle wombs and between you man shall see the light of day and sorrow of night! My heart melts open and consumes the infinite—the infinity of my self! Ha haa!"

Poul shook his head, his mind chanting: "No. No. No." His small brown eyes stared longingly at the figure over the fire. All his dreams.... "No, Mendel. Not just when I was coming—"

"Life is—"

"—to give you a new life—"

Mendel fell to the ground and lay still.

Poul gasped and for the first time in his career, lost control. "No! Not now!" He started down the hill toward the still figure. "Not now! Not when we were so close to—." He was halfway down the hill when Mendel's arm rose. As if using his last bit of strength, the aged composer reached out toward the sky. Like an unfolding flower in the April dawn, his fingers slowly uncurled until they stretched out in longing toward the heavens. A moment later the fingers relaxed and curled inward, and like a drying, withering flower, fell.

"Oh God...Oh God...."

Poul's mind was blank. "Mendel...damn it! Mendel...." He couldn't control the tears. It was over. Why had he waited so long? If he hadn't left Mendel this last time...if he'd come back sooner...his own life was over. He felt no reason to be alive.

Just as Poul's mind was arranging itself for mourning, guilt and self-pity, Mendel slowly sat up and pulled the hair back away from his face. "Some old fools seek to become the children they envy—and fail," Mendel muttered. He picked up a few scattered papers and fed them slowly to the fire, still shaken with his last vision. It was all coming too fast. He picked up his bag. "Well, old friend, time to part ways."

He paused and stared at the bag, remembering when it was new, ages ago. His eyes watered again with memories and the rush of years. A lifetime is so long at the beginning and so short from the middle onward. But he had no time for ruminations. Those bound in time felt its brevity. He squeezed the bag one last time and tossed it into the flames.

"Goodbye."

Poul sat paralyzed, wondering if he was going crazy. His mind was doing strange things. He wasn't sure if he was in or out of his body. He wasn't sure anymore how old he was or even who he was. He couldn't swear if Mendel was dead or alive, or dead and risen, or even real.

Mendel was silhouetted against the fire, singing a wordless, almost tuneless song over the ashes of his final number.

Poul was drained of everything—emotion, energy, thought. Numbly he stood up, swaying slightly with dizziness, his mind saying, "I can't take it any-more. I can't. I just can't take anymore." He turned, and though it was night, stumbled back toward the city. The song was gone.

It was over. Beasely was dead. The song was gone. Mendel was lost and it was over. Behind him a full-bodied laugh echoed over the mountain. It was the laugh of a man sitting in a comfortable chair in front of a fireplace, sipping brandy after a good meal and deeply happy with a long, rich story whose humor was enriched by undertones of pathos, adventure, tragedy and discovery.

It filled the darkness, mingling with the breeze, rising toward the moon, sending chills through Poul and making his stomach tighten. Nothing now could bring warmth to his numb mind. He never slowed his pace and he never looked back.

CHAPTER 19

Phillips handed Poul the paper that showed Poul what he was worth in hard cash.

Poul studied it, trying not to show the shock he felt. He had no idea he was worth that much. "I could walk out of here with this much right now," he said, glancing up at the younger man.

"Yes, sir."

Poul nodded. "Okay. The Mendel Trust Fund I asked you to set up will work this way." He outlined the plan.

"Any person in the world who thinks he wants to be an artist, regardless of sex, race, age, religion or anything, is eligible," Poul said with quiet authority. "The Mendel Trust Fund will give that person a stipend to train for an occupation, whether it's carpentry, business management, or ferret husbandry. It doesn't matter. Anything but art. The person will then go out and try his hand at the new profession."

The tape recorder was running, but Phillips made notes besides.

"If it doesn't work out and the man or woman still wants to be an artist, the fund will give him one more stipend to try another line of work. If the person gives it a sincere try and *still* wants to be an artist, he or she will receive a small amount of cash on a monthly basis. It will be enough for the artist to exist and create his art, no matter what the quality of it. It won't be a lot but the artist will then be free to exist without worry about food, shelter or the judgment of the benefactor."

"Okay," Phillips said, putting down his pencil.

"I'm not through," Poul said, irritated.

Phillips nodded and picked up the pen.

Poul continued. "Two stipulations. One is the artist not take another job. If he believes strongly enough in his work, food and shelter will be enough. The second stipulation is that the artist take his own path, follow his unique vision and dream no matter where it leads or how stupid it might seem. Okay?"

Phillips nodded curtly. "It's your money."

"Right," Poul agreed. "Now for the second item." He waited until Phillips looked up from his notes. Poul leaned down to look the man in the eye. "Mendel is dead."

Phillips started slightly, the strongest reaction Poul had seen from this breathing piece of clay since he first met him. The young man adjusted his glasses with slightly trembling fingers. "Dead?"

Poul gently touched Beasely's gold Mendel lighter, knocking the little figure on its back. "Dead."

Phillips studied the man on the other side of his desk, this bald, wizened shell in smelly clothes and maddening serenity in his beady eyes. He was a demented old fool who had just given up a huge fortune to feed a new generation of artists, of all people.

"Might I have some proof? In all due respect, of course."

Poul's smile was an exhibition of worn, yellowed teeth, a mouth sacrificed to a life on the road. "As a matter of fact, you might not. The only proof you had of his existence was my word. And now," he shrugged, "I say he's dead." He smiled again. "It's as simple and clean as that."

Phillips straightened his back and regained his composure. "Would you put it in writing?"

"No!" Poul exploded. "No I won't! I said he's dead!"

Phillips took a deep breath and bit his lip. "Yes, sir. At any rate, we have planned for the event."

"What a surprise," Poul said with a slight sneer. "Are people still looking for me since your little announcement about my existence?"

"Uh, yes sir. We've had many—"

Poul held up his hand, cutting off the younger man. "I'm dead, too. That will be included in your general announcement. I was alive, spent fifty some years hauling in songs and now I'm demised."

He crushed out his cigarette. Phillips stared at him, finally understanding. "It's your life."

"Thank you, Phillips. I knew you'd understand." He thought a moment. "We've gone over everything the last few months. I've signed everything that needs my signature, I'm sure." He turned and started for the door.

"Uh, not quite," Phillips said. "Before you, mmm, die, would you sign off on the royalty rights to the music? Just for legal purposes."

Poul turned and smiled. "You couldn't find the agreements between Beasely and me, could you?"

"As a matter of fact, we couldn't, but I've had some documents drawn up that will relieve—"

"Phillips, you dim wit. Beasely was honest and I was naive. I've never signed a thing—except those documents right there that just turned all my money into a fund for crazy young artists." He thought a moment. "Oh, and that other paper that says you'll pay for my apartment and living expenses for the rest of my life." He shook his head at Phillips' chalky face and his confused silence. "You got out of it real cheap."

Poul shut the door behind him for the last time.

❦   ❦   ❦

He sipped a glass of wine and wondered what he would do now, what Mendel would do. Damn, it could have been a nice last few years. The life Mendel lived would drive anyone mad, though. It was no wonder the old coot finally fell off the edge. He stared out the window which glowed with city lights. He would try to settle in, become a hermit and write his memoirs. The world should have the true story, although Poul was the last person to take a firm stance on what was true and not true. Every piece of information that society had about Mendel was a lie or a fabrication. But it was the information that society had accepted and further reinforced until it became its own truth.

His mind returned to Mendel. Had he left the man too hastily? No. No, he had waited. He just couldn't take anymore. Every man reaches his limits and must make a decision. But that was easy to say now in the comfort of his apartment. Mendel was out there alone, truly alone, without even his songs. He'd burned his entire life. Poul had watched it.

He looked around his bedroom, resting his gaze on a few Mendel clippings taped to the wall. Mendel had nothing to show for his entire existence—no family, friends or possessions. He didn't even have a comfortable place to die, and if he had lost his mind, as it had appeared, he didn't even have himself.

The traffic outside rushed back and forth, like rambling sentences, jabbed with exclamatory honks and human yells. "Mendel moves in silence to the music of the years." Poul smiled to remember the line he'd created himself so long ago. Another cigarette, glowing softly in the darkness. Another glass of wine. He couldn't force Mendel to come back. He wouldn't. Mendel had lived his life free. Better he die alone than have the world see him as an aged, babbling idiot. Poul grunted heavily from the bed and paced to stretch his aching back. He turned on the television, hoping it would lull him into sleep. He had forgotten the order he'd given to Phillips.

"...world tonight mourns for an artist who gave his life in quest of the perfect song. Mendel is already recognized as one of the world's great artists for the beauty of his music, the breadth of his subject matter and the images that have become a part of American and even world culture.

"Mendel is responsible for legions of imitators who drew upon his works and his individualistic way of life for inspiration. But he is perhaps most dearly remembered for giving art back to the people, for bringing millions together in a common cause. That cause was a dedicated quest for beauty, truth and perfection. Running throughout his works was a sense of the earth as a living, feeling and caring spirit. Though he apparently never found his perfect song, Mendel's life itself can certainly be called a beautiful and glorious quest. He will be missed."

Poul switched channels where an announcer paused dramatically. The camera cut to a scene of crowds in the streets. "At this moment, thousands of people are crowded around the Beasely Publishing company with lighted candles, singing lines from Mendel's works, works that will live in the hearts of men and women forever."

Poul snorted. "Yeah, milk it for all it's worth." He fought to contain his emotion as the camera moved in to show faces filled with shock and despair. Record sales were an indication of an artist's popularity, but these thousands of mournful, tearful faces, God. This was a scene of love and loss that few men ever earn. Poul shook his head.

"Christ, Mendel, if you could only see."

"The circumstances surrounding Mendel's death are, like the man's life, sketchy," the newscaster continued. "One report claims that he took his own life in the Rockies. Another source claims he died of head wounds at the hands of a mugger in Chicago. Yet another report says he died of a brain hemorrhage in Death Valley...."

Poul switched to another channel. Apparently all shows had been pre-empted for this news. Another reporter in front of yet another weeping crowd spoke grimly into the lens:

"...perhaps the most reclusive of any artist, Mendel never once made a public appearance. Indeed, while many claimed to have met the man, only the equally mysterious man named Poul could prove Mendel's existence. Poul's sole proof was the regular delivery of Mendel's songs. Poul's unwavering dedication spanned half a century. We just learned that Poul is also dead of apparent heart failure after learning the news of his friend's passing."

Poul nodded and muttered, "Clever."

He switched to another channel. "...while the songs made billions of dollars, Mendel rejected the money to continue his quest. Poul, who spent his life gathering and saving the songs, gave his earnings to charity and also died in poverty."

Poul angrily clicked off the set and shook his head. Not one person in the world knew the truth. Not one. He picked up his bottle of wine and sat on the bed, pondering the power he had held throughout his life. He was the link who gave the man's art to the world. With a word he had given Mendel existence; with another he wiped him out of it. Clutching his bottle like a drowning man holding a floating board in a churning sea, Poul wondered if there ever was a shore.

Now that they were both safely dead, Poul wondered what had happened to Mendel. What was that night on the mountain all about? How could Mendel have lost his mind so suddenly? Sure, he had his moments of passion, but overall, Mendel was the essence of stability, locked by fate and attitude to his quest for the perfect song. Even on that final evening, Mendel sat by the fire touching his song parts as if they were cherished parts of his being.

He lay back on his bed, still holding the bottle, to better rerun a couple scenes. He saw Mendel handling the papers with a mother's gentle touch, fitting and refitting each piece with other parts as he hummed its growing tune.

As his mind relaxed and opened, Poul saw the image of a child working intently with a set of blocks, building an elaborate castle. The larger it grew, the more unsteady it became until the sneeze of a fly could toppled it. He saw the child back up ever so carefully, his eyes reflecting pride in his accomplishment, knowing it was imperfect but the best he could do. He saw the child's excitement with the castle's precarious condition. He saw the child step quickly toward his masterwork and give a mighty kick, laughing as the blocks splayed in all directions. Laughing as the castle's core tumbled inward.

Mendel reappeared in his mind, sitting on the mountain, putting his life's gatherings together into one huge song. He saw Mendel stand and pull the huge roll of paper toward the fire—

"Damn!" He jumped up and tried to hop from the bed, caught his foot in the sheet and fell in a heap to the floor. The room spun with alcohol and realization. "Damn! I'm the world's biggest fool!"

He pushed himself up to his hands and knees and crawled toward his clothes. It was not easy. They were spinning too. "I've been an idiot!"

He sat on the floor and tried to aim one foot into a spinning pant leg, trying to focus and make it slow down. The pant leg was too small. "Now I know why drunks leave their clothes on."

Mendel wasn't mad at all. He was *culminating*. The word entered Poul's drunken brain. Culminating. He got his foot in the leg hole and shoved till he saw it emerge from the other end. He began on the second leg. This was harder because his first leg was trapped.

No. He had never seen a man so full of…what? Spirit! Yes, he had witnessed it and it confused him and he ran away from it. Or maybe deep down he knew Mendel shouldn't be bothered. He knew…no. Be honest. He had run away in fear.

Focus, he told himself. Focus. Victory! The other leg went in. Now if he could just stand up. He crawled to the dresser and began the slow climb upward.

Who has ever looked upon a man who knew himself so completely and who was so openly joyous? Who has ever experienced such a man and not felt disoriented and scared? How many men and women have been locked away for no other crime than knowing themselves and fully accepting the joy of total existence? No matter how free or liberal a society is, no matter what its politics or religion, the underlying belief is that life is hard, sad and heavy. It is filled with tragedies, guilt and punishment. A man who steps out of these confines is "mad" and punished for breaking out of society's spiritual prison. Mendel, however, entirely escaped society and was revered.

He was now upright. The world was spinning, but he didn't care.

✤   ✤   ✤

Poul ran drunkenly through the streets clogged with weeping mourners, anxious police, radios blasting Mendel music, and the voices of large groups holding candles and singing Mendel choruses. The whole world was a wake.

Some mourners glanced at him with shock, wondering why this shrunken bearded old man was not paying tribute to the country's greatest artist and his silent companion.

A passionate young woman called to him as he passed: "Pray for Mendel!"

"Pray for Poul!" Came another voice.

"Stop and feel their goodness, old man!"

He pushed his way through the crowds who swayed under the hypnosis of death, prayer and song.

"Insensitive bastard!" Someone screamed after him. Bonfires of peace burned on every block. People sat in the streets stopping traffic to force drivers to halt and think of Mendel and Poul. A block north a large groups of AM's chanted with exuberance: "Mendel is dead! Mendel is dead! Praise God! Mendel is *dead*!"

"Oh Mendel, damn it, I'm sorry." He stumbled over bodies of passed out mourners and headed for the mountains that now seemed a world and a lifetime away.

CHAPTER 20

Mendel was gone. Poul scoured the site for papers, knowing it was futile. He searched for any kind of clue, walking in widening circles in his usual Mendel-hunting posture, hunched over, nose downward, eye on every blade of grass. There was nothing.

Finally he sat down on the stump where Mendel had perched all those months. "Mendel," he sighed. "Where in hell are you?" A wave of fright rippled coldly through him. He jumped up. "Mendel! Mendel! MENDEL!"

The next day he found half a footprint and sat beside it for hour trying to understand it. There was no other sign of the man. With a sigh and only hope to guide him, Poul set off in the footprint's direction. Heading into this vast unknown without Mendel before him Poul again felt the split desire to follow the man at all costs, and to call it quits and go home. But he had nothing to go back to. He was a walking dead man whose primary attachments to life were now fear and hope. Where the hell was Mendel when he needed him? He was always there for Mendel, for Christ's sakes. No. He shook his head to clear it. Poul was simply there. Mendel didn't need him, ever.

Poul made a mental note not to let his mind wander. He tacked it up on a cerebral bulletin board and made another note to refer to it if he felt confused. Don't let the mind wander. He needed all he had for this search.

As time passed he grew angry and bitter, which was better, he figured, than fright and self-pity. "Some men give their lives to God and get by pretty well. Some guys give themselves to their jobs or to women and families. I hand myself over to the whims of a rootless artist who spends his life trying to create something impossible." He stopped walking, as if to help still his mind, which was, with increasing frequency, refusing to hold onto single thoughts. The trees around him shimmered through a watery blur. He sniffed and wiped his eyes and stumbled onward. Damn it all.

The beauty of Mendel and his lifelong quest passed before his eyes. The man had given his whole life, everything he had. He had sacrificed everything that other men consider valuable. He had given it all up to strive for the truth of all truths, the song of flawless beauty.

And he had failed.

He had given the world everything but the perfect song.

Poul held his tears. Through the shifting perceptions of watery eyes, he stared toward the sky which suddenly seemed to reach down and meet the upflung trees whose swaying leaves flowed into the swirling clouds. The clouds in turn rolled downward into the ground, coursing through the rocks and soil and water until all was a gracefully spinning ball, humming its momentary way through existence.

When he cleared his eyes, the vision vanished and objects resumed their normal positions, cut off from each other by space. But the instant was enough to give Poul a feeling for the depth and sweeping breadth of what Mendel strove to capture. His cast-off songs, written on this journey, brought others a little closer to his vision as he led them to it in fragments, as if it were the way he had planned it.

Poul resumed his search, traveling through cities, plains, wheat fields and cattle ranges. He climbed mountains, stared into stores, walked the edges of lakes and farm ponds and waded through swamps. He stopped at every cemetery he came to and checked for new tombstones.

Mendel's stone would be unmarked, but Poul would know. He checked the records at hospitals, courthouses, and police stations. He became depressed with the ungodly number of people imprisoned, dying and dead. The graveyards, especially, reminded him of his shortening time. In all recorded history, which has proven there are always exceptions to the rules, death was the exception to that rule.

It made no exceptions.

In another vision, which he only vaguely understood, Poul saw that man partially circumvents his mortality through his art and his works, but his breath, that one meaningful gift, is always taken away. It is retrieved by the great force that loaned it to him. Life is a short-term loan with lots of interest.

Poul was not afraid of dying. He was afraid of dying alone, without Mendel at least near him. He grew angry again. Here he was, a bent old man who had been around the country, made tons money, now painfully limping around the country once more looking for a man to die with.

He sat down on Imperial Beach. "Damn it to hell! Mendel, where are you?" He picked up a handful of sand and heaved it, noting how it felt vaguely familiar, as if from a dream or a deeply felt passage in a story he'd read.

As if in answer, a nearby group of youths began dancing to a lively version of one of the early Springtime songs that blasted from a portable CD player. It carried Poul back to the young, passionate Mendel who pushed through the countryside, rambling in a world of natural, romantic songs. He smiled at the memory of the long dark hair that covered Mendel's face as he scribbled away, and he felt pride that he, Poul, was the only man on earth who had seen these songs being created.

The youths at his side laughed as they danced, their joy tuned to the song that celebrated new life, young bodies and the clean lust of a new season. A girl wore a T-shirt with Mendel's face on the front. Beneath the songwriter's beard were the words: "Mendel saw all." On the backside was Poul's likeness, clean-shaven and the words: "Poul Gave All."

A pretty young blonde girl, maybe 18, trotted over to Poul. At one time he could have bought someone like her for the evening. Now he simply envied her youth, grace and energy. "Are you okay?" She asked.

"Yes," Poul nodded. "I'm fine. Thank you."

The girl studied him. "You look like Poul, the man who followed Mendel."

He smiled sadly. "Poul is dead."

Her expression fell into true sorrow. "I know."

"You sound sad," he said.

She sat down beside him, a wistful look now on her face. "It's like, Mendel is everything. He's mythic. But Poul's my hero," she said. She looked out at the waves.

"Why?"

"If it hadn't been for Poul we'd never have Mendel's songs." She shook her head and the thick blonde hair waved like the sea. "What Poul did was…I can't imagine it."

Poul listened to the music coming from the radio and the music of the ocean. "Mendel spent his whole life writing those songs," he said matter-of-factly.

The girl nodded. "Mendel gave his life to something he had to do. Poul gave his life to something he *didn't* have to do. That's what makes him heroic." She looked at him again. "Does that make any sense?" Poul thought that she was not as innocent as the young blue eyes would have her seem.

"Yes, it does. I wonder if Poul knew that?"

She shrugged. "I guess we'll never know." She smiled and jumped up. "Well, nice talking to you. Have a nice day!" She trotted back to her friends.

Poul studied the t-shirts. Maybe he understood before, but now the full significance sank in. He thought about this a long time, then turned and headed eastward again.

Wherever Poul journeyed, Mendel's music played and magazines screamed headlines about Mendel's and Poul's adventures. Their ghosts appeared everywhere. People claimed to have talked with Mendel or Poul before the men died. Some communicated with them after death. Mendel's demise created books of revelations. Poul's death created speculations.

❦   ❦   ❦

One night months later Poul stopped in a Louisiana swamp and listened to the cypress trees whisper a song Mendel had copied and revised years ago. Poul remembered the time well, especially the morning he had awakened to find a large copperhead nestled cozily beside his warm body. Poul had lain motionless with terror, trying to calm himself, until the snake slithered off in search of mid-morning sun.

Now he lay on the warm, damp earth staring up into the night sky. The man in the full moon smiled coldly, the arrogant bastard.

The world felt strange. Loneliness and fright overtook him again and he clenched his jaw against the tears, scratching his chest as he stared into the night. He felt like a child, small and abandoned on a dark road. The child, terrified, conjures up creatures in the darkness and shakes in horror, and the more he shakes, the larger and more terrible the creatures grow until he finally screams, and the louder he screams, the larger they expand and the closer they come, and the child falls into a swoon, hypnotized by his own horror, feeling that life is a nightmare like no other.

He gave way to tears and wept beneath the trees until he fell asleep. At some point he dreamed that Mendel appeared in his tattered gray-white clothes. His white hair swayed freely about his shoulders and his snowy beard fell below his chest.

"Slow down," he said cheerfully. His eyes glittered like stars on a clear December night. His voice was old and deep but full of youthful power. "I'm with you. Just slow down."

"Where?"

"Here," he laughed. "Closer than you can imagine."

"Why can't I find you?"

The figure bent backward in laughter. "You have! I'm here. That's all you have to remember."

"Can I go with you?"

Mendel smiled. "You always have."

"I want to be where you are."

Mendel leaned forward and nodded. "You control your destiny."

"Now, then." Poul saw himself reaching outward and upward, an emaciated, begging figure.

"When you're ready." The words came from everywhere in the sudden blackness.

The morning sunlight stabbed his eyes open. He instinctively looked for snakes and rose when he found none. He didn't remember the dream but he felt better and ate a quick breakfast of soup. He turned from his northern route and headed for Texas. He wasn't sure why, except that he hadn't looked there. As it once was an effort for him to track down the hundreds of bits of paper Mendel liberated, it was now an effort just to walk. His muscles were stiffening and the very act of motion required concentration.

He wished he had cigarettes and maybe some wine to ease the pain in his joints. In the long hot days he sometimes saw Mendel ahead of him, or thought he did, and each time he concluded that if he thought he saw Mendel, that was enough.

If the hard years had weathered him, the past few months had transformed him. Poul was unrecognizable now, even to himself. The dirty white hair that ringed the bald crown fell below his shoulders and his thin, splotchy beard straggled far below his chest. His watery brown eyes that drooped toward the long sunburned nose were the eyes of a mystic and a madman—the eyes of a man persistently pursuing a singular vision. He fashioned a cane from an old maple branch and used his free hand to shield his eyes from the sun. He accepted the probability that he was slightly daft, but even the burden, or liberation, of dementia would not stop him. "I'll find you, Mendel. God damn it, I'll find you." He resembled, and indeed knew that he was, in the deepest sense, an old beggar.

Sometimes during the middle of the day when it was warm and humid, or at dusk when shadows spring upward into tricky life, Poul saw his friend. It was always a fleeting glimpse, caught as the elusive master rounded a curve ahead or vanished over a small hilltop.

Each time Poul smiled and nodded. His pace quickened slightly, not only because he was close but because he also felt the sighting was proof that Mendel was still searching for the perfect song. Maybe Mendel would invite him to sit down beside the campfire to sing a tune before Poul rushed the new songs back to the city. Time is money! People are waiting! You know that damned Beasely, how impatient he is…old fart's going to work himself to death.

He continued walking. Mendel's with Mara, Poul. He's forgotten you, his best friend in life. No! Don't cry. He's not really with her. He's up ahead. Just up there….

He's with Harry. Harry who? I was Ha—Harry's dead, long dead.

Mara's…I knew her…I loved her….

They're tricking me. Harry's dead. Mendel's alone. He hasn't given up the song. I'm right behind you. Ha! We're alone. All of us together, en masse, we're alone….It's the sun. Christ, all mixed up. Out, out, damned sun!

❦   ❦   ❦

A few days later he saw Mendel more intensely than ever. He saw every detail of the man just before he disappeared behind a boulder up ahead. Poul nearly laughed, infused with a youthful energy he hadn't felt for years. But when he made the turn around the corner of the huge rock, stillness greeted him like a faceless watch. Poul's full weight slowly sank upon the cane and he knew he couldn't go a step further. He just couldn't. His body was heavy and tired. His mind had no fences, no boundaries; it just meandered like an old cow, lost in an empty field.

Sitting beside a small fire that night, Poul listened to a coyote howling miles away, its desolate cry growing, then shrinking in the still air. Stillness knows no distance, he thought. Neither does loneliness. He touched the earth for comfort.

Did Mendel invent the harmonica? Why, yes…no…no, he created the sound of the harp that blankets the harsh silence with gentle feminine waves. Poul dropped his gaze to the fire and with effort blinked himself back from the distance. He coughed. He was so tired. "Mendel, where are you? Damn it."

He squinted into the nervous blaze, fighting to keep his thoughts together. What did Mendel do with this business of loneliness? Surely he knew loneliness better than anyone. Poul, during his travels, viewed Mendel as a companion, but for all Mendel knew, he was alone.

Poul's mind floated upward with the little flames. Surely he wrote about loneliness…. Mara…he created Mara to stave off loneliness. No. Mara was created as a gift. Poul strained until it felt as though his brain would crack like a dry walnut shell. He felt the vibrations of a sidewinder searching for a rodent. A small spider shook the rock over which it scuttled.

His aching body was heavy but his mind was so light, as if it were beyond the body. He gazed from afar at his fingers, once so adept at snatching the liveliest of papers. Now they were twisted and could barely grasp his stick. Long ago, on Mendel's trail, Poul had ridden the blazing chariot of his friend's lifelong drive. He had spent his own life preserving the songs that now would survive them both. It all seemed so simple. As long as the songs came, they would survive, Mendel waiting to create, Poul waiting to gather and Beasely—Beasely! He broke the charmed circle. The son-of-a-bitch died and left them as unbalanced as a two-legged tripod.

He straightened up, catching himself again. Poor Beasely. No, it was he, Poul, who had miscalculated. He had left Mendel in fear and the perfect song was lost. No, that wasn't true either. Mendel wouldn't have left without the song. He would battle death itself until he had it in his possession. He would defy Satan and God until he knew he had it.

He shivered. The only warmth in him were tears. He closed his eyes and swallowed. "Come and get me. I'm too damned weak to go on. I'm…ready." The night air's weight pressed upon his chest and all his strength focused on drawing breath. Mendel made the sound of the wind. Poul made the sound of the wind dying.

Something whispered. The sands? A bat. He listened for the sound that had passed like one of his shallow breaths. The darkness cut into his eyes, seeped into his ears and entered his nostrils.

"Poul…." Stillness grew inside him. His body swayed with the effort of his concentration. He lay on his back and fell into one of those dreams he could never remember and he and Mendel walked together as if they had known each other forever and their separation during their brief lives had been no more than a candle flame's whimsical flicker.

❦   ❦   ❦

"Hey!"

Poul opened his eyes and shielded them against the odiously cheerful morning light. Dark forms cast shadows over him.

"Hey, old fella, you okay?" Four young men, ruddy and muscular, stared down at him. He nodded, angry that they had broken his sleep. He struggled to remember the dream. It was something about Mendel. It was gone. "I'm okay," he said, shivering with the night's leftover chill.

"Look at him," one of the men said. "He's shaking."

"He doesn't look too good," a man with a pleasant voice said. He set his camping gear down and knelt beside Poul. "What are you doing out here alone?" He asked gently.

Poul heard music playing. Damn, was he hallucinating again? No. It was coming from the radio in their camper. It was a Mendel song. He smiled wearily. Mendel was always so close, yet so out of reach.

"What's your name?" The man had a kind face and Poul decided to answer him.

He swallowed and licked his lips which were cracked from exposure, age and lack of water.

"Poul." He scratched his neck to hide a hand that wouldn't stop shaking with the chill.

The men looked at each other. The kneeling man stared at him. "Poul? The guy who followed Mendel?" The men smiled patronizingly.

Poul nodded. "Yeah. My whole frigging life."

"Poul's dead," someone said.

Another man laughed softly. "Dead? He was never alive, just like Mendel. That was all media hype. Marketing stuff."

Poul's chest tightened in anger. Who did this scummy little punk think he was? Smart young assholes. If he could just get his breath, he'd beat them senseless. He shook his head as the figures before him became shadow forms, unreal shapes on a swirling canvas. He wasn't sure if he was awake or dreaming.... He swallowed again and tried to stand. His legs were weak. "He is too real, you goddamned idiots! He's...real!"

Damn it, he thought, give me some strength to stand up and knock some sense into these cocky snots. .

"I always heard about people who believed he was real," another said conversationally. "I just read something last week about guys who spent years trying to track down Mendel."

"He's real!" Carried by the strength of his rage, Poul made it to his feet. His beard was splattered with dew and spit and his eyes focused and fuzzed like a single lens sans reflex. "And he's around here, by God." The ground was rocking back and forth. Christ, he could live to be a hundred and nature would still find some new trick. "He's real and you'd better believe it."

The cocky man shook his head. "It was all a story. Nobody ever saw him. Logic tells you—"

"I saw him. Me! Poul! I saw him!" The men were quiet and looked down at the ground, smiling. Poul fought to control himself and stay upright. "If he wasn't real, who wrote the songs? Who was great enough to write the damned songs?" He snorted and scratched his rib. That shut them up, the smart asses. Goddamn kids don't even think anymore. Don't believe.

The nice man gently took Poul's arm. "Look, come with us and we'll get some help. Okay?"

"No!" He yanked his arm away and nearly fell. The damned ground kept floating. "I'm searching for—"

"Just come with us." Poul was grabbed gently from both sides.

"If you stay out here you'll die. Quit struggling. We just want to help—"

"Christ, he hasn't had a bath in a year."

"Strong old fart."

Mendel was near. He knew it. They would take him to a hospital and he'd be drugged and mess his pants everyday and finally die. He was almost to Mendel and these demons were trying to tear him away. No. No.

"NO!" The amount of strength it took to yank loose from two young men blanked his thoughts and in the darkening sky and the slow motion rise of the ground, he heard someone call his name. He recognized the voice and smiled, knowing as synchronicity's final crashing blow freed him, that his search was over.

And he realized in the brightening dream what Mendel must also have known. The perfect song was the journey itself.

"The passing is always painless," the voice said. Poul sighed. The illusion of these men faded as a smiling figure moved toward him in the muted light. It was almost as if an old friend, a part of himself, laughed as they moved together, quickly, toward wholeness.

❈   ❈   ❈

After radioing for help, the young men sipped beers to calm their nerves and held their eyes self-consciously away from the blanketed body.

"Poor guy," said one. "You suppose he really was Poul?"

"Check his wallet. Must be some ID there."

The kind man leaned down and pulled the wallet out of Poul's pocket with quiet respect. "Strange. Nothing here but a little money and a note."

"What's the note say?"

The kind man unfolded it and they all read the single line:

Perfection is perception

The police arrived and wrote their report. The coroner took the body that would be buried without identification.

And the songs played on with a joyful life of their own.

0-595-31274-8